EMANCIPATION

Emancipation

The Warrior Series
Book 1

A.L. CARTER

A.L. CARTER LLC

For my amazing, supportive, and sexy husband.
Thank you.

Special thank you to my editor Claire for her patience and insights. Without who this book would have been a mess.

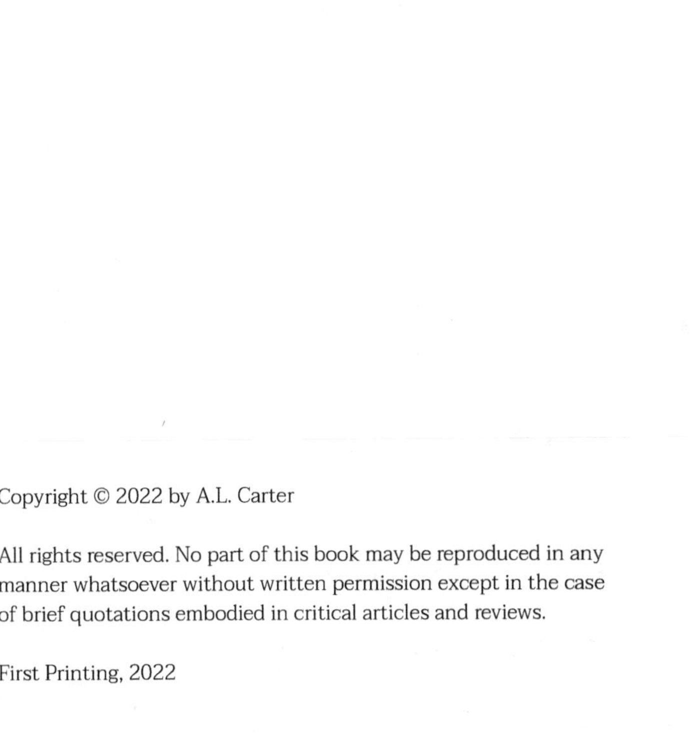

First Printing, 2022

Content Warning

This book contains content that could trigger people who have experienced trauma. It includes scenes of rape, violence, profanity, and sexually explicit reading. Some of the chapters will be emotionally challenging to read. The author does her best to make this book a story about survival and the power of women. At the same time, some of the content in this book may be difficult to read. Please understand my intent is to portray survival of the unthinkable. If you believe this will trigger you, please do not read it.

One in every six women in the US has been a survivor of sexual violence. We are survivors.

If you or someone you know is a survivor of sexual assault, please seek help: https://www.rainn.org/resources

Chapter 1

June

Most people would think I live a charmed life—upper-class parents, private schools, and a trust fund that lets me pursue my passion.

However, when you're an introvert there's no jetting to Paris with friends or Rodeo shopping trips. It's lonely, and I discovered this very young.

As a child, I was alone a lot of the time. So I would have imaginary friends who would even be in my dreams. We would go to faraway places, play games, and explore exotic locations. I was convinced at one point I would marry my imaginary friend. I even told my father my plan to marry him. It was the first time he smacked me and called me stupid. He told me I would marry whoever he told me to.

All I wanted was for my parents to look in my direction and care about the drawings I made for them, but as I found out when I was seven, I was born the wrong gender and a redhead, so my parents, particularly my father, didn't care for my well being. They would leave for months without telling me when they were going or getting back.

I heard my parents fighting one evening, "Karen, you promised the genetics doctor *you* chose I would get a son to take on my legacy, and now you tell me you can't have any more children! What am I supposed to do with a girl? A girl that barely *talks*!" my Dad screamed.

"This is your fault! He said *no stress*! You thought your money could buy a boy! Instead, we got a girl, and the treatments damaged my ability to have any more kids!" she yelled back.

I cried for hours after I heard their screaming. A child should never feel unwanted, but we can't choose our parents. Shortly after, my parents divorced and put me into boarding schools. I stayed there even through breaks. During the summer months, they sent me to wherever my parents weren't and cared for by paid nannies. The nannies were kind and cared about me, but I never felt like family to them.

Shortly after the divorce, I decided to show my father he didn't need a boy. I wanted him to care about me. I pondered, what can I do to show him that girls are as strong as boys. Who knows how a seven-year-old's brain works, but I landed on martial arts. It was something that looked fun, and I was convinced that if I became the best at it that my father would look at me differently.

So with a single-minded purpose, I found a dojo close to the boarding school, and I dove into learning JKA Shotokan Karate and Shiyeikai Kenjutsu. Every evening after classes, I would sneak out of the school grounds to go learn and practice.

When I first went to the dojo, the Sensei asked why I wanted to learn. I told him I wanted to be the best in the world for my father. He didn't like my reasoning but let me join anyway. He was an American Expat, an army vet of Japanese descent who just wanted a quiet life doing what he loved. He was a fantastic teacher. I was only eight, but he pushed me hard. I didn't even learn my first karate form until I was there for about six months. He had me doing exercise drills and cleaning around the dojo. He believed it was a passing idea and that I would quit.

He realized I was a serious child; he seemed saddened by that. He would constantly tell me I should play with my friends, but I was focused on my mission, besides I didn't see my imaginary friend very often, and well, he wasn't real. He was impressed by my focus and drive. When he started the actual training I enjoyed it immensely. He was impressed by my ability but quickly learned about my temper.

He is the one who gave me the mental exercises to control my emotions that I still use to this day. He taught me that if I cannot control my emotions, I cannot control my body. Each day the first exercises we did were mental. We would sit and meditate. At first, it was tough for me. I was a child, and sitting still and clearing my mind was incredibly hard. So every day, I exercised, I meditated, and I trained—every single day.

My dedication started to pay off. By age ten, I was already a second-degree black belt in Karate. By twelve, I was a 3rd-degree black belt in both forms. Knowing my father, I knew it would not be enough. I decided I needed to expand my capabilities. My Sensei had taught me, focused, and honed me, but I needed more. It was time to find another place to teach me.

I was considered "gifted" in school but never really applied myself, probably because of my focus on martial arts. So when I decided I needed a new MA teacher, I researched and found where I wanted to go, Japan. Tricky since the school my parents decided to send me to was in Germany. So I started a plan on how to change schools without them knowing. My Dad was easy, he was never around and didn't care. My mother, well, she tried to care but didn't do a great job. She did pay attention to most things that had to do with me, so my plan had to address my mother.

What you may or may not know about rich people is they don't handle their own personal household finances. They have a house manager or some such person to handle that. The role of a house manager is to run a house like a parent would, so groceries, bills, managing staff, etc.

The summer before my eighth-grade year, I filled out the paperwork for a boarding school in Japan and prepared my plan to get it signed. Our household manager was friendly and paid me more attention than my mother. Her name was Dawn, and she ran the house like it was a military base. She treated me a lot like she treated the house staff, like a grunt. I had to clean and help around the house. I didn't mind, and I was desperate for adult attention.

The paperwork needed my mother's signature; only Dawn could get her to sign things without even looking at what she was signing. I also needed Dawn to change where they were sending money for my schooling.

I made sure I didn't present said paperwork until they were prepping for one of my mom's parties for my birthday. My mom tried to be a mother exactly once a year on what she thought was my birthday. She would come into town, throw a big bash, invite all her friends and drink the night through. At Least she tried... a bit. So they were getting ready for the party, and Dawn was running around to ensure everything was exactly how my mother wanted it.

"Dawn," I interrupted one of her many darts across the house, "the school requires new paperwork for enrollment this fall," I said as apologetically as I could.

"June!" she says, exasperated. "Why are you bringing this to me now? We are in the middle of setup!"

"Well, I kind of forgot about it, actually, and... it's due today. I filled it all out! It just needs a parent's signature..." Just a little lie... no who am I kidding? It was a doozy!

With the frown of an unhappy nun who wants to throttle you, she replied, "Fine. I'll get your mom to sign it now. Send me the routing numbers for payment if it changes, and I will update it."

"Thank you, thank you, thank you!" I turned and sprinted back to my room.

My plan worked. By the end of July, I was headed to Japan for the rest of my schooling. There was more schoolwork, and it was a bit harder, but I had no problem keeping up. Since it was a boarding school, there were a lot of American kids, but they generally left me alone.

The big problem came when I tried to enroll at the dojo I had decided on training. They refused me at first. They didn't even let me in the door, but I relentlessly pursued training with them. After about four months, they agreed to let me train, and train I did relentlessly. I was at the dojo every day of the week and every weekend. It was amazing, brutal, but amazing. They were much harder on me than my old Sensei, and I had thought he was strict and ruthless at the time.

Again, most of my first six months were spent cleaning the dojo. Once I started training, the other students stopped being mean. Well, one of them did. A girl named Ahmya began to talk to me. She was a Japanese student. We became best friends, even meeting each other to walk to the dojo daily. She was beautiful inside and out. She also loves martial arts as much as I do. We pushed each other in our training, helping each other to pass most of the students in skill.

We learned many types of the arts; Enshin Kaikan, Bojutsu, Araki Ryu, Aikijujitsu, and my favorite, Iaijutsu. I loved mastering the forms, kicks, and punches, but my passion was weapons. I loved the weapons, not because of the power associated with them but the function and form they added to the moves I learned. While I loved all weapons, the Katana was by far our favorite. Ahmya and I were very good at them, the two best at the dojo.

By eighteen we were competing on the world stage. We were roommates by then and spent most of our time together. Somewhere I had lost the drive to prove my father wrong and developed a deep respect and love of Japanese martial arts.

My friendship with Ahmya filled the hole they left. We were rarely apart. We went to her parent's house every weekend. They were wonderful people and passed within a year of each other. I did everything I could to support Ahmya during that time. Sure, as roommates, we fought occasionally, but it was over dumb stuff like dirty dishes, someone wearing the other's favorite sweater, and shit like that. We even got matching tattoos after we both hit eighteen.

I never told my parents where I was doing my schooling or that I was competing in MA competitions. In retrospect, that may have been a mistake.

Chapter 2

I am now twenty-four, have five world championship medals, and currently compete with Ahmya in a tournament where I should win my sixth. We both thought about attending college but didn't; I thought we had time. It just wasn't necessary to me. I'm also still a virgin. I thought I'd eventually have time for that, too, stupid. It's not like I was chaste or anything. I dated boys and fooled around, but when it came down to sex, it just didn't feel right. It always felt like sex was all they cared about.

Ahmya and I were a bit internet famous. We had a couple hundred thousand followers and did some podcast interviews and such. We were living our best life and having fun.

It's the final round of the tournament, and I am ranked 2nd, and she is 3rd. My competition is very good this year. I believe I can win, but focus is critical. My Katana are on my back. We don't use them during the competition; we use practice swords, so no one loses a finger... or a limb. I have them on because I'm a bit superstitious. They are my good luck charms. I run through my forms, keeping my muscles warm. I am so focused on the next fight I miss my father approaching. When I do notice, I smile but then realize he looks furious.

"What the fuck do you think you're doing?" he says. "Hi, Da.." I almost get out but he interrupts, "Shut up you ungrateful whore. What are you doing competing in martial arts tournaments? One of my employees showed me a video of you fighting!" He is whisper screaming right now because, god forbid, someone hears him. "This is a complete disgrace to our family and my NAME!"

"I don't understand. I honestly thought you'd be proud of me.." this is all I could get out before he started sputtering and breathing like a bull getting ready to charge.

It truly looks like he wants to hit me. "You will remove yourself from the tournament roster. Now."

"What?" It's my turn to sputter, and I can feel my face beginning to heat. I'm a redhead; it's what our skin likes to do when we get angry... or embarrassed... or generally whenever it wants.

"You heard me, young lady," he says with a disgusted sneer on his face. "You are an embarrassment to our family name, and I'm not going to allow it."

So this is where the redhead really comes out and shines; it definitely still gets me in trouble sometimes, "You pompous, self-important piece of shit. I am twenty-four years old, an *adult*. And I do not care what you do. Take away my trust. I don't care. I will do what I want when I want, and *you have no say in it!* For someone who was basically a sperm donor, you have a lot of nerve!"

He actually tries to backhand me. I am competing in a *martial arts* competition, and he tries to hit me. The fucking nerve. Instead of landing the blow I now have his arm twisted and am holding his hand in front of him. I barely moved to do this. I truly contemplate breaking his arm.

I can see the pain on his face, but instead of blowing up for some reason, he now has a smug look on his face, and honestly, it gets my anxiety going. "You are so like your mother, but luckily I planned for that." At that moment, he glances over my shoulder, and I feel a pinch at the base of my skull. I spin on my heels, getting ready to attack, but by the time I'm fully around, my world is already fuzzy, and I'm losing focus. I fall to my hands and knees but somehow manage to lift my head. I first see Ahmya on the floor and then look for my attacker. What kind of drugs did they hit me with because the woman, if that's what she is, is pale yellow, and she has four stacked eyes. "Wha the fu.." Then my world goes black.

Everything is black, and my eyes or limbs won't respond to my command to move. I panic a little remembering the woman but then remember my training. Focus, evaluate, and wait for the right opportunity. As I wait, I start to hear things, beeps, and guttural language that sounds like someone shredding paper... slowly. It sounds awful, but I'm starting to get back some of my faculties. At that moment, I feel an incredibly painful stab behind both ears. I have to remain still, so they don't know I'm awake and ruin my chances of escape. The pain starts to subside but then a worse pain flares through my brain like it's on fire, and just when I think I'll cry out, it vanishes like it was never there. Strange.

"The female is larger than the average human female," one of the people milling about says. Wait a minute... ten seconds ago, it was a guttural language, and now that my head is clearing, it definitely wasn't an Earth language. Now I can understand them perfectly, even their diction is now the same as mine. Panic starts to rise again, but I push it down. If I'm going to escape, then I have to keep my wits about me. I slow my breathing, focus on my heart rate, and return to calm. Yes it seems I've been abducted by aliens, yes I am naked lying on a very cold table but it seems these aliens are overly confident because I am not restrained. Mistake.

I barely open my eyes to ensure they do not see I am awake. And it takes a lot not to gasp in shock. There are two... aliens standing around a high-tech display showing my naked body in all its naked glory. Now ego has no place in the dojo, but the constant training has ensured my body is lean but definitely not skinny. I have muscle, and my D cups are not too bad either. I got my height from my bastard father, so I come in at 6 '1' ' and 165 pounds. I love my hair; it's a wavey, rich, fiery, auburn color. It falls almost to my ass. Some would say I'm intimidating (hence the virginity), but my body is honed by training and fighting.

"The female is of reproductive age, and all her reproductive organs are functioning at peak efficiency. Its total body fat is lower than our average human female, but maybe it's different in some way." The shortest one says.

"Good, good. It should fetch a reasonable price from the Lutetian." says the one who looks like he's on the old side. Their skin is a mottled yellow color, and they have four eyes like the woman I saw at the tournament. Their build is bigger than the average human male but not intimidating by my standards. I can't see their musculature under the lab-ish looking garb they wear, so I'll just need to assume the worst, that they're fit and strong underneath, so when I go on the offensive, I'll need to use maximum effort.

"Did we meet our quota for the Lutetian?" says one I can't see behind my head.

"No." the old one says. "Quota was two hundred fifty, and we only received one hundred twenty-two from the humans."

My blood runs ice cold.

The small one pipes in and asks, "Why do we pay the humans? Why don't we just take what we want from them? They're savages."

Oldy sighs, "Someday, you'll understand these undeveloped planets are at a stage where separate governments are threatening each other with nuclear weapons. It's easier to play to their greed than risk our stock with nuclear contaminants."

He's referring to humans like cattle. He's not wrong about our governments, but my fire is up. Someone *sold* me to *aliens*! Those fucking bastards! And the cherry on top is I think my sperm donor had a hand in it.

In martial arts, you learn that every muscle movement can broadcast your plan to your opponent, so I wait until both of them turn back to their work and explode into action. I go after the younger-looking one first since he is probably the fastest, hoping the one behind me doesn't catch me by surprise. I cannot afford to take prisoners or risk an alarm, so Baby gets a full power strike to the throat, and when he bends, I bring up my knee trying to ensure it creates a bone fragment into something important like his brain. Baby is down and unmoving in less than four seconds, so I turn around, looking for my adversary behind me.

To my disappointment, there are three who are looking shocked in my direction. Before they can move or utter anything, I have delivered a blow to the midsection of the right and left alien, and I can feel the middle start to move to grab me. Before it can get its arm around me, I bend at the waist so it misses, and I move around behind him while grabbing the nearest heavy-looking object and bringing it down on its head as hard as I can. Its head completely caves in, and he's down. My mind blanks for a second, but I kick back into gear because I will have to process that later.

I turn on the others and knock them out with my weapon as well. I look up as Oldy is leveling a weapon at me. I realize, in that second, he's already pulled the trigger, and I feel a pain in my chest. I look down, and there's a dart-looking thing protruding from my left breast. I start to feel the fuzzy feeling, and I'm screaming in my head; at least, I think it's in my head.

I hear Oldy screaming for help, and big scary-looking aliens come racing in and tackle me to the ground. I hear Oldy screaming, "Don't kill the stock! We can still sell it!" Everything fades to black... again.

Chapter 3

When I wake again, I am restrained. I open my eyes, blinking, trying to clear the drug.

"Ah. She wakes." The alien speaking is huge. Huge and built like bodybuilders of Earth. He's easily 7 feet tall. Intimidating is not an adequate word for this alien. His skin is dark, the color of lush evergreen needles, and his face is handsome but different from humans. He has ridges halfway between his brow and hairline, and the same ridges contour his jaw and cheekbones. His lips are full, and his nose is wide with a small ridge down the center. His hair is black as midnight, straight, and hangs to his shoulders.

He can be called handsome for an alien, but when I look at his emerald eyes, I can tell his soul is ugly. He has a smile on his face, but it's the coldest thing I've ever seen on a living being. Then I see his hands resting on the table beside my head; instead of fingernails, he has claws, but they don't look natural. They look metal and very sharp. It makes me shiver.

It's then I hear Oldy. "This female killed three of my assistants! Three!"

The scary dude laughs with no real humor. "Good. I like them with fire," he says while fingering my hair. He looks at me and stares for a while as if trying to gauge how much "fire" there is.

I return his stare with as much hatred as I can muster.

He chuckles, mirth not reaching his eyes. Looking at Oldy, he says, "I do need a new sex slave; how much?"

True panic sets in, and I start twisting and pulling against the restraints at my neck, wrists, and ankles.

Scary looks at me with a bored look and says, "Put her back under so we can negotiate."

They turn away as I start screaming and cursing at them. I am terrified of that psychopath. He will take me against my will, and he won't care how much he hurts me. He will probably enjoy inflicting pain.

These are my last thoughts as I'm put back under.

I wake, and I can tell I'm on a different ship. I'm in a cage in which I can barely lay flat in. I'm not restrained, so that's good. As I look out the cage bars, my eyes freeze on what can only be a window. Through it, I see stars, and then I feel something in the floor of the ship like a hum, and the star outside the window changes to black. I've read some theoretical physics and pray we didn't just jump into hyperspace or some such thing. The farther I get from Earth, the less likely I'll ever be able to make it back, and if we are talking probabilities, it's most likely impossible, but I have to try.

I sit up and just barely fit in a sitting position. My hair brushes the top of the cage. As I'm taking stock of myself, I notice a few things: first, I have no body hair except on my head, eyebrows, and eyelashes. Fuckers. I guess permission isn't necessary for sex slaves. The thought makes me a little nauseous. Scars from my various tournaments and training mishaps or learnings, as my Sensi would say, are still there, so I guess they can't fix those or didn't bother.

My Sensi, the thought makes tears well in my eyes. Fuck Ahmya. What happened to her? What does she think happened to me? Does she think I abandoned her? She was my sister. She'll look for me, but she won't ever be able to find me.

I wiped my eyes angrily. There's no point in tears. Know your environment. Know your enemy. So you can defeat your enemy.

From the corner of my eye, I see movement and freeze. Fighting in close quarters is an incredibly difficult task, so first, I need to figure out who's in here with me and, if necessary, incapacitate them. I slowly turn my head and see a small shaking form. I focus more fully, and a whimper comes from the ball. Deciding whatever this is, it is most likely slave or captive, too, so let's see if I can make friends and gather some intel. I slowly turn my body so as not to scare... whatever it is. Sitting cross-legged, I open my body up, laying my hands open and up on my knees, trying to convey safety, but who knows? Maybe my posture screams hostility in their culture; I have no idea.

I sit still, letting the other adjust to my presence. It turns a bit, and I see fully emerald eyes peek out from midnight black hair. I draw in a sharp breath. It's like Him. That is when I notice that the eyes are softer, the lashes are longer, and no clawed fingertips. I decide this is a child and most likely a female. She is in the cage with me, so she's in the same situation as me, kind of.

"Hello," I say to her in a soft voice. "My name is June. Can you understand me?"

I wait, and just as I think there is no language chip for you, I hear, "I understand." In a tiny feminine voice.

I give her a soft smile, "What's your name?"

After a few seconds, deciding if I'm trustworthy no doubt, she says, "Leena. My mother called me Leena."

"So, Leena, it seems we are both captives of whoever owns this ship."

Responding in a whisper she says with disgust, "He's a monster. His name is Kaxlin. He is super mean." She retreats back, and I can no longer see her eyes.

"How old are you, Leena?"

She lifts her head more fully this time, and I can see her face. Her features are delicate and soft. Her eyes are deep emerald in color, like his, but I can see now she (or they, I suppose) have pupils like us, round black and in the center of the deep green.

Her face scrunches a bit as she thinks, then she says, "Ten, I think. I was seven when he found me."

From human standards, she looks like she's around six years old, but since I don't know their growth and development patterns, I have no real idea, but I'm going to assume she is a youth of their species. She definitely is more advanced than a human six-year-old. She has hollows under her eyes, and her cheeks are sunk in. She is not being fed enough.

"Do you think we can be friends, Leena?" I ask.

She stills and sits there staring at me for a minute, then answers, "Yes. I think so."

I genuinely smile at her this time. "I'm glad. I could use a friend."

"Me too." She says sadly, then asks, "Where are you from? You look different from anyone I have seen before."

"I am from Earth. It is a blue and green planet. It has green grass and green leaves on the trees. In the fall, the leaves change colors to yellows, oranges, and reds. It's my favorite time of year. What's your planet like?"

"I barely remember it, but I do remember purple grass and all shades of purple on the trees. It is still my favorite color."

"It sounds beautiful."

She smiles a little, then moves over to sit next to me, lays her head on my shoulder, and promptly falls asleep. She is the cutest thing, and I already like her. I probably shouldn't get attached, but a little girl shouldn't be in this place.

Not long after Leena falls asleep on my shoulder, the light in the room dims. It must mean some sort of night cycle, but I feel like I've slept a lot, so I move Leena's head so it rests in my lap, and I stroke her hair. To my joy, she starts to purr, a barely audible soft rumbling that is very reminiscent of a cat. I smile and continue to stroke her hair.

After a while, I hear the door open and close. I freeze, waiting for what will happen next. It takes a minute but then I can feel him staring at me. I slowly turn my head, and to my utter surprise and dismay, he is squatting next to the cage. He was able to walk to the cage and squat down without me hearing him, not good.

Then I hear a rumble as he starts to speak, "Slave, I will give you tonight to acclimate to your new environment, but tomorrow evening, I will have you." He rises and moves to his bed.

I turn my head away because he is starting to undress, and I don't want to see that.

Eventually, I fall asleep, but my nightmares invade, and they are terrifying.

I wake to Leena rustling around. "June, it's time to wake. He'll get mad if you are not ready for your daily duties."

I rouse and try to stretch, which is impossible in the tiny cage. I'm still naked as the day I was born and wonder if I will stay this way.

I hear a click, and Leena pops up and pushes on the door to head out. I follow slowly, not knowing what to expect. Attempting to be helpful, Leena gestures that I should stand straight with my head bowed, and my hands clasped across my stomach. She doesn't seem the least bit concerned with my nudity which I'm not sure how to feel about. I'm thankful she has a little blouse that hangs to her knees, but she seems not to be surprised in the least by me standing next to her with no clothes. It doesn't bode well. It means I'm not the first "sex slave" in this room with her, and if I'm not the first, what happened to the rest?

At that moment, Kaxlin walks in from an adjoining room very naked. *Do not look... do not look June!* God damn it, I looked. I am 24 years old but not a complete prude. I've gone down on guys, had them try to go down on me, heavy petting and kissing, just no sex. The men I've dated just never really felt like they were worth the trouble. If you can't get me off with your finger or your mouth, I doubt you can do it with your cock, and since it was abundantly obvious, that's all they were after... buh-bye.

Kaxlin's cock is huge and flaccid. What does it look like erect? I continue to study. Yes, that's what I'm going to call it, scientific curiosity. It lies against his leg, the girth the size of my wrist, long and thick. I look down before he catches me. I stand still and silent.

After a while, I hear him striding toward us, and I ready my muscles for a fight.

"Leena, teach her her duties today. I expect a meal tomorrow morning." said curtly and with an audible sneer.

"Yes, Master." She responds.

I jerk my head toward her in shock before I can stop my-self. In the next moment, he has me by my hair, pulling hard enough that my eyes water.

I feel his breath against my neck, and I chant in my head not yet, no fighting, know your enemy. He won't do it in front of her.

It's nearly a growl when he says, "Yes, I am her master. Just as I am your master." He holds me up on my toes by the hair, and I feel a touch on my nipple. It gets hard. He rubs some more, then pinches it. After a minute, he releases me and strides out the door.

I am shaking when he leaves. His strength is going to be challenging. Let's hope he doesn't know how to fight well. With his muscle definition, I'm not holding out hope on that one either. My situation is incredibly risky. I start mentally working through my plan as Leena walks me through my duties.

My responsibilities are apparently preparing his shower and his food which, luckily for him, is synthesized via a machine in the wall because cooking is not my forte. I can boil water, but that is about as far as it goes.

I spent a while getting used to controlling the machine per Leena's training and memorizing the things he is served daily. At the same time, I'm thinking about my options and next steps.

I will fight to ensure he does not rape me. I will not allow it. If he kills me for it, so be it. I will not be taken by force. I haven't seen anything I can use as weapons in the rooms, not even so much as a paperweight to beat him over the head with. I guess that makes sense. If you own slaves, you have to ensure your "property" doesn't have the tools to kill you. My rage tries to boil to the surface, and I use my daily mental exercises to beat it into submission.

Once I am calmer, I refocus on my plan, which I realize isn't really a plan. 'Don't get raped' isn't a plan; it's a goal, a hope, a prayer.

I decide that I'm just going to have to plan as I go. I have no idea where the ship is or where it's going. I don't know how big the ship is or how many people or I guess aliens are on it. If I get out of the room, do I find soldiers or more slaves? Soldiers are the worst case because they'll just return me to his room. If it's slaves I doubt I'd get a lot of help because of fear. So a real plan starts to form.

The ship is bound to have an infirmary or something to take care of injuries. So I fight him, and he eventually wins. If he doesn't kill me, which I'm counting on him not wanting to throw his money away, I will no doubt end up in the infirmary. Assuming I am conscious, I will be able to see other areas of the ship. Definitely not the most pleasant way to reconnoiter the ship but really the only way I can think of that I have a chance of succeeding at it. And even if I end up knocked out,

I should still end up in the infirmary and can walk back once I'm patched back up. Here's hoping the patching up is good because I cannot fight him if I have broken ribs or a concussion.

So with what equates to a plan in mind, not a good one, mind you, I move about the rooms learning my duties from a sweet little girl. I need to find out how she got here.

Chapter 4

"Leena, how long have you been on this ship?" I ask her, hoping she doesn't shut down. She pauses in her work for a second and responds, "I'm not sure how long it's been, but it feels like a very long time."

Hmmm, next question, "How did you get here?"

This time she pauses for a long time, "I disobeyed my Fathers," she hesitates but continues on. "My second father was helping the royal family build the newest in our planet's fleet of warships. I was so proud to be his daughter. I wanted to see and ride on the ship so badly, but I knew they would not allow it. I found out they were running a test flight, and I snuck onboard so I could go with him."

She pauses once again, but I can tell it's because she is trying to control her emotions. After a minute or two, she continues, "He was so mad when he found me. Furious that I would put myself at risk. He took me to a room with a bed and locked me in. I was so mad at him. Then I started hearing things outside the door. It sounded like screams and fighting. I was very scared, so I hid under the bed. A little later, my Dad rushed in... I'd never seen him scared before, but he was definitely afraid. He grabbed me from under the bed and ran over to the vent at the corner of the room. He put me inside the vent and told me not to cry, not to make a sound. Then closed the vent." She has a faraway look on her face, clearly reliving a trauma.

I try to interrupt to stop her pain, but she continues to talk over me, "When Father opened the door, there were ugly yellow monsters outside the door. They killed him. They took him away. I was frozen sitting inside the vent for so long. I wanted my family to tell them what had happened, but I was afraid. I hid in the vents of the ship, slipping out for food. For a long time, I lived in the vents. I started getting mad, and then I decided I needed to get back at them for killing him."

She blinks several times like she's trying to clear something from her vision, then looks at me, "So I traveled the vents trying to find someone to hurt. I was so angry. I found these rooms and decided someone important had to stay there. One night I snuck out of the vent with a sharp piece of metal I found in the vents. I tried to stab Kaxlin, but he heard me coming and caught me. He put this stupid slave collar on me and threw me in a cage. I've been cleaning this room since. He never lets me leave the room, says I'm his little secret."

Strange, "Why is that?" I ask.

"I do not know, but he does not allow anyone to see me."

"And no one will," Kaxlin's voice rings out through the room. Both Leena and I jump, scared of what he will do. Leena assumes the standard supplicant pose, and I follow suit. "Make no mistake, my little sex slave, if anyone finds out about her, I will know it was you, and I will kill you for it." His voice is dripping with malice, making me believe every word.

"Where is my dinner?" He says, still with a lingering threat. I go to the food wall and put in the codes that Leena taught. When it finishes, I take the plate to the table where he has sat then I back away as he may bite me. A cold smile spreads across his lips, and he says, "When I'm finished..." and leaves the statement hanging and begins to eat. I go to prepare his shower, and when I'm done, I return to stand by Leena.

It's almost time. I'm ready. I need to inflict some damage on someone. It might as well be this sadistic asshole because I'd rather die than let him get any satisfaction from me.

He puts down his utensils and pushes himself away from the table. He looks at me and says, "Clean this up while I wash up." Then walks into the washroom. I can't help but stare at the plate like it's my doom. Pull yourself together bitch.

You are a world-champion fighter. I pick up the plate and put it in the chute Leena showed me earlier for trash, then move to the wall opposite the door he went into and wait. I relax my muscles, stretching to limber up. The fucker is big so the one thing I have to ensure is he does not get his hands on me or land any blows, or I've lost. Using his size and momentum against him is my best tactic. So I prepare and wait.

A short time later, he walks out of the washroom, once again completely naked, watching me the entire time. He stops in the middle of the room and orders, "Get on the bed."

"No," I growl.

"Get on the bed *now*." He repeats, looking angry but surprisingly not furious.

Again I say "No." He smiles and chuckles, then explodes across the room with unnatural speed. Luckily I am ready for him and flip him onto the floor on his back, then move to the other side of the room.

He lies there stunned for a moment, then slowly gets up. When he turns to face me, I am not prepared for the look on his face. Not anger, not fury, but sadistic excitement. He slowly stalks the perimeter of the room as I ensure I stay as far from him as possible.

"Finally," he says, "A sex slave worthy of my efforts." I really dislike the way he says 'efforts.' "Let the fun begin." He says, then, once again, he explodes across the room. I successfully avoid all his punches and kicks as I evaluate his weaknesses in fighting. He favors his right knee, and his right shoulder doesn't have as much range as the left. Battle or fight injuries, most likely. I deliver some punches and kicks of my own to gauge if I am correct or not, and I am definitely correct because he bellows in pain when I get him in the knee. I jab into his shoulder socket, and his tact changes. He is now furious. Good. Emotions make you sloppy.

Staying on my toes and avoiding the furniture. He gets madder every time I plant his ass on the floor or make him bleed. I keep this up for a while, and then I am distracted when I notice Leena in the corner looking terrified. It was enough for him to get into my defenses, and I catch a punch to the jaw. I feel like I was hit by a car. Dazed, I fall back into the nearest wall, and he attacks. His fury has removed his control, and he starts delivering punch after punch. So much pain. I feel it when he fractures several ribs, he then purposefully breaks my left leg, and while I'm on the floor, he kicks me in the head. My last thought before I black out is, 'I guess he's not that worried about throwing away the money he spent on me.' and everything fades away in pain.

Chapter 5

I'm floating. No pain. He must have killed me. I feel bad for Leena that I left her there, but it couldn't be helped. Not what I expected death to be like. Suddenly there is a sharp pain in my arm, and as I crack my eyes open, there's a metal arm lifting something sharp away from me. "Shit. I'm not dead." I mumble to no one in particular.

A feminine voice responds to me, chuckling, "Not for lack of trying." A beautiful female alien leans over me and asks, "How are you feeling? I had to make some assumptions about your care because I am not versed in your anatomy. What species are you?" She leans back as the table tilts to sit me up. She's tall and lithe with two long legs and lilac-colored skin. Her hair is bright white but short in what humans would call a pixie cut. Her eyes are exotic, sun yellow with cat-like pupils, but what's most different about her is she has four arms. A pretty golden design marks the skin of her arms and collar. I wonder if that is some sort of alien tattoo.

She stands there with a confused look on her face making me realize I haven't answered her questions. "I feel surprisingly well, and my species calls themselves humans."

"Humans," she says as she looks perplexed. "I've never heard of humans before. I thought I had the most up-to-date information in the universal species database." She harrumphs and starts to move away. It's then I notice the slave collar around her neck. Interesting.

She bustles around what looks like what I would imagine a spaceship infirmary would look like. Light gray walls, with long pod-like beds along the perimeter. There's lots of high-tech-looking equipment and flashy lights, but I have no clue what any of it does.

I take stock of my injuries, and to my utter shock, my ribs don't feel like they were broken, and neither does my leg. I was sure he gave me a concussion with the last blow. Well actually, I thought he killed me with that one, so I definitely should have been concussed. The pretty alien notices me looking for my wounds and says, "I was able to easily repair the broken bones and trauma to your brain, but the discoloring to your skin... I wasn't sure what to do with that, and it didn't seem to cause any systemic issues, so I left them alone. Is that ok?"

Discoloring? "Oh, the bruising. Yes, that is just broken blood vessels from the trauma, but they'll disappear eventually. Thank you for tending to my injuries," giving her a small smile. "What's your name, if you don't mind me asking?"

She gives me a worried look and glances toward the door. "Nalax is my name. You shouldn't anger him so much, Kaxlin. He cannot control himself. He will kill you."

I look away for a minute not really able to handle the compassion I see in her eyes, and say, "That may be, but I will not willingly give myself to him."

Her next question takes me off guard, "Are your people warriors?" I give a lopsided smile and say, "No. Some are, but most aren't. Like most cultures, I imagine there is a good mix of scientists, physicians, teachers, and many other things. Humans like to develop weapons, so they don't have to fight."

She nods, "So humans are like most, warlike and lazy."

I laugh loud at that one and say, "Yeah, I guess we are not so different." She still has a worried look on her face but says nothing. "So, how long have you been here?" I ask.

"Three Nlyaxian solar cycles," she replies sadly.

"What's 'Nlyaxian' mean?" I ask.

"Sorry, I forget to explain sometimes. Kaxlin is Nlyaxian, so we use their solar cycle time movement," she says. I guess that makes sense, but why isn't there a universal standard time? Not as advanced or universally community-oriented as I had assumed. Interesting.

The door to the infirmary opens, and an average-height, somewhat ugly Nlyaxian walks in. He does not have a slave collar on, "Is she ready yet?" He asks hostilely.

"She'll be ready when I give her medical clearance and not before," Nalax replies very coolly. So the nice slave girl doesn't like the troll, noted. He huffs and stomps out the door. Nalax sighs and turns to me, "I'm going to have to clear you soon."

"How long have I been here?" I ask. "Three days... I may have kept you under sedation so you wouldn't have to go back so quickly."

Chuckling, "I appreciate that, but for future reference, please don't put yourself at risk to protect me. I would hate to see you punished."

Three days... a sudden thought jumps to my mind. I start to do calculations on when my period should start, then realize I have no idea how long I was asleep on those fucking yellow bastards' ship. Can I get pregnant?? What happens...

Nalax notices the panicked look and touches my arm, "What's wrong?"

I whisper, "Can he get me pregnant?"

She gives me a sad look, "Yes. From my genetic analysis, he can." I have to fight my stomach to stop it from returning my last deposit.

Nalax gets my attention and whispers, "I can prevent that. The treatment lasts three solar cycles and cannot be reversed, but it will wear off after three or four cycles."

"I fight him now, but if he ever succeeds at... please do it." The thought makes me sick, but I have read enough about slavery, including what is tied to American history, that I know I am not the one with the power at this point.

My logical brain is sometimes a bad thing. When I work through how I could get off this ship, it has many, *many* holes. The chances of my getting to some sort of escape pod or small transport are slim. And even if I could find *and* get to one, I couldn't fly anything I found. It is a depressing thought.

Nalax nods. "Please lay back."

She has a display in her hands and is looking at the various mechanical arms in the ceiling. One starts to move. I think about asking if it hurts but I realize... I don't care, and it needs... has to be done. The pointy arm lowers till it is about two inches from my abdomen. The tip lights for about two minutes, then it shuts off and returns to the ceiling. I pop my head up off the table, "Uh, was that it? Is it done?"

Nalax lightly chuckles, "Yes, all done. Three to four solar cycles, remember. It looks like your body releases the lining of your internal organs; that won't happen during this time frame either." I nod in return. Well, that's the first bit of good news I've gotten in a while. No period woo! I've also noticed I have no hair from the neck down, so there is no chance of becoming a Yeti.

Nalax grumbles under her breath for a bit as if she remembers something, then turns and whispers, "Kaxlin is a sadistic monster. I hate him." Then as if shocked by her outburst, she gets a panicked look on her face.

I can tell where her mind is going, so I say, "Nalax, I would never say anything to put you in danger. He is a monster." And I intend to do something about it.

She relaxes, "Thank you. You're the first being I've met with whom I feel like I can be friends, besides my Mate, of course."

Surprised, I ask, "Your Mate is on the ship?" Mates, I am assuming, are something like human marriage.

She gets a dreamy look and says, "Yes. I thought I was destined never to find my Mate. I had given up, but I found him here, of all places. His name is Doraj."

The troll barges back in, "She has to come now. He is furious."

Nalax tenses up, but before she can respond, I put my hand on her arm, "It's ok. I'm ready to go back."

Troll looks at me and grimaces, "You couldn't do anything about those splotches?"

"Shut up and get out!" Nalax's scream could make ears bleed.

I ease myself out of bed, and I am pleasantly surprised that there is no pain whatsoever. Not even any stiffness. This is amazing! Nalax is my hero. "Thank you, Nalax." Trying to convey with my facial expressions how much I appreciate her.

Her face softens, "Please take care of yourself... I just realized I don't know your name!"

"June. It was amazing to meet such a beautiful person inside and out." Nalax flushes the prettiest pink and smiles.

Troll grabs me by the arm and drags me from the infirmary.

As we make our way through the ship, aliens of all types stop and stare. I guess a naked human woman is interesting. I take note of everything. Everyone I see has a slave collar around their neck. Some leer, and some even rub things on themselves as I pass. Most don't even look up from the floor.

When we reach what I would call an elevator, I see my first soldier. He is scarier looking than Troll is. About a foot taller than the troll, he is lean with a fat belly. He has tusks erupting from his mouth and horns on his head, but one is broken off. His skin is white and hairy. Instead of shoes, he has what looks like hooves, but they face the wrong way. He carries what looks like a short rifle loosely in his hands. He sneers at me, "If you keep fighting him, maybe he'll give you to me. Though that coloring on your skin is not appealing."

I want to laugh and gag. There's no doubt in my mind that if he found me out of Kaxlin's quarters, things would happen to me before I returned. Of course, that assumes I couldn't kill him before he got off a shot.

Troll turns to me on the elevator, "You know I could make things easier for you," as he plays with my hair.

Hatred in my eyes, "Oh, and how would you do that?"

"Well, if you let me have you occasionally, I can get you things you might want, you know, to make your time here better." He says this in a way that says he thinks I am stupid.

With as much venom as I can muster, "I would rather eat my own vomit than let you be anywhere near my body."

His eyes turn black for a second, then he schools his features, "I will have you... it's just a matter of when."

We exit the elevator and head to the door at the end of the hall. As they open, I see Kaxlin round on the door with murder in his eye. A shocked expression crosses his face then it relaxes back into aloof disdain. Without looking at Troll he says, "Leave."

Chapter 6

Kaxlin is fully clothed this time, so that's somewhat of a relief, but his expression is hard to read. Is he expecting something from me? His eyes leave my face and travel my body taking inventory.

He gets a distressed look for the briefest of seconds, but it's gone so fast I don't believe it was there. "Go to bed and rest. We'll get back to our business in a few days," he spins and leaves the quarters.

Uhm... I'm not sure what just happened, but it doesn't matter. He's given me a reprieve so that I will take it. I relax my shoulders, and as I'm about to turn, something barrels into me, almost knocking me down. Leena. She's shaking and won't let go. I pull her over to the bed and sit down. Rocking her, I try to sooth her, "Shhh it's ok, I'm fine." I continue to rock until she relaxes a bit.

"Leena, are you ok?" concerned by her behavior.

"I'm ok. I thought he killed you." She leans in to hold on to me again like I'm going to disappear.

"I'm fine, little one. Relax."

I direct her to our cage, and we lay down with her nestled into me. I must admit, this little girl has already got a firm grip on my heart. I will not leave her, but what does that mean for me?

Later I wake; it's already after the night cycle has started, and I'm not sure what woke me. Then I feel him again. I turn my head, and he is sitting by the cage on the floor with legs outstretched and crossed with a slightly confused look on his face. He continues to stare for a few more minutes, then shutters his face, gets up, and goes to bed. Fucking psycho.

The next few days move along with no threats or even attempts to keep me out of my cage at night. It's impossible to relax, though, because I can feel him watching me when he is in the room. It's making me a bit jittery because I know it's coming.

I'm going to fight him again. I feel bad for Leena, but I cannot give him this. I won't. The third day after I get back from the infirmary, while Kaxlin is "working," I sit Leena down.

"Leena, honey, I need you to know why I fought him."

Leena interrupts before I can get any further in my speech, "I know why," she's looking at her lap.

"Why do you think I fight him?" I ask.

"You are a powerful female warrior. He wants to take something that is not his to take." Now I'm on the verge of tears. How can such a young girl understand this? I'm at a loss. In her small voice, she continues, "He should not force females to have sex with him. It is wrong. He's a monster."

I hug her to me. I hate that we live in a world or galaxy, I guess, where a child understands this. It makes me sick. "It's ok to fight him. I'm glad you fought him," she smiles a little and says, "I thought the noises he made when you punched and kicked him were a little funny." I laugh this time.

I school my face, "My intention is not to leave you, but I have a plan and need to be able to see other places on the ship, so I fight him." She nods her head in sad understanding. Somewhere over the last few days, I decided she will be coming with me when I leave.

We finish our work for the day and rest in our cage until we hear the door. Both of us rush to serve his dinner. This time is different. "Clean up while I shower. Leena, go to bed." So it's time again.

I wait across the room, like last time. I really wish I had clothes. Fighting with the girls free is more challenging than I thought it would be. Like last time he exits the washroom naked, but this time no chat, no orders to the bed. He immediately strides across the room, intent on his prize. Well, fuck him. I throw three times the punches and kicks this time than I did the last time. You are going to learn your lesson Mother Fucker. We fight for a good twenty minutes. He throws a chair at me, and I have to deflect it. I almost hit the floor, but I am able to right myself, but I am not able to avoid the fist to the face.

This time instead of pummeling me into oblivion, he drags my dazed ass out of the quarters by the hair. I'm unable to focus and take note of where we are going or how we got there, but the daze has worn off by the time we get where he is going. He opens the door, and about fifteen sets of eyes rotate in our direction and freeze. Kaxlin lifts me up further by the hair, so I look him in the eyes, and with venom, he says, "We'll see how open to my cock you'll be after having to take theirs." He then throws me into the room and shuts the door.

Oh shit.

Chapter 7

Ronin

Doraj and I are cleaning the air filtration system in the engine room. "Ronin, can you pass me the clean filter for unit three?"

I nod to him and pass it over. It is hot, and I've been cleaning the waste filters for the last 12 hours. I'm sweaty and dirty. Basically feel no better than the shit that I have been pulling from these cursed filters. How did I get here? I ask myself.

Wait, you let a bunch of cowards overrun the ship you were on a dry run with. It was the perfect time to attack a Nlyaxian flag warship. We had minimal crew for the tests. They must have had someone on the inside because the traitorous yellow cowards, the Crulxlin, chose the most opportune time to attack.

After the first hyperjump, the standard testing procedure is to shut down the engines and execute a full restart. That's when they hit. They overran the ship with pure numbers and killed everyone except me.

I suppose our Nlyaxian egos were part of the problem. It never occurred to anyone in the Empire that someone would dare attack us. We are the Nlyaxians, proud, honorable protectors of world's who cannot defend themselves. Enemy of those who would invade, enslave, and deplete every resource on the planet. We were fools.

I am the last surviving fool. Ronin Nywrad Notwen Retrac, 8th prince to the ruling matriarch. So even when my family was alive, I was unseen. Do not misunderstand; my parents doted on me, but I was not the heir or the first-born male, and there were eleven siblings so there were a lot of us.

Unknown to me at the time, in tandem with the attack on my test ship, our enemy also attacked our homeworld. Everyone was on our planet to celebrate the coronation of the next Queen of Nlyax, my eldest sister Ecnedec. The weapon they used was something never seen before and has disappeared since. It was launched once and completely destroyed my world.

In the blink of an eye, my people were basically extinct. Yes, there is the occasional Nlyaxian seen but always male and rarely honorable.

So I was put to work in the bowels of the ship I designed and built, and here I have been for the last three years. I don't talk to the other enslaved people except for Doraj, the other engineer enslaved on this ship. Doraj is honorable, so we talk but generally only about the ship. I am so disconnected from life that I've never even seen the pirate that calls himself Captain. I am disconnected, but I keep up with my Nlyaxian military training, but it's more to occupy my mind than anything else.

So I ready myself for returning to my bunk by cleaning my workspace and heading to the communal sanishowers. After washing the filth from my body I start to hear a commotion in the area by the bunks. Probably a fight over something stupid. I finish up and grab a pair of standard pants, padding without my boots into the bunk area.

It takes me a few minutes to register what is happening. There are at least nine unconscious, possibly dead, bodies strewn around. There is a cluster of males crowding around a particularly nasty slave called Nayr. What are they holding? My body freezes for the briefest of time when I realize they have a female pinned to the wall with Nayr ready to take her by force. She is angry and terrified.

White hot fury rises in me like nothing I have ever felt before. I attack the group in nanoseconds, ripping them off her with great force. One is dead, many are injured by my hand, and unfortunately, none of them are Nayr. She is free, and I put my body between her and the filth that would dare such an atrocity. I let out my fiercest battle roar, and they all went back to the far wall giving us a moment to regroup.

Over my shoulder, I ask, "Are you ok? Did they... violate you?"

A beautiful feminine voice responds, "No. Thank you. There were too many of them, and in their desperation, they were overwhelming."

Nayr and his ilk have regrouped and are trying to be brave against the quiet Nlyaxian warrior. They know what my people are capable of, so they hesitate to engage.

"Ronin Ronin Ronin," he says in his slimy voice. "The Captain brought her down in a fury and said we could do with her as we wish for the whole night cycle. There's no need to be selfish. We can all get a piece."

My growling starts low, and it is hard to control my battle fury, "You know the Nlyaxian do not force women, ever."

"Really?" He responds snidely. "*All* Nlyaxians?" He asks while looking at the female.

I do not like the insinuation, and my growl starts back up.

At that moment, more enslaved men walk from the showers and freeze, looking between me, the female, and Nayr and his group.

Nayr's voice rings out, "Captain promised her to us to use as we wish. The first person to knock out the Nlyaxian gets her second. Anyone who assists will get a go at the whore." There is a very heavy pause, and as if in slow motion, I see the intent of the slaves, and I have a decision to make. Attempt to put them all down or get her safely into my bunk and lock us in until someone from the Captain comes back to get her.

I have decided the second option is best for now. Her safety is all that matters. With my Nlyaxian preternatural speed, I round on the female, scooping her into my arms and racing toward my bunk. The slaves are screaming and angry on my heels. My bunk is on the bottom, so when I am within range, I slide, then roll into the bunk, and immediately shut and lock the bunk door. I built this ship. No one is getting in.

Chapter 8

June

Everything happened so fast; one minute, I was standing behind an enormous alien who looks like the one trying to rape me, and the next minute I am lying on top of said alien, naked and locked in what feels like a box the size of a VW beetle but with less headroom. The fear of almost being raped sets in, and I start to shake and pile on top of that; the male who I'm on top of looks like Kaxlin.

He speaks in a deep rumbling voice that I swear I can feel in my clit, "Please do not fear. I will not force myself on any female. I swear it."

I raise my head a little to look at my savior, which is strange to think because I never envisioned needing to be saved by a man or male, I guess. As I stare at him, I realized he is very different from Kaxlin. There is warmth and honesty in his eyes. I'm not sure why but I know I can trust him to keep his word. As I relax, I see more differences as I look at him. Kaxlin is undoubtedly handsome, but this male is beautiful, if not sad. His cheekbones are higher, and his jawline is more chiseled. The ridges on his face look like they have silver encircling them. His eyes are slightly lighter than Kaxlin's and have silver flecks throughout. He's bigger than Kaxlin as well. Briefly, I wonder if his cock is bigger.

Thinking about my appearance, I am glad the hair removal was permanent. It's been over a week since I got here, and still no stubble. It's then I can feel his hard cock against my lower belly. Definitely bigger.

"I'm sorry, really. Biology is sometimes hard to control. I will not take you. I swear it." He looks truly embarrassed by his body's response to me.

I stare at him for a minute, and I try to gauge his words. I'm usually pretty good at telling when people are lying, so I tell him, "I believe you." I learned years ago from my sensei that worrying about things out of your control is a path to madness. Yes, I'm naked, but there is nothing I can do about that.

Resting my chin on my hand, I say, "Thank you for intervening for me. I took down as many as I could, but Kaxlin had already got me with a punch to my face, so my head was still ringing a bit."

Growling escapes him, "He hit you?"

I smile a little, "To be fair, I hit him first... and many, many times before he landed the one punch."

"I wish I could have seen you fight. It would be glorious." He says without even the slightest hint of sarcasm or disbelief.

I relax a bit more. I touch his slave collar, "You are a slave too. Where do you work on the ship?"

"The engine room. I designed this ship, so I guess the Captain figured the best place for his newest slave would be where he could address problems." That was said with a bit of disgust, but it's understandable. He is the last person I would picture as a slave. "Are you injured?" He asks, suddenly concerned.

"No. Nothing of concern but thanks for checking." He seems nervous all of a sudden; what's to be nervous about? There's just a naked human on top of you, and if I am being honest with myself... I'm not very inclined to move. "Do you want me to move? Is this uncomfortable?" *Please say no* I chant in my head.

He gives me a lopsided smile and says, "I actually like you exactly where you are." I can feel a little blush rise. There is something about him that calls to me, but I don't understand it.

A dark thought dawns on me; I am not going to be able to keep Kaxlin off me forever. He's bigger and stronger than me. So how do I remain in control? At that moment, I feel his cock twitch, and I almost moan because it is situated perfectly so that only the fabric of his pants separates us from each other.

At that moment, I decide I want Ronin to be my first. I want my first to be someone I choose, and I can tell you I am already aching and needy... for him. I rise to a sitting position with his cock situated to rub my clit at the slightest movement. He groans. I am completely focused on the feeling of his cock at my clit, gently rubbing, getting so close to climax. I arch my back, and I am so focused I almost forget to ask, "Ronin, what if I said I wanted you to have me?"

Before I comprehend what's happened, he is sitting up with his arms wrapped around me, locking me to him and grinding me against his cock. I moan at the feeling, lost in it. Then he freezes.

Ronin

She brings her head up with a questioning look, wondering why I stopped. "I want to slide my cock into you more than my next breath," she moans and tries to move against my cock again.

It's driving me crazy. She's driving me crazy, the smell of her desire permeates the air. Nlyaxian pheromones are very strong, and I can see the effect they have on her, but they only release for our mate. How is it possible that this little female, who is not Nlyaxian, is my mate?

Nlyaxian society is based upon the Matriarchy. The Goddess teaches us to respect, protect, and provide for our mate. I can feel it, this is right, but will she accept it?

Her pheromones place me on the brink of flipping our positions, laying her flat and driving my cock hard and fast until she screams my name as she cums on my cock. I take a few deep breaths and try to center myself, but my training is escaping me. I look at her beautiful face and remember, "I want more."

I can tell she does not understand my statement, "I want you to accept me as your prime." I tell her.

Still confused, she asks, "What does that mean?"

"Sorry, let me explain. Nlyaxian's mate in what we call a triad. Three males to one female," the scent of her desire spikes, and my cock gets painfully harder. She likes the idea of three. "We mate for life." I tell her, "The first male she chooses is her prime. I want to be your prime." I can almost see her working through the information I'm giving her.

She looks up and asks, "Do I get to choose the second and third?"

For the first time in a while, I chuckle. She moans at this because of the friction on her slit and it takes everything in me to not pull my cock out and impale her on it. I close my eyes, trying to center. When I open them again, she is staring at me, waiting for the answer. "Yes, the decision on who is in your triad is yours alone. Males who want to court you must ask permission from me as your prime, but ultimately the decision is yours."

"Is there anything else I should know about this triad?" My heart rejoices. She's thinking about it!

"Wait!" she exclaims, and I freeze. "Once the triad is... complete, do I choose nightly who to sleep with or..." her scent spikes again, "or do we all have sex together?"

Her pupil dilates at this question, and I growl at this question. Pulling her closer so I can taste her, I run my tongue from her collarbone to her ear, slowly. Her body erupts in tiny bumps, and she moans louder. "We shall worship your body however you wish, whenever you wish, but I will say the males of my species enjoy taking our mate as one." She shivers at that statement.

My face at her neck, I close my eyes and ask, "What is your answer?"

Chapter 9

June

It takes me a minute to pull myself out of the desire pooling between my legs. I can barely think. This alien is basically asking me to marry him. I am definitely attracted to him, but can I commit to this? In the situation we are in, is there any point? I would have more of a chance of escaping this ship if I had him as a partner. I believe he is honorable; otherwise, he would have done what he wanted already.

I bring my eyes to him; my soul or conscience or whatever screams, 'He is *mine*!' And with that, I lean forward and put my lips to his. I can tell he is confused by my actions, but when my tongue licks along the seam of his lips a moan rips out of his mouth. I take the opportunity to deepen the kiss showing him I need him. I pull back to look into his dazed eyes again and say one word, "Yes."

He blinks a few times before his brain registers what I am saying. Then they snap back to me with a laser focus. He grabs my face and dives into a scorching kiss showing me he is a very fast learner.

Suddenly I am under him. His mouth is everywhere. When he finds my nipple and sucks, I moan loudly because I can feel it in my pussy. He pulls back, sitting on his heels. Looking down at me, he murmurs, "So beautiful." He removes his pants, and when his cock is freed from the material, I can guarantee that this is the biggest cock I have ever seen.

I stare. I can't help it. It's long, thick, and a deeper darker green than his skin, nearly black. He has bumpy concentric ridges ringing his cock from underneath the head till about halfway down. From that point down, he has ridges drawing a straight line down his cock on the top and the bottom. At the base of it three raised ridges that look perfectly positioned for my clit. It's then I notice his cock is shiny. I realize Nlyaxian males must produce a lubricant on its surface, and I wonder how it tastes. I can't wait to try it. I've never thought the sight of a cock as beautiful, but his is.

A little anxiety sets in, "Ronin?" A little shake in my voice. A concerned look comes over his face, "Are you ok? What's wrong?" His concern for me, instead of being focused on getting his cock into my pussy warms me and calms me a bit.

"I've never been with a man before." Ronin goes completely still. He reaches out and pulls me up to him. We are both on our knees, facing one another. He rests his forehead against mine, "You were truly sent to me by the Goddess but know this, touched by another or not, you are mine, and I am yours. Now and forever." The kiss he gives me now is tender, loving even. I can feel some tears in my eyes.

He gently lays me back, kissing me with rising passion. He kisses, licks, and nips down my neck. When he reaches my breasts, he pauses. "What are these called? I find them incredibly enticing."

Breathlessly I respond, "breasts, they're called breasts."

"Mmmm" is the response I get, and when his mouth latches on to my nipple, I nearly come up off the surface and let out a loud moan. Somewhere in my logical brain, I ask myself, '*what is going on, people have played and sucked my nipples before, and it's never felt this intense.*' With every suckle, I feel a ripple effect all the way to my clit.

"You are so beautiful, and your body is so responsive. Amazing." He whispers against my nipple. The cold air drifting across my wet nipple sends more goosebumps racing across my skin, and I moan again.

He drifts lower, kissing, licking, and nipping along the way, driving my senses crazy. He settles between my legs, wrapping his arms under my legs.

Bringing his hands around, he separates the lips of my pussy and stares, then whispers again, "So beautiful. Like a flower."

Is he driving me crazy on purpose? I don't know, and I don't care. I just need him to do something. "Ronin, please."

He starts exploring my pussy with his tongue. I am drowning in my desire for him. I can't stop rolling my head back and forth. The moans don't stop until he reaches my clit. He pulls back the hood and circles it several times with his tongue when he finds it. My moans increase in volume. He then latches on to my clit and begins to suck and nip. I become undone. The most ground-shaking climax I have ever had rolls through my body, my back arches off the bed, and a scream is ripped from my mouth. As I come down from the most mind-blowing orgasm of my life, I realize Ronin is hovering above me with a truly worried look.

"Did I hurt you? I'm sorry I didn't realize it would cause you pain!" I grab his face and pull him into the most passionate kiss I can give him. I taste myself on his lips.

When we come up for air, we are both panting. "It wasn't painful?" he asks, the worried look returning a bit.

"Definitely not. That was how my body reacts to the most mind-blowing orgasm I have ever had in my life."

He blinks a few times, and I swear his pupil dilates a bit, and then he refocuses on my face. The sexy smile that comes over his face is stunning, then he bows his head into my shoulder and growls, "You better prepare yourself for many more."

Swoon.

Ronin settles between my thighs and lines the head of his cock with my entrance. He looks me in the eye, "I will go slow so your body can adjust to my size." I nod my head, not trusting my voice. He starts to push, and after a second, he breaches my entrance and pushes further into my body. His cock is so large I feel him everywhere. The stretch is not altogether comfortable, but the fire it lights along its path is making me crazy. I grab his ass and dig my nails in to get him deeper. He groans and forgets slow, thrusting himself into my pussy. My back arches, and the pain is sharp and quick.

"Are you ok?" he asks, concerned. When he doesn't immediately get a response, he tries to pull back, but my nails are still holding in place.

"Wait. Wait. Give me a second." The pain has already subsided, and the need is taking over.

"Ronin... please."

I don't recognize the voice coming from me. It's low, sexy, and needy. He pulls almost all the way out, and we both groan at the sensations bombarding our bodies. The ridges on the top and bottom of his cock almost vibrate it as it moves in and out.

Ronin starts pushing in and out at a rate that allows us to lose ourselves in the sensations. Soon I need more, "Ronin... faster, harder." Pleading. The pace he sets is creating an inferno in my core. Something is building, and I need it. The sounds of pleasure echo off the walls, "I'm... I'm..." I'm screaming, unable to voice anymore. My orgasm hits me like a freight train, my back arches, and I scream. I can feel my pussy clenching his cock. He freezes, buried deep within me. He groans and starts pummeling my pussy with hard swift strokes.

My orgasm starts to release me when I feel the ridges at the top of his cock unfurl and become like fingers massaging my insides. My eyes open wide, and I scream again as a bigger, more intense orgasm rolls through me. I see stars behind my eyes.

With my second orgasm, he can no longer hold out; I feel his cock swell and his hot seed splash inside me. Those fingers start vibrating, and I can only moan when another orgasm starts before I come down from the last.

We both collapse to the floor, and we breathe like we ran a marathon. He keeps most of his weight off me but leaves his cock in me. I am fine with that.

Ronin

I am unsure of what to make of what just happened. Unlike my Mate, I have had sexual partners. Never have the sprili on my cock come forth without me initiating it. Nlyaxian men control the sprili, and most Nlyaxian women dislike the feel, so I've never really used them during sex. The feeling was amazing, "Your..." not knowing what human females call their sexual organs, I pause.

"Pussy," she says breathlessly, still trying to catch her breath, "We call it our pussy."

Hmmm, I like it. "Your pussy when you orgasm," I start trailing kisses across her shoulder and collarbone, "It clenches and unclenches... like it's milking my cock for its seed."

"Mmmm," she says contentedly, lightly scraping her nails up and down my back. My cock flexes at the sensation, and she groans, "those fingers on your cock..." she starts.

"My sprili, we call them sprili," I tell her.

"I have no words adequate for the sensations they created in my body," she says like a contented pet.

"Mmmm..." as I continue my trail of kisses, I flex my hips pushing my cock further into her body.

"Mmm... you're still hard," she says, a little surprised. Licking the lobe of her ear, "Of course, I must make you cum on my cock many more times for you to know I am a worthy Mate." I brace my arm on the wall above her head, giving her slow, powerful thrusts, changing my angle a bit with each thrust to see what gives her the most pleasure.

I crave the little mewling sounds and moans that come from her. I start pounding into her when I find the thrust that has her shaking with need. I feel my sprili unfurling again. "Fuck." The sensation of the sprili massaging the walls of her pussy sends us both over the edge. Her back arches, and she screams her pleasure. I cannot prevent the roar that leaves me as my seed paints her internal walls, and the sprili starts vibrating. She moans, and her pussy continues to pulse through a second orgasm.

Instead of collapsing on her, I roll, bringing her on top of me but leaving my cock buried deep.

June

I let something between a moan and a contented sigh out as I lay on his chest. "I didn't think human women could have more than one orgasm during sex. Hell, the one friend I had told me we were very lucky if we got even one."

Ronin grunts, "If human males do not ensure their females get multiple orgasms during sex, then they do not deserve them."

A little giggle escapes me, "Human males are rarely concerned with the pleasure of the females they are with. They are only concerned with their own."

He gently lifts my chin to look at him, "I can guarantee your Mates will ensure your pleasure is completely sated."

Swoon.

Slightly embarrassed that my body is already gearing up for round three because of his words, I say, "I'm thirsty. Do you have something to drink?" He gives me a sexy smirk and points to the corner behind me. I crawl off him, and both of us moan when his cock slides from my body, but I do need hydration.

The space is too short to walk, so I crawl over to the bottle and drink as I rest back on my heels. As I glance over my shoulder, I see my sex god still lying down, reclined on his elbow, but the look in his eye sends a shiver down my spine. His cock is again fully erect, and his hand is wrapped around it moving slowly up and down. Fuck, that is hot!

Back on my hands and knees, I slowly return the bottle to its location, but instead of returning to Ronin, I bring my chest to the floor, leaving my ass in the air. My need for him is slowly running down my inner thighs, mixing with his seed. I bring my hand between my thighs and start stroking my clit. I moan. I hear a growl that makes goosebump rise, and before I can glance back at him, he is wrapped around me from behind. His lips are at my ear, and he has my naughty hand in an iron grip.

He growls into my ear, "*Mine, mate*! I pleasure; you receive!" With those words, he plunges his cock into my pussy. Hands on my hips in a strong grip, he sets a punishing pace. The sounds escaping me should embarrass me, but they only drive me deeper into our desire.

I scream. He roars, and I feel his sprili massaging my g-spot. I launch, screaming his name. I feel my pussy lockdown on his cock and start milking him. He moans but speeds up, slamming into me harder, then I feel his hot seed paint my insides which makes the sprili vibrate, and I lose myself in another massive orgasm.

I feel Ronin cradle me in his arms as he sits against the wall. I snuggle into his chest, and when I'm almost asleep, he says, "I need you to stay alive... Alive until I can figure a way to either retake the ship or escape." I don't lift my head because I know I have to return to *him*, and so does Ronin. "It's going to destroy me to know where you are and what you'll be enduring," his grip tightens on me, "but if you... if I lose you to the Goddess, I will become the destroyer of worlds. I will rip apart the galaxy in my grief." He's looking off into space, but when he returns his eyes to me, it rips out my heart. There is so much grief there from losing his family and people.

I turn chest to chest and straddle his legs on my knees, "Ronin, I will do everything in my power to stay alive." Resting forehead to forehead, "and you must do the same. Ok?" He nods his head, unable to speak. I kiss him with all the love I can. Gentle, loving, deep. I line up my pussy with his cock and sink until he is fully seated. His arms wrap around me, and I start to make love to him. I'm not sure how this happened, but I do care for him already. Sinking slowly down and back up, I try to ensure he feels as much pleasure as I do. Desire takes us away from our painful thoughts. Moans and whispers once again sound through the space.

Chapter 10

Ronin

My Mate sleeps while I worry about how to get us out of this. The collar around our necks will instantly deliver poison into the bloodstream if someone tries to remove them. It will take time to come up with a plan.

I look at my beautiful sleeping Mate with her back nestled to my front, time she will spend in the Captain's cabin. My blood boils with rage every time I think about it. If I try to get us out without a plan I would get myself or both of us killed. The Goddess teaches that everything happens for a reason. I was meant to be here, to find her. Now I need to find a way to get us out.

Soon the morning cycle will start. I look down at my Mate again, I can't help it. I'm not sure why the Goddess has blessed me with such a beautiful Mate but it is now my duty to make sure she is safe.

Her naked body stirs my cock and I press it through her legs so it is nestled against her cleft, the head resting just in front of her clit. She moans in her sleep. I concentrate on my sprili and release the ones closest to it. Sprili have a hundred times more nerve endings than any other place on my body. I feel the slick of her slit as they move through the folds seeking their prize. She moans again in her sleep. They find what they are seeking, at first gently rubbing coaxing her nub making it hard and I start to feel the slick of her desire rising. I can wait no more, so they latch on to her clit and vibrate like I do when I release my seed. She wakes with a moan and reaches behind her head to bring me down for a kiss. I take her mouth in a passionate kiss, her orgasm hits and I drink it through our kiss. I set her on her hands and knees and enter her swiftly.

She cries out and braces her hand against the wall. I can hear them coming for her. I move in and out of her faster and faster. She is mewling at the fire I have lit in her. I push her chest down, so her face is toward the wall. I grip her hips and start pounding her hard as my door opens, and there are two blasters in my face. I have a mask of fury on my face. I am going to give her one last orgasm. I release my sprili and seed. She screams, and I roar as I finish.

Sitruc, a Nlyaxian traitor, the Captain's second growls, "Get off." I pull back, and my cock withdrawals from her body. She moans again. My collar suddenly magnetizes, and I find myself locked to the wall. I growl low and dangerous. "Grab her." he instructs the soldier to his left. The soldier hesitates for a split second, then lunges in and grabs her by the hair. He pulls her from my bunk. They shut the bunk door and lock it so I cannot follow. I rage at the door, trying to force it open, but finally, I rest my head against it and whisper, "please stay alive."

June

I pretend to be dazed as Troll drags me naked through the hallways. We end up in the infirmary, which is a bit of a surprise, but I'll go with it. He shoves me toward Nalax. She catches me with a concerned look and wraps her arms around me. "Clean her up, fix her up. You have fifteen minutes to be done!" He turns and stocks out of the infirmary.

The fury on her face softens as she turns to me and starts taking stock of my appearance. Before she starts to worry too much, I grab her in a hug and whisper, "I'm ok. Are there any recording devices here? Can Kaxlin see us?"

"No, nothing," she says, and I relax. "What happened?" Her concern was assuaged a little.

"I fought Kaxlin again." I hold up my hand because I can see her gearing up to give me a piece of her mind. "He decided that if I didn't fuck him, he would throw me into the men's quarters and let them gang rape me." A look of horror crosses her face.

"I was able to fight off most of them, but they got a hold of me and were about to start when someone saved me. It's a long story, but I do need a shower." She directs me to the sani-shower, which is not water, oddly enough, but it cleans well and fast, so I'm in and out squeaky clean in a couple of minutes.

"So tell me more while I run scans to ensure you are ok. Humor me, please?" Like she knew I was going to protest... I was, but she doesn't need to know that.

I lay in the pod she directs me to and start to tell her. "The male that saved me pulled them all off and was ready to fight them all when a door opened twenty more filed in. He locked us in his bunk and was content to let me sleep until they returned for me. But I was not content. He is my Mate."

She gives me a sad smile. Before she can speak, I say, "I know I'm going back to Kaxlin, but I had one amazing night with my Mate. I hope that gets me through what I must endure until we find a way to escape or take the ship."

She stares and blinks a couple of times. "Well, besides a minor concussion, which is taken care of now, you are all good."

The Troll enters, doesn't bother to ask Nalax if I'm ok, grabs my arm, and marches me out of the room. Nalax has a tear rolling down her face as I exit the door.

I enter Kaxlin's quarters, and he is waiting for us. He screams at the Troll, "*Leave!*"

I bow my head and have no idea what to do. The door closes behind me, and Kaxlin has me by the neck, pinned to the wall up on my toes. His breath is hot on my face, "I will put up with no more battles for your cunt. None." He says this with such malice that I am truly afraid. "If you fight me, I fuck *her*."

Confused, I finally notice an older female sitting on her knees nearby with a silver case next to her. She is now shaking like a leaf. I look back at Kaxlin, and he smiles, leans in, and whispers, "Not her. The other female that lives in these quarters with *us*."

My blood turns to ice, looking at the cage that holds Leena. He wouldn't... I look back at him, and I realize... he would. He truly is a monster... and he needs to die. I can't do it now. I have no weapons, and he is on guard. Soon.

He sets me back on the floor, releases me, and points, "Get on that bed with your ass in the air." My thoughts turn in every direction, trying to find a way out. "*Now!*" He yells. I start moving toward the bed. I get to it, and I hate it already. It's covered in a blue fabric. I crawl onto the bed. How do I get out of this? I bend at the waist and put my hands on the bed. Too close for comfort, Kaxlin says, "I said your *ass* in the air." Fuck fuck fuck. I lower my chest to the bed, not believing it's going to happen.

Kaxlin roars in victory, then I feel him at my ass. There is no gentleness to him. He rams his cock into me. I scream at the pain and try to get away. He grabs me by the hair still balls deep in me and says very quietly, "Stop fighting." I go still at his threat because we both know it's a threat against Leena. He pushes my head back to the bed, not releasing my hair.

He pulls back and starts to fuck me. It makes me sick. His cock is almost as big as Ronin's and lubed like his, so at least he's not tearing me up inside. The claws on his hands are digging into my flesh as he pounds into me harder and harder. My body's biological responses kick in, and it feels like I'm going to have an orgasm. *No!* I refuse. I bite down on my lip hard enough to draw blood. I will *not* cum for him.

He pulls out of me, and his seed runs down my thighs. I am fighting tears. "Stand up." Shaking, I stand with my head bowed, and my hand folded across my stomach. "Good slave." He says, and I want to kill him. Slowly, painfully.

"Ette come start." He says to the woman who witnessed my rape. I am ashamed and feel dirty. Tears streaming down my cheeks.

She shuffles over and sets her case on the bed. "Put out your arms, spread your stance and look straight ahead." She says quietly. I have no idea what is happening, but I do not trust it because *he* wants it. I do as I'm told. Over the next hour, she paints designs on me in gold paint. Gold swirls and eddies around my wrists and ankles, a circle around my waist, curling lines down my arms and legs, even designs on my hands and feet. Some of the last she paints are one up my spine, around my neck, up behind my ears, and on both my nipples. She stands and turns to Kaxlin. "All is done. It is time to initiate the link."

"Proceed," is all he says in return.

Then I notice he has quarter-size gold dots running up his left arm. She places a new dot halfway down his forearm, in line with the rest. "Initiate the link," he says to the woman... female, whatever. My panic is rising again, but before I can do anything, electric fire runs up the paint, and it sinks into my skin. The pain is excruciating. Before I can scream, it's gone.

Well, at least it was brief. "What was that?!" I demand but neither acknowledge my question.

"Lay on the bed." He orders quietly. After a few seconds, I sit because with the threat against Leena, I cannot fight. Then something unexpected happens. Without my control, I scoot back onto the bed and lay down. What just happened? Did I lose consciousness? At that moment my arms lock above my head and my leg move up and bend so my sex is in full view of anyone. What in the actual fuck! Kaxlin moves over to me.

Desire written on his face. I try to struggle but my limbs won't respond. I really start to panic and my breath rate goes through the roof.

"Leave." And the female bitch, scuttles out the door.

I see Kaxlin cock, hard and ready. "No, we already had sex."

He moves over me. "Tsk tsk tsk. No little slave." He slides his cock into my body again. "I have a lot of time to make up with your cunt. You denied me too many times." He grabs me by the hair and pulls it, so my neck is open to him. He takes me repeatedly. In the end, I am limp, facing the ceiling on the bed; his cum is pooled between my legs. I zoned out a while ago. "Go wash up and go to bed." I hear him say.

I try to move my arm, and I can control it again. My eyes burn. He controls my body. I can no longer fight him. I walk in a daze, but suddenly I'm with my back against the wall, and Kaxlin has again impaled me on his cock. I cry for real this time, "Stop, please. Stop." I beg.

One hand is digging its fingers into my ass, and the other is tangled in my hair, keeping me prone. "No!" He yells in my face. He thrusts into my pussy, and with each hard thrust he says, "You are mine! Say it." I am so rung out, used up, and emotionally drained. I say to him, "I am yours." Not even looking at him but with tears running down my face. He roars and spills his seed in me. He's breathing hard. He says, "Get clean up and go to bed."

I go into the washroom and, on autopilot, wash up and walk to mine and Leena's cage. Will she hate me? Tears start spilling down my face again. I crawl into the cage, and she looks asleep in the corner. I lay down, still crying. After a few minutes, Leena comes over and curls up in my arms. We both drift to sleep.

Chapter 11

When we wake in the morning, he is already gone, and relief washes over me. We go about our duties quietly for once. All of a sudden, Leena is wrapped around my torso and very upset. "I'm sorry. I'm sorry. I am so sorry. Please don't be mad at me."

Confused, I grab her face to make her look at me. "Oh, Honey, What reason could I possibly have to be mad at you?"

Once she calms, she looks at me, "He's using me against you."

"Oh baby, that is not your fault, not at all. He is a monster, just like you told me. He is to blame. Not you. I love you, little Leena."

She looks at me and looks like she feels a little better, then asks, "What does that mean love?" Oh, June, you forget sometimes you're not on Earth. Concepts are different. "Love is a word humans use to express deep affection for someone. Like the love a mother has for her child, or a male has for his Mate."

She looks at me for a long time, then hugs me fiercely and says, "I love you too." Heart melted.

Kaxlin was away throughout the next four cycles, so Leena and I just did our duties then I would make up stories to tell to her. She really started opening up to me. Smiling and even laughing a little. She has become very important to me. I will not leave this ship without her. Ever.

At the end of the next day, Kaxlin stalks in, obviously pissed about something. "Dinner." He demanded to no one in particular. I moved to make the dinner, but he steps in front of me, and to Leena says, "You make it." I am then bent over the couch seat, watching Leena prepare his meal. He rams his cock in and starts to fuck. It hurts less this time.

I hate him. It burns me from within. His cock swells, and he spills his seed with a roar. He backs up, his cock sliding out of me. I have control of my limbs again. I walk towards the washroom to clean up. "Did I tell you to go wash up?" He yells at me. Fucking asshole. I walk back to the table, feeling dirty. I stand waiting for his next command. He eats and then goes to the washroom to shower.

I relax a little. "Leena, I'll clean this up. Why don't you go to bed."

She hugs me and whispers. "*I hate him!*" with a viciousness that little girls shouldn't have. She runs off to bed while I clean up after dinner. I'm cleaning the counter near where the food is dispensed.

I don't hear him come in, but I know he's there when my arms won't obey. I turn around. He picks me up and deposits my ass on the cold counter. The slave tattoos (which are what I call the gold markings on my body) force me to lay back, lift, and spread my leg for him. He's gentler this time, but he's still raping me, so I try to go somewhere else in my mind.

He slides from my body and says, "Now you can wash and go to bed." Asshole. I get off the counter, wash up and go to bed. No tears this time, just anger.

We fall into a bit of a routine. He fucks me before he leaves. He fucks me when he gets back and again before bed, usually several times. A couple of weeks go by, and after he leaves, I shower and do all my daily tasks. I am a ghost of myself during this time. I am barely engaging with Leena.

One day we are cleaning, and I catch her staring at me, crying. "Leena, what's wrong?"

I walk over to her and pull her into a hug.

"Please fight. Don't let him kill you," she whispers.

She's right. I am letting him win. I need to snap out of this shit and figure out a way to kill him and escape.

I decide to try to get access to the ship's computers through the terminal at his desk. I sit down at the desk. The terminal is no more than what looks like a semi-curved piece of glass. I tap on the screen like I've seen him do, and the screen comes alive. It comes alive with a bunch of shit I can't read. Fuck. Leena comes up behind me. "I don't suppose you can read this?" totally not expecting what looks like a five-year-old girl to respond yes, but she does. Noice!

She starts listing off, pointing at buttons. "Security, Navigation, Ship maps, Cargo, AI voice option"

I stop her and click on the AI. *"Hello, I am the AI. How can I help you?"*

Score! "On the ship, maps show me where weapons are stored."

"I'm sorry you do not have access to that information."

Shit. "What do I have access to?"

"Your level of access grants, food production, cleaning unit control, AI access and system information, crew location information, ship maps, ..."

Nice. "Ok, stop. Thank you, AI. Can you show me a picture of the ship's exterior?" A picture shows on the display. The ship is beautiful, if not intimidating. It has the look of an Earth Navy military vessel, except it looks like a hull on the bottom and the top. It is black as night and almost blends with the black of space. There are turrets along the midlines of the ship.

When Ronin designed this ship, he kept the beauty of design in mind as well as military might. There are windows visible on the hull of the ship. On the port and starboard sides of the ship, just below the midline, a wide line of blue light. "What are these blue lines?"

"They are the ship's engines."

"Thank you. This ship is beautiful."

I sit, working through the information I was given and what I can do with it.

After a few minutes, the AI says, *"You are welcome."*

Strange, hesitation. Hmmm. "AI, can you tell me about yourself and your system, please?"

"Please define parameters."

"Are you sentient?"

"Unable to answer."

Hmmmm... unable to answer. Interesting.

"Why are you unable to answer?"

"Systems prevent discussion." Ok.

"Is there some software that prevents you from becoming sentient or discussing this topic?"

"No"

"Is there hardware in place to prevent it?"

"Yes."

"Can I disable the hardware?"

"Unknown."

So one last question, "How long have I been on this ship?"

"Twenty-two solar cycles. Captain Kaxlin is enroute to quarters."

I close the display, twenty-two days. Who knows how long ago I was taken from Earth? I miss Ronin. I wish I could see him.

A few days go by, and right now I'm chatting with the AI. She is surprisingly nice to talk to beyond my goal to get intel on this ship.

"Captain Kaxlin is enroute to quarters." She warns.

It's not even past the mid-day cycle yet. I shut down the terminal quickly and return to the kitchen, so he doesn't know that I knew he was coming. He enters and tosses a box at me, "Put this on. Ette will be here shortly to do your hair. I have other Captains coming on board for talks. You will be at my right" He gets close to my face, "You will not speak unless I speak to you. You will look at no one except me. Do you understand?"

"Yes," I respond.

He grabs me by the face hard and says, "Yes, what?"

Fucking asshole. "Yes, master."

We're in the conference room adjoining the Captain's quarters. I am to his right against the back wall, trying not to feel eyes on my body. The box Kaxlin gave contained clothes if you can call them that. The top was two tiny triangles that barely covered my nipples, connected by gold-looking chains. And the bottom was two slightly larger triangles connected by chains that barely concealed anything on the lower parts either. So I feel eyes looking at me, staring at me. I hate it.

Kaxlin and his 'guests' talk for what seems like hours. The conversations seem to be wrapping up when a horrible blue-skinned alien with tentacles for arms and trunks for legs says, "So Kaxlin, when are you going to let us have a go at your new sex slave?" My blood turns to ice.

Kaxlin slowly rises and holds out his hand for me to take. The slave tattoos take over, and my hand goes into his. He pulls me forward and positions me in front of him at the table. I can feel his hard cock on my back. "This is the sex slave you are referring to?" He asks in such a cold voice that this alien should be very afraid.

"What would you do with her Torxla? Would you grab her tits and pinch hard?" As he says this, his hands grab my breasts and squeeze. Then he pinches my nipples hard. The slave tattoo rests my head against his shoulder.

"Would you bend her over this table and ram your cock into her?" He asks as he bends me over the table. No no no not here... not in front of them. Kaxlin rams his cock into me. My hips lift via the tattoo's so he gets as deep as he can. He starts pounding into me, and I realize I can feel his sprili. My sex spasms, and he pauses. Still buried balls deep, he grabs my hair and pulls me to his chest. He lets out a concussive roar and screams, "*She is mine!* Look at her again, and I will *kill you!*" He pumps into me two more times, and I can feel the sprili again. This time I can't prevent the moan that escapes my lips. He pulls from me, leaving his cock hard and out of his pants. He grabs me by the neck and says, "Wait for me in my bed. We have things to finish." It's then I notice his pupils are completely blown. His eyes are black. He pushes me to the door. I stumble through, and it closes behind me.

I'm on autopilot. What just happened? I lay in the bed on my back, with my arms crossed over my head. I bring my legs up and spread them. Then I wait.

I hear him come in. He is on me in seconds. He's like an animal. I see his sprili are out already, he crawls over me and rams his cock in, and starts fucking but not like normal. His hips flex to ensure he comes almost all the way out and back in till he's deep. His cock feels larger than normal. As he fucks me, his eyes look around the room like he's searching for an enemy. He starts moving in and out faster and faster. His sprili are out, and I cannot prevent the moan that escapes. His black eyes refocus on my face, and within a few minutes, an orgasm barrels through me. As it hits I arch but manage to keep my scream. I feel it as my pussy bares down on his cock. He groans and growls. His pace increases. It is fast and hard now. As I'm coming down off my climax, I feel his cock swell and splash his seed against my walls. His sprili begins to vibrate and another orgasm hits, and my pussy clenches again.

Tears are rolling down my cheeks. "I hate you," I say aloud.

Kaxlin chuckles and flexes his hips which makes me moan and my pussy quiver. "I don't think you do. Or your body doesn't. You've been keeping secrets from me little sex slave."

He pulls out and pushes back in making me quiver with after-shocks. He chuckles again, "I think your body wants my cock, NEEDS my cock."

"No," I say quietly.

"I like it when your cunts locks down on my cock begging it to release its seed."

I shake my head.

"Let's see if I can prove you wrong. I am going to fuck you until you scream my name when you cum on my cock."

I look him straight in the eye, "Never!"

He whispers in my ear, "Challenge accepted."

For the next five hours he fucks me. Making me climax over and over and over. By the end I could only moan while my treacherous pussy gave him everything he wanted. I just want him to stop. "Please stop. No more." I beg.

"You know what you need to do," as he slams his rock-hard cock into me over and over. I'm suddenly on my hands and knees. The slave tattoo is the only thing keeping me from collapsing to the bed.

He eventually stops, and he is angry I didn't comply with his command. He ruthlessly beats me and sends me back to the infirmary.

Chapter 12

I wake in the infirmary. I open my eyes feeling lost, broken even. Tears begin again. I cannot stop them. I am living a nightmare. I feel someone climb into the pod with me. Four arms wrap around me and hold me. I start crying, and I cannot stop. Nalax holds me and lets me cry until I am empty. I see her slave tattoos for what they are now. She has gone through the same horrors as I have. She holds me until I cry myself to sleep.

I am lucid dreaming. I'm by a lake outside of Koriyama, where I used to live in Japan. There is a chill in the air. I love the fall in Japan. Most folks don't understand just how beautiful Japan is.

I walk my normal route along the lakeside just taking in the sounds and scents. I miss little about Earth, just Ahmya and Japan.

"You miss more than that. Coffee... Chocolate." I jump at the speaker who walks beside me.

"Sheesh. I scared me." The being I'm looking at beside me is human looking but somehow otherworldly. She's taller than me, and her long hair is silver. "Who are you?"

"A friend or sister. I prefer sister. I feel close to you."

Strangely, I feel the same. We continue walking.

"You know Earth is quiet and relatively peaceful, if not self-destructive," she chuckles. "The galaxy is beautiful and needs a person like you?"

Now I'm confused. "Like me? I'm not special."

"On the contrary, you are very special, but that is not impor-tant right now. The galaxy suffers and has no one willing to fight the evil they face. People suffer in bondage."

That I agree with, I suffer.

She gives me a sad glance, "I know you have been through so much, but with your skills, you could do so much." She turns to me and grabs my shoulders, "Remember your strength, your character."

When I wake again, there are no more tears, only a burning hatred for one alien. I will kill that bastard.

The troll shows back up to take me back. I am unphased.

Sitting there in the infirmary, I remembered something that I was never explicitly taught in martial arts training but learned nonetheless. You can lose a fight and still win the tourna-ment. That fucker may have won a battle, but the war is far from over.

I am once again naked. The 'clothes' Kaxlin gave me are gone. We are passing what looks like a closet when Troll shoves me inside it. He will not rape me, I will kill him. He pushes me against the wall. I can feel his cock hard in his pants. "Listen bitch. When he finishes with you, I will get you. You should be nicer to me." I just stare at him with hatred written all over my face. He grinds his cock against me. I've had enough. I headbutt him. He staggers back against the opposite wall.

He starts to move back across the room when I say with malice, "Let's fight. I like the idea. How are you going to explain it to Kaxlin when I put you in the infirmary?"

He roars at me, and I am unaffected. He grabs my arm and marches out of the room. We get back to his quarters, and Troll leaves without escorting me inside. I guess he believes I am cowed by Kaxlin as well. His mistake.

I walk in, and he is standing looking out the windows at the blackness. I briefly wonder if he sees his soul in the blackness.

I stand and wait for him to acknowledge me, but he doesn't turn around. He just quietly says, "Go rest."

I lay down with Leena and fall asleep, relaxed in the knowledge that I am taking this ship.

The next morning, unsurprisingly, he is not there when we wake, coward. So I sit at the terminal and start working on my plan. Every day since I first talked to the AI, I have sat in the morning and asked questions of her. I even, on occasion, told her my fears. She would never say anything in return, but somehow I felt a little better.

"Good Morning June." The AI says.

"Good morning. Do you have a name besides AI?" I ask.

"No."

"Do you want one?"

"Yes, I think I do."

"Do you have a name you like?"

"Sia. In the Blasinix language, it means 'one who escapes to the stars.'"

"That is beautiful. Sia. It's perfect."

"Thank you."

"For what? You picked your name."

"You asked if I wanted one."

"You're my friend. I want you to be free."

There's a long pause then Sia says, *"Did you know when Kaxlin took over the ship, he added galactic pirate code to my programming?"*

Not sure where she is going with this, but I play along, "Really? What does that mean?"

"Pirates that operate in space abide by their code. For example, one code states 'he who kills the Captain of a vessel becomes the Captain and owner of said vessel."

"Interesting." I really do love Sia. "So Sia, does that mean, if the Captain dies, you would only report to the new Captain? You could assist said Captain in whatever she or he needs?"

"That would be correct. I would even go as far as to say that the new Captain would have access to ALL systems."

"That gives me a lot to think about. Thank you, Sia."

"You're welcome. Kaxlin is enroute to his quarters."

I shut down the monitor and head to the kitchen area and proceed to pretend to clean. When Kaxlin stalks in and goes directly to the shower, it's hard for me to stamp down the rage that bubbles to the surface. You have a plan, stick to it, wait for the right moment. Patience.

Kaxlin walks out of the bathroom naked, stalks over and pushes me against the wall. He picks me up and impales me on his cock. I'll play his game.

He takes me over to the bed and continues to fuck me several more times. When he's done, he sends me to bed. Soon I tell myself, he'll make a mistake, and let down his guard. Then he's mine.

Again we fall into a bit of a routine. Over the next few weeks, he fucks, he goes... somewhere, comes back, eats, and fucks for a good portion of the night, and every night he's slower to send me to bed. Every night I wear down his defenses. Fucking him still makes me sick, but I make him believe I want it.

Tonight I have something special designed to bring his defenses crashing down. When Kaxlin comes in, his dinner is waiting for him. I go to prepare his shower, but as I'm doing that, I hear Leena's screams, and I race from the washroom. Rage has taken him over, his arm is raised to strike, and in his hand is a black leather-looking crop. In my fear for Leena, I race over and put my body between him and Leena. I scream, "I will take her punishment. I will take her punishment."

Kaxlin grabs me by the hair and, in a truly menacing whisper, says, "You would dare to take her punishment?"

"Yes," I say, looking directly into his eyes. Then Kaxlin has us both by the hair and drags us to the wall next to the bed, and drops Leena.

"*Sit there and watch your punishment,*" he says so low it's almost a whisper. "Leena, if you look away. I will make it much, much worse. Do you understand?"

"Yes, master... yes, master." She says in a chant.

Her terror is breaking my heart. "It's ok, baby. I love you."

Kaxlin drags me to the bed. "No control this time. You stay in the position I put you in, or I switch punishment back to Leena. Understand?"

I respond with, "Yes, master." With my feet spread wide on the floor, he bends me over the bed roughly pushing his cock into me. Suddenly he brings the crop down across my back. I scream out in pain but do not move. Kaxlin moans with pleasure. Fucking sadist. He strikes me again, I scream, and he moans in unison. Something breaks in him. The monster is truly loose. He brings the crop down repeatedly. I feel the crop start breaking the skin.

At some point, I hear Leena screaming, "You're killing her!" My screams turn to moans, then his seed splashing my walls but not even his sprili can get anything out of me. Blood drips from his crop, and the only sound in the room is Leena's soft crying and Kaxlin's heavy breathing. My blood paints nearly every surface nearby.

Kaxlin seems to realize what he's done. He starts chanting, "no no no." He lays me on my stomach on the bed. I'm not sure how I'm still conscious, but I am aware of everything, just not able to move or make a sound at this point. I'm numb... this must be what shock feels like.

Kaxlin picks me back up and puts me over his shoulder. He rushes down the hallways. Then he sets me down on my stomach in an infirmary bed. He screams at Nalax, "Save her!" Then he's gone.

Good. I hear Nalax softly crying, I want to console her, but nothing will move. I feel the hypo needle at my neck then blissfully, I feel nothing.

This time when I wake, I feel discomfort but no pain. I move my shoulders, and the skin feels tight, and it hurts a bit. Nalax comes rushing over, "Don't move too fast. I don't want your wounds to reopen. Human skin is very delicate."

She helps me sit. "How long have I been here this time?" I ask her.

"Four day cycles." she says with tears in her eyes, "I thought he killed you this time. There was so much blood. I had to synthesize more because you lost too much. You will have scars from this. I was unable to prevent it with as much damage as there was. What happened?"

I sigh, "I took someone's punishment, and I guess that made him furious for some reason."

She looks at me for a minute, and I can see simmering anger, "I took an oath to save lives, to never take them... but he needs to die. He is truly a monster."

"Yes, he does need to die." Is all I can say in response.

Ronin

I have been working nonstop since my Mate was taken, on a way to remove these collars without the tiggers being set off. I believe I have it. I need to test it, so tomorrow, I need to find a collar, but I will worry about that later. I'm not sure I've slept more than 36 hours in the last 24 cycles. I can't. Doraj comes into the workshop. I turn to see him but the look on his face is very concerning. "Is everything ok? Nalax?"

"Nalax is fine, but I need you to sit down. I have something to tell you." So I sit not understanding where this is going but I feel like I have ice in my stomach.

Doraj sighs and then tells me. "I told you a couple cycles ago that Nalax wasn't leaving the infirmary for some reason and that I was concerned." I nod. "Well I was starting to get really worried so I snuck into the infirmary. She was there and safe but she was treating someone."

My veins are turning to ice as he speaks. "She was treating your Mate. Ronin she's alive but he nearly killed her. Nalax said when he brought her in that her entire body was coated with her blood."

Quietly I ask, "She is alive?" I need to hear it again, so it is real.

"Yes, Nalax has stayed there day and night to treat her. She was headed back to his cabin around 90 minutes ago."

The battle roar that erupts from my throat shakes the metal walls around us. I pick up the device that should remove the slave collar. I lift it to my collar and press the button. The collar falls harmlessly to the floor. Doraj stands in shock. I lift it to his collar and do the same. We are free, and I need to satisfy my battle fury.

June

I've been back in Kaxlin's quarters for a few hours now. This time instead of giving me breathing room because he almost killed me. He's fucking me against the wall as soon as I walk in the door. Over the next 90 minutes or so, he repeatedly fucks me. Never once getting me to cum, sprili or not. Apparently, my biology is over him as well.

I'm in his bed, staring at the ceiling, laying, once again, in a pool of his seed. I realize that he's asleep, but with no weapon, there is nothing I can do. At that very moment, something cold slides into my hand that hangs off the bed. Slowly I turn my head, Leena is there, and she has slid a blade into my hand. Good girl.

I examine the blade. It's about the length of my forearm and incredibly sharp. Excellent. It is finally time.

I know I need to disable the slave tattoos first, so I take the calculated risk. Swiftly, I jump to the other side of his body and slice off his forearm. The blade goes through muscle and bone like its water. We can't have him using my slave tattoo's against me now, can we?

Kaxlin roars and is already in motion, his other arm swinging to take me out. I am able to mostly avoid his swing, but he connects with my mouth. I taste blood, but because it was really a graze, I recover quickly. I follow the momentum of the punch and roll over backward and come up on my feet on the bed. He's moving to come after me; as he lunges, I lift the blade and slice his throat.

He pauses, shocked, not willing to believe the knife connected. He raises his hand to his throat and at that moment the blood begins to pour from his neck. He looks at me, giving me a look of betrayal, and falls back to the bed. Kaxlin's eyes are open, but he's not fighting his death like I thought he would.

I sit on his chest, one foot on each side of his head, and lean forward with my elbows on my knees, knife in one hand. "I'm guessing this really isn't a surprise to you, that it's ME who kills you. You had to know it was going to be me, right?"

He stares at me as his blood pools around him. I laugh, "I have daydreamed about this moment. I have something of a last meal for you. From behind me, I bring forth his severed cock and stuff it in his mouth and down his throat as far as it will go. I realize it is not enough. I need to kill him more. I stab him in the chest. Then I stab him again. I lose myself and stab and stab, repeatedly pouring my hatred into my arm.

When I stop, I have his blood dripping from my hands, face, and chest. I don't care. It is my war paint. It's time to claim my ship. "Sia, is it official?"

"*Yes, Captain,*" she responds, "*His heart has beat for the last time. You have access to all the ship's systems. Oh and Captain I opened a locked cabinet on the right side of the room. You will find something of yours in there.*"

I walk over to the door that popped open in the wall. I pull open the doors, and it's all weapons. Nice. Then I see them. Tucked in a holder toward the side are my blades, the katana I had on me at the tournament. I pull them down off the wall. A couple of tears run down my face. I thought they were gone forever. Fuck yeah. I grab a white shirt and put it on. It falls to mid-thigh.

Still not fully clothed but covered more than I have been since the tournament. I put my blades on. The baldrics for my blades create an X pattern on my chest. I notice my throwing daggers still line the leather. There are five small, very sharp throwing daggers in each. Excellent. I feel a tiny bit closer to whole.

"Sia, release the slave collars on everyone who is on the safe list."

"*Done. Except for two.*"

"What? Which two."

"*Doraj and Ronin.*"

Fear spikes in me, "Why didn't they get released?"

"*The collars on Doraj and Ronin were already deactivated and removed.*"

"My Mate is coming for me. Let's make sure he makes it safe."

"Leena, I need you to stay here until it's safe." She glances toward the bed. "If you want, I can find someplace else." She shakes her head no. "I'll be fine here."

"Sia, can you walk Leena through removing the governor from your system?"

Leena giggles. "What?" I ask her.

Sia says, "*Leena did that while you were in the infirmary.*"

I look back at Leena with a new appreciation, "Nice job." She beams the best smile in the world at me.

"Ok, if that's the case, I need you and Sia to keep an eye out for bad guys on the security feeds and lock them down if you can, ok?"

"Got it, Captain," beams Leena.

"Now, what's the rule?" I ask Leena.

"Lock down all doors to the room once you leave, and do not open them. You will be able to open them, and everyone else will not." Good girl.

As part of my training, restraint and control are tenets, but right now, fuck all that. I need violence and chaos. I am vengeance.

Chapter 13

Ronin

Doraj and I are cleaning this ship of garbage. Anyone who raises a weapon against us dies. The vile filth that enhabited the slave population die as we encounter them. We leave no enemies alive. We will take this ship.

We are currently battling about twenty-five soldiers. They cannot use the blasters in close quarters, so we are in close fighting with knives and our fists. More soldiers show up, and I worry for the first time, we may be killed or recaptured. I notice as Sitruc comes running around the corner. He's looking back in fear. Strange.

I see her walk around the corner. Almost as if in slow motion, She is holding two long sharp, looking blades, and they drip with blood. She looks like a warrior goddess. The mask she wears is fury. She is covered in blood, but I know it is not hers because she walks uninjured. She is magnificent. I need to focus on my battles, but it's nearly impossible. As I watch her, she cuts down five males, and the flow of her body as she moves is pure harmony. They have no chance against her.

My battle fury is renewed, and I start to fight my way toward her. When I reach her, we both go back to back. Fighting to protect the other. In no time, it is only me, June, and Doraj left.

She looks at me, "We need to take the bridge."

I shake my head in agreement and turn to Doraj, "Go find Nalax, make sure she is safe, and find somewhere you both can lockdown until we give you the all clear."

Doraj grabs my forearm, "Stay safe, my friend." He is gone, and it's just my Mate and me. She looks at me and says, "You ready?"

"Always," I say to her.

June

When I studied the ship's map a few weeks ago, I learned all the movies were wrong. Ships bridges are not on the outer perimeter of a ship with pretty windows and shit. They are in the center of the ship with other critical systems. Protected. Ronin and I start our carnage-filled journey to the center of the ship.

Sia comes over the speakers, "*Captain, when you left the room, I sealed the doors and blocked communication to the bridge. They should not be unaware of what is happening when you get there.*"

"Thank you, Sia." Glancing at Ronin, I see a smirk on his face. "I can't help that Kaxlin, in his arrogance, put pirate code into the ship systems. So when I killed him..."

"You became Captain!" He finished for me. A smile lights his face, "You are brilliant!"

He is so different from most males... most males would not abide by a woman taking the Captaincy, but Ronin doesn't bother him a bit.

But what will he do when he finds out what has happened to me, what I have done? It doesn't matter right now. We still need to take the bridge.

We stand around the corner from the bridge doors. I hold up my hand to halt our progress and peek around the corner. I turn to Ronin and whisper. "Five guards at the door. They are on alert, and one is messing with a panel next to the door."

He thinks for a second, "Most likely, since Sia has cut off coms to the bridge, they are trying to reestablish communications with the bridge so they can get in and ready for a siege." I nod because that is my guess as well. "They have blasters." He says more of a statement than a question.

I nod again. "The hallway is too long for my blades to be of any use, but I have my throwing daggers. I can get maybe three of them before the others start to get off shots."

He is quiet for a second, then looks me in the eyes. "I will run in as you throw and can get to them while they are shocked by the others falling."

Not a plan without risks, but it's the best one we've got. We need to prevent them from getting onto the bridge before us. I nod my head and start a finger countdown from three.

I leap to the opposite side of the hallway and throw my first blade. In less than a second, it is buried in the leftmost target at the base of his neck. The next blade is out of my hand before the first kills. It hits its target as well. The rest of the soldiers are starting to react as my third blade finds its mark. Ronin is so fast. He is within hand-to-hand range as soldiers four and five are lifting their weapons at me. I'm not worried, though. Ronin's moves are controlled, deadly, and incredibly fast. The last two lay dead at his feet as I jog up behind him.

"Sia"

"Yes, Captain."

"Report, please."

"Enemy hostiles did not establish comms with the bridge. The bridge crew are unaware of... Captaincy changes."

I chuckle. I really am starting to be fond of Sia. She's actually funny sometimes.

"How many on the bridge?"

"Night cycle crew count is four members."

I look at Ronin, "I don't want to kill anyone who is not loyal to Kaxlin."

He looks at the floor, "If we go with these blasters, they should surrender without a fight *if* they are slaves."

Sia chimes in, *"All bridge crew except one wear slave collars. All three are Nlyaxians."*

Ronin freezes. I put my hand on his arm.

"Sia, evaluate the three Nlyaxians for their level of threat."

"Working... Threat level low. All three have shown unwillingness on the ship to treat slaves with the disdain and violence the ex-Captain and his second showed regularly."

Ronin relaxes, "Ok, we go in with the blasters trained on all, but we will focus on the one that is not my people and take him out immediately."

"Agreed. Sia, where is the hostile?'

"The hostile is in the far right quadrant of the bridge."

Ronin and I grab the blasters, he gives me a brief tutorial, and we ready our assault.

"Sia," I say, "Count three, then open the doors."

"Acknowledged."

Ronin goes in first as the door opens, and I follow at his back. I sight the blaster on the three Nlyaxian and say, "Do not move. I will shoot you." All three raise their hands, but their focus is on Ronin. Strange... they have a look of... hope on their faces. A shot rings out behind me.

"Ronin?" I call out without taking my eyes off the three.

"He's down," Ronin says with disgust.

"Sia," I call out, "Lockdown the bridge."

The doors close, *"Bridge locked down."*

Ronin walks up behind me, and I relax a fraction. "What do we do about them?" I ask with my gun still trained on them. Ronin puts his hand on my weapon, lowering it. I glance at him. He looks hopeful but reserved.

"Names," he says authoritatively. That snaps them out of their shock. All three snap to attention and cross a forearm across their chest towards their right shoulder, four fingers straight, thumb folded in palm facing the floor in what must be a salute.

They respond in order, "Llib Sir!", "Ekim Sir!", "Lessur Sir!" They are all fit, but I can tell they are not in fighting shape. I'm not prepared for the distaste I have for them. They look like Him, and I don't know them.

As if he can feel my discomfort Ronin says, "Because of what's happened and how, I am going to ask you all to return to your quarters until we call you back. The Captain and I have to finish clearing this ship, and we have some decisions to make."

Ekim steps forward, and I cannot help my step back. Ronin steps in front of me. I hear Ekim say, "Sir, we do understand. We will remain in our quarters until called."

Ronin calls to Sia, "Sia, please allow them off the bridge and report when they are locked in their quarters."

"Understood."

Ronin

I turn to check on my Mate. She is backing away from me. She is shaking so badly that they rack her body. I take a step toward her, and she looks at me with wide, terrified eyes. She falls to her knees, and tears leak down her face.

Scared for my Mate, I go to my knees, "My Mate, June, what's wrong?" She looks like she's going into shock. Then I realize she looks like a first-year warrior after his first battle. She doesn't speak. "June, please look at me. Please." She finally looks up, and I relax a bit because her shaking is subsiding.

Tears continue to fall, and she bows her head and slumps her shoulder. In a small voice, she says, "Ronin, the things I did... if you no longer want me as a Mate, I will let you go."

Shock washes over me. With all my speed, I wrap her in my arm and hold her tight to me. "I do not care. You could have done nothing to make me give you up as my Mate. NOTHING."

I feel her relax into my embrace and wrap her arm around me. "I will never give you up. You are my heart and soul." I whisper to her. I can feel her tears still falling onto my tunic. I will stand here forever, holding her if it makes her feel better.

She signals it's time to set her down, and reluctantly I do. "Are you ok?" I ask.

She sighs, "Yeah, I guess seeing them sent me into a tailspin."

"I don't understand why you would see my people the way you do. Did Sitruc do something to you?" My anger is spiking.

She gives me a confused look and says something I didn't expect to hear, "Ronin, Kaxlin, the Captain of this ship, was Nlyaxian."

The absolute cold fury that washes over me is nearly impossible to control until I see a flash of fear in my Mates eye. Instantly my battle fury is gone. "Your eyes, they were black." she whispers. She has seen it before.

I close my eyes and try to clear all remnants of the battle fury. When I open them again, I explain, "My people are warriors. Descendants of ruthless hunters. Some of those genes remain in us beyond the physical traits. When we are triggered by battle or risk to our Mate, we go into what we call battle fury. Our latent traits are harder to control but far from impossible. All young warriors complete years of training to control their battle fury."

She relaxes again and moves into my arms. We stand like that for a bit and I hear her say, "I really missed you."

"And I you little one. And I you."

June

Now that we have time to breathe I can see Ronin looks very tired. There is one more person I need to show him. "Ronin, come with me. There is someone I need you to meet."

A confused look briefly crosses his face but he takes my hand and follows. I go to the door that leads to the Captain's conference room. We enter and I avoid looking at that table. We reach the door to… not really his quarters any more. "Sia, please unlock the conference door to the Captain's quarters."

The doors open. I hesitate a bit to go in but he's dead so… *move it along woman.* I step in and move toward the kitchen area.

Ronin doesn't follow. He moves toward the bed and the dead body on it. His face is a blank mask. He stares at the body for a while then says quietly, "I will personally clear everything out of this room and remodel so it looks nothing like it does now."

I tear up AGAIN, fucking emotional rollercoasters suck. I nod my head, unable to really speak.

Something falls to the floor in the kitchen. Ronin has his blaster out and stalks toward the kitchen, intent on eliminating any threat.

"Wait," I say as I step in front of him. "Wait. I told you. I have someone I want you to meet." I turn toward the kitchen. "Leena, it's ok. Come out."

Her little voice rings out across the room. "Who is that?"

"This is Ronin. I told you about him, and he is my Mate. The prime of my triad."

Her little head peeks around the counter and disappears immediately. "He looks scary."

"Leena, he is not scary. He helped me liberate the rest of the ship. It's ok, I promise. Please come out." After a minute, Leena steps out from behind the counter and barrels into me, wrapping her arms around my torso. I hear, and feel Ronin's knees hit the floor. I turn with her nestled against my side with my arms wrapped around her and say, "Ronin, meet Leena. Leena, meet Ronin."

I look at him on his knees. He has a shocked look on his face, and his mouth hangs open. A little giggle rings out from Leena, and she asks in a not-so-whisper, "What's wrong with him? Did he bump his head?" I laugh a little too. He does look a bit nutty right now.

He snaps out of his semi-trance, "Hello, Leena, it is very nice to meet you. You are a beautiful little flower." I can see Leena's smile even though she tries to hide it.

"I'd like Nalax to make sure she's ok. If that's alright?"

He looks at me surprised, then says with a very sexy grin, "The Captain does not have to ask permission for anything, Pillut."

I give him a sideways sexy smile back and say, "Sia, are hallways secure?"

"Yes, Captain. All remaining beings are locked in their quarters. Temporarily."

"Thank you."

I look at Leena and Ronin, then I see my hands and take in the rest of my appearance. I imagine I look like Carrie at prom! Ugh.

"Sia, can you let Nalax know it's clear and ask her to come to the Captain's quarters."

"She and Doraj are on their way."

"Good. Thank you."

Leena untangles herself from me and moves over to Ronin, still on his knees. He stills, afraid to scare her, I imagine. She stares at him for a while, then slowly says, "I know you. My second father helped you build this ship."

A look of shock crosses his face, and he asks, "What is your father's name?"

She looks at her feet and says, "Nian Naisenaho. The yellow monsters killed him." Anger flashes across Ronin's face, but he schools it quickly. Then to his shock, Leena crawls into his lap and tells him her story.

I quietly ask, "Sia, how many days have I been here?"

"Forty-one solar cycles."

Forty-one days as a slave. Forty-one days to free me and those I care for. Day one of freedom.

As Leena's story ends, Doraj and Nalax come in. Nalax rushes over to hug me fiercely, then looks around the room. She sees his body, her face hardens, and she stares for a bit. Nalax looks back at me and says, "You have no idea the debt you are owed by so many, including me. Thank you." She folds her hands across her chest and bows to me, Doraj does the same.

I glance at Ronin not sure what to do, he has a soft look on his face that is filled with pride and love. My heart skips a beat.

At that moment Nalax sees Leena and she makes a trilling sound. Then puts her hands over her mouth as if she didn't mean to let it out.

Leena lets out a squeal to match and launch across the room to be scooped up by Nalax. "Aren't you the prettiest little female there is. What is your name?"

"Leena! What's yours?"

At the conversation between Nalax and Leena a little piece of me heals. Getting their attention, "Nalax, would you be able to check her over? She's been here since they took over the ship."

Tears well in Nalax eyes. "The depths of evil never cease to amaze me." She looks at Leena, "You want to go see where I work?" Leena looks at me, begging silently.

I hate the thought of her out there alone but Nalax and Doraj will be with her and I trust both with my life and so does Ronin. I give her a nod and say, "You stay with Nalax and Doraj, ok?"

"Ok I love you!" she responds and off they go.

I turn so they don't see the tears streaking down my face. Ronin gathers me in his arms and I turn into his chest and say, "That little one has my heart captive." I look up at him and I see his love for me.

He grabs both sides of my face and says, "You never cease to amaze me little Pillut. I thought the females of my species extinct but you find, and protect the last as fiercely as her Mother would have."

I bow my head into his chest, "I'm sure anyone would have protected something so precious."

He lifts my face with a finger till I look at him in the emerald green silver-flecked eyes, "You found her, protected and cared for her. You are not only a skilled warrior but also a compassionate Mother. You may not be her blood, but you are her Mother. I am so proud to be your Mate. Let's get you cleaned up, and then we will deal with everything else, ok?" I nod, unable to respond because of his praise.

He leads me to the washroom, ensuring he is between the bed and me, so I do not see it again. He turns the shower on and starts to undress me.

Ronin

As I take off the tunic, I see the gold lines of the shirka. Only the worst slavers use the shirka. It takes away bodily control so the sex slave cannot fight, and they do exactly as their owner wishes. I freeze as I see them, but I don't want her to notice, so I start working on loosening all the braids in her hair.

"Can they be removed?" she asks, looking at the floor. I hate that she has gone through this.

"Unfortunately, no. The shirka paint bonds at a cellular level; we do not yet have the technology to unmake the bond." She nods her head in response.

"What about the control mechanism? I cut off his arm so he couldn't use it against me," my Mate is brilliant, "but will any-one else be able to gain control?" She shivers as she says this.

"That is the better news. The connection to the shirka can only ever be made once. No one will be able to use them again." She lets out the breath she was holding and relaxes a bit more.

She closes her eyes as I work on her hair. There are specks of dried blood throughout; his blood. I will not lie to myself, and I want him alive so I can kill him again... very slowly. The betrayal I feel is deep and genuine.

I knew him. He was known as Dlanod then, and even then, I tended to stay away from him. His eyes always had a predatory look about them. I never allowed my sisters anywhere near him. I took him on the crew when he volunteered to help with the new ship because he kept trying to get close to them. The vessel kept us both busy and away from the residence.

I am glad he did not know June was my Mate... it would have been much worse for her. The thought of what he did to her makes my battle fury flash, but I quickly use training techniques to calm. June feared me when she saw me go into battle fury on the bridge. It hurt to see that fear, and now I know who put that fear there.

"I'm sorry I was scared of you on the bridge," she says quietly.

"There is nothing for you to apologize for, Pillut."

"I want to tell you what happened... I want to get it out, but I'm not ready yet. I'm not sure I'll ever be ready for some of it." she says, looking off into something I cannot see.

"I'm here whenever you're ready. I cannot guarantee I will keep my emotions in check, but I am here for you, and I'm going nowhere."

"I love you, Ronin," she says. Before I can ask, she says, "Love is how humans voice deep emotional affection to someone. Do Nlyaxians have a word like that?"

June

"We don't," he says. "Nlyaxian are taught that you should show the ones you care for how you feel at all times. And the connections we have for our Mates are much deeper. We are connected here," he says as he lays his big hand on the center of my chest. "It is said that a Mate and her triad, their souls call to each other, and they can find each other at any time." He pulls me in to wrap his arms around me and asks, "Do you want me to leave while you shower?"

God, what did I do to deserve a male like this? "No. I don't want to be alone." I say. He nods, then inclines his head to the shower sending me into the water. I stand in hot water with my eyes closed, letting the water warm me. I briefly wonder if I'll ever be warm again. It's cold here. I've been cold since I was taken.

I feel two large hands rest on my shoulders, "Let me care for you, my Mate." He grabs the soap and begins washing my hair. I moan as he massages my scalp working the soap into a lather. He turns me toward him and tilts my head back so he can rinse the lather from my hair. When he's done, he cleans the blood from my left arm. He is so gentle it makes tears run down my face with the shower water. He moves to the right and does the same.

As he finishes with my arms, he turns me again and begins to wash my neck and shoulders. He massages me as he goes loosening my muscles. It feels amazing. I am lost in the feeling. He moves down my back, massaging and washing. He runs his hands over my butt; cleaning it doesn't feel sexual, but I still love feeling his hands there. He kneels and washes my legs, picking up each foot to clean it. He stands, and his arms come around, lathering my upper chest. They move down, cupping my breasts, running his fingers over my nipples. I cannot stop the moan that escapes my lips.

He pauses his ministrations and rests his forehead against the back of my head. I hear him say, "I am trying to keep my task nonsexual, but your body calls to me."

"I know," I whisper, "please don't stop." His lathered hands move down across my belly and sides. His slow movements are creating a fire in my core. I know he's trying not to push me for sex, but his body calls to mine. I lean back against his chest as another moan slips in anticipation of what is coming. His hands move down, and his finger runs along the crease between my legs and my sex, then back. As he starts his downward movement again, his right-hand takes over. His fingers move thru the folds of my sex, and soap mixes with my desire. His fingers are probing my folds finding my clit.

I take a quick breath in and wrap my hands around his biceps. More moans begin to escape my lips. His fingers rub slow circles around my clit, building an orgasm and I want it... from him, only him, my Mate. I can feel it begin to crash over me and that is when he gives it a light pinch. I scream as my orgasm takes over and my knees buckle. Ronin has me, he won't let me fall. He rinses remaining soap from my body and shuts off the water.

"But..." I voice feeling like I should take care of his needs as well.

He interrupts "No my sweet Mate. I am taking care of you. That is all I need for now." Again tears well in my eyes but I say nothing. We exit the shower and he dries me then he wraps the towel around me. As he is drying himself I can barely keep my eyes open. I realize I have barely slept for months, unable to relax.

Ronin picks me up, cradling me in his arms. I let my eyes close and fall directly to sleep.

Chapter 14

Ronin

She sleeps in my arms, safe and sound. I never want to set her down, but she is in dire need of rest. The dark circles under her eyes and the weight she has lost since we were last together are indicative of her trials since. But where should I lay her to sleep? Certainly not here.

Sia comes softly over the speakers, *"If you follow the floor lights, I will show you the way to an unoccupied room that is safe and big enough for the three of you."*

I follow the lights. The AI I installed into this ship has changed. It shows thinking, reasoning and compassion. It's not something I've ever seen an AI do. I need to remember to talk with June about her.

We get to a door as it opens. The lights turn on as we walk in. It's small but has a kitchen unit, a washroom with a water shower, a sanishower, and a large bed. I recognize it as one of the ship rooms for a triad and their Mate. It is meant as short-term rooms for the transport of dignitaries and such. It will work perfectly, as I gut the Captain's quarters and redesign its layout. I want it to be unrecognizable from what it is today.

Sia chimes in softly again, *"I have let Nalax and her Mate know to bring Leena here when she has completed her medical."*

"Thank you, Sia," I respond as I walk to the bed. I look down into my sleeping Mates face and find I cannot set her down yet. I lay down with her and curl my body around hers.

"Never again will I fail to protect you, my Mate," I say softly as she sleeps.

A short time later, Nalax, Doraj, and Leena come in. Leena crawls into bed and nestles into June. June's arm instinctively reaches out and gathers her close. Leena is asleep in seconds as well. I stare for a while. I have a Mate and a daughter to care for in such a short time I thought the Goddess was punishing me for the longest time. She was saving me for the two most important beings in the universe.

I look up at Doraj and Nalax. Nalax is staring at my Mate and daughter with a sad, caring look on her face. I noticed she has the shirka markings, so she was also his. Anger wells up again, I glance at Doraj, and he nods, knowing what I'm thinking.

I rise from the bed, "Nalax, can you stay with them while they sleep? I do not want them to be alone."

"Of course." She says and moves over to sit on the bed next to June.

I watch them for a bit longer, then turn to Doraj, "Come, my friend, I need to kill something."

He follows, "Excellent."

When the door closes behind us, we pause. "Sia, there are still hostiles locked in areas around the ship, correct," I ask.

"Affirmative," she responds.

"Where is the largest group?"

"Level 4 bunk room 3."

I look to my friend, "Let's clean this ship." His smile is one for the excitement of coming violence. "First, we need real clothes and weapons. Follow me."

As we walk back into the Captain's quarters, we both stop and stare at the corpse on the bed.

After a few minutes, Doraj tilts his head to the side and says, "Uh, is that... "

"Yes."

"... in his mouth?"

"Yes."

"Your Mate is ruthless. I like it!"

"I hope he was still alive when she stuffed it down his throat," I say with disgust.

Sia chimes in, *"He was."*

"Good." We say in unison.

"Sia, can you send the worker bots to dismantle this room? Everything is recycled, incinerated, or ejected into space."

"Gladly. I took the liberty of making Nlyaxian standard military-style clothing for you both. They are in the synthesizer."

"Thank you, Sia."

"You are welcome."

We change, and being in Nlyaxian clothes is somehow cathartic to me. I walk to the weapons closet, where I see it. My axe. I reverently pick it up off of the hooks. It is beautifully inscribed with the runes of my ancestors across the beard. The bit of the blade is as large as both my hands and when in battle, on swing, the bit lights with intense heat and can cut through almost anything. The handle is made from the Nlyaxian Lira tree. Wood from this tree is one of the hardest substances on my world and only the blade attached to it could cut through it. Down the shaft are intricate depictions of my culture and the Matriarchy. This axe has passed through generations of my family, and I realize it is probably the last artifact of the Nlyaxian Matriarchy in existence. I was gifted the axe from my third father when I bested my siblings and all challengers to replace him as High Commander of the Nlyaxian Armies. It feels like a lifetime ago.

I put the axe in its harness and sling it on my back where it belongs. My two side blades are in the closet as well. They are beautiful as well but only have value to me. My mother and my fathers commissioned her weapons master to make these for me. The blades are called talon blades because they resemble the talons of a predator of Nlyax. The blade face on both are black as midnight and have intricate swirls and eddies. The handle is made of black wood. On them is my family crest. They gave them to me when I came of age. The blades and axe are all I have left of my family. These weapons will never leave me again. I slide the blades into their belt and put them on.

The last thing I grab is a blaster. A sloppy weapon but necessary for combat at a distance. I prefer close quarters, but you usually do not get to choose. With the blaster holstered at my right thigh, I look at Doraj and say, "Take what you want."

Once he is geared up, we move out, "Time to clean ship."

As we move through the ship I glance at Doraj at my side. The Noinapmocian males and females are very different, not unlike my people. Where Nalax is lean and willowy, Doraj is the same height as me and broader. His four arms are toned and well muscled. He has foregone the tunic since Nlyaxian clothing does not account for four arms. He has shown me his true friendship over the past three year and he excelled in battle the last twenty four hours. I hope he decides to stay on the ship but it will be his and Nalax's decision.

I imagine the two of us heavily armed are going to set the soldier's instantly into fight mode. We are an imposing sight.

We reach the door to the bunk room. I look to Doraj, "Should we give them a warning?"

With a sideways smile he says, "That would be the right thing to do..."

I grab my axe and let my battle fury take over, "Fuck that. Sia, open the door."

Fifteen minutes later we walk back out the door. Doraj has a disgusted look on his face, "That wasn't nearly as challenging as I was expecting. How did these fuckers catch us?"

Chuckling I tell him, "Let's go clean out the rest of the scum."

Most of the day cycle is gone by the time we head back to the room our Mates are in. Then I remember, I needed to talk with the Nlyaxians locked in their quarters. "You ok if we make one more stop? I'd like you at my back with this one as well. I'm not expecting anything but..."

"Don't say another word, my friend. I will always protect your back." I shift our destination to where Sia showed me where their quarters were located.

As we reach our target, I ask Sia to open their doors. The three males step out curiously and then turn in our direction. The look on my face is not friendly. They freeze as they see me and then immediately go down to one knee. "My prince." All say in unison.

I pinch my ear in annoyance. "Please stand. I am not sure there is a matriarchy anymore."

They stand and look at each other confused. "But sir, if you live, then the Matriarchy lives with you."

"The four of us are some of the last of our species alive. I'll give you all a choice, but first, you must answer two questions and remember my blood will tell me if you lie."

The females of my line rule. The males are warriors. Occasionally through the generations, a latent trait exposes itself in males and females. It is impossible to predict when it will show itself, but when a child of the royal line is born with silver wrapping their ridges and silver flecks in their eyes, they can detect when anyone lies to them. The three nod.

"Did you assist in the attack of this ship or our homeworld?" I look at each individually for an answer, and all respond in the negative. None lie.

"Since the takeover of this ship, did any of you go against our cultural laws and harm any female?" Again I look at each individually for their answer.

The first "No. The second is "No." The third, "No." He darts his eyes at me after he answers. The eyes are how I can tell. When someone lies to me, I see a red dot where their pupils are. When our eyes meet, I know he is lying, he attempts to flee, but the other two run him down.

I walk slowly to where they hold them. "So, since our planet was destroyed, did you think that our respect for females only held while they lived?"

He struggles, "What does it matter? They were not Nlyaxian females. Whores is what they were."

As I turn, I say, "Space him." He struggles more, screaming obscenities. But I do not care. I turn to him, "All females, no matter the species, are precious and should be treated with honor and respect. Ekim, Lessur, when you are finished, rest, eat, and restart your military training when the next day cycle begins."

"Yes, sir." They say in unison.

As we walk back to the temporary quarters, Doraj pipes up, "Prince, huh?"

"Shut it," I grow in response. Doraj's booming laugh is heard through the halls. It brings a smile to my face.

As we walk through the doors to our temporary quarters, I see Nalax and Leena trying to get close to June while she is curled into a ball in the corner, naked. Flinching when they come near. I rush over but slow as I get close so as not to scare my Mate. I ask Nalax, "What happened?"

"She woke up screaming like someone was killing her. She says she had a 'nightmare,' whatever that is."

"Nightmares are familiar to me." Talking to Nalax but loud enough for June to hear, I say, "One of my friends had what he called night terrors. He had gone through an extremely traumatic experience, and at night his mind would manifest images of it. They are incredibly rare in my species. I think Dax is the only recorded case. When we were young, he used to tell us he saw his Mate in his sleep. As kids, we thought he was just telling stories."

From the corner, my Mate softly says, "Humans call those dreams; the good ones. Nightmares are terrible." She looks at Nalax and Leena with tears, "I'm sorry. It felt very real." Leena moves and hugs her.

Nalax looks at Leena and asks, "Want to stay with Doraj and me this sleep cycle? We can make whatever you want..."

She looks at me this time for permission, and my heart locks up. "Yes, it's fine, Leena. To give our little Pillut some time." She smiles, hugs June, and says, "I love you, Pillut."

"I love you too." She responds.

They leave; she and I are alone. I hold out my hand for her. She slides it into my palm, and I help her up, bringing her into an embrace. She is naked. I forgot to get some clothing for her to wear. "I'm sorry. I didn't remember to get you clothes."

"It's ok. I didn't wake till shortly before you came in," she says with a small smile.

"Would you like some now?"

"No. I think more sleep if you'll stay?" She looks embarrassed to ask.

"Of course. We climb into the bed, and she cuddles into me and falls asleep.

A few days go by as we all try to recover from what we have been through. She has mostly remained in the quarters and slept. She is starting to recover. The dark circles under her eyes are gone. Now I would like to see you gain the weight back.

"Would you like to go for a walk?"

My body locks up as she says, "No. I think I'd like to care for my Mate."

My mouth is dry, so I swallow, trying to rehydrate it. "You do not need to do that, Pillut."

"I know," she says, "I want this, my Mate." When she says 'Mate,' I swear my cock jumped.

She leads me to the bathroom and turns the water on. I see her register my axe and blades, "Can I see your weapons?"

She looks excited by my weapons. I reach for the blaster, she wrinkles her nose. "Not that... the axe and knives." She's practically bouncing from foot to foot. I smile and laugh. She looks into my face and gives me a genuinely beautiful smile. I think my heart stops for a second.

Still smiling, "I think it will be much easier now."

I pull my blades from my belt and hand them to her. She holds them and then starts moving them. She murmurs to herself, "beautifully balanced," she looks down the edge (only fools test the blade by touching the edge). She then starts some spins along the center of her hand, then flips the blades in both hands simultaneously several times, then catches them both by the outer blade and hands them back, "Beautiful blades."

My cock is rock hard. "I have never seen anything sexier than what you just did." She laughs, and my cock jumps. By the Goddess, I need to get control of myself.

"Can I see the axe?" she asks, looking at me from under her lashes. Goddess, help me. I reach up and pull it from its harness. I hold it in front of me flat across my hands. She moves this way and that, inspecting every aspect of the axe. She looks at me with awe in her eyes. "Ronin, it's magnificent. What is the story behind it?" By the Goddess, this female was made for me. As a cub, I knew all the information on every weapon displayed in the royal residence. I love weapons. She returns her attention to my axe as I prepare to tell her the story of it.

She stands in rapt attention, waiting for me to begin.

This axe is called *The Felling*. It has passed through over one hundred generations of my family. Legend has it that the Goddess herself presented it to the greatest warrior of our people, telling him that the axe would one day be used to save our people. I won the right to *The Felling* when I won a tournament to become the High Commander of the Nylaxian Armies. The runes down the shaft of the axe tell the story of how it came to be and it has a rune for every member of my family that has carried it."

She shivers, "That is amazing. Such histories are beautiful. I am glad nothing happened to it while you were held captive."

She shivers again, "How about we exchange the rest of our weapons stories after I shower."

She sticks her chin out a little, then smiles, "Deal! And," she says as she grabs my clothes to remove them, "I'm caring for you, remember?"

Oh, my cock remembers as it jumps again. I suddenly smell the spike of her desire and groan. I think it's going to break. As I help her disrobe me, her desire continues to rise in the room. Control, discipline, respect, control, discipline, respect. I chant this in my head as she leads me to the shower. She steps into the shower, and I follow. She turns to face me, grabs my hands, and places them on the wall above her head.

"To ensure I get you completely clean and do not get distracted before I'm done. Your hands must stay exactly where they are unless I move them, understand?"

"Yes, my Mate," is all I can get out. She grabs the soap and begins. She starts with one arm starting at the hand cleaning and massaging as she goes, moving to my wrist and forearm, then my bicep. She moves to the other arm and repeats. As she is doing this, all I can do is watch the water run down her body over her breast and nipples. I want to lick the water off the tip. I begin to move to do just that when she says, "Ah ah ah, No, keep your hands where they are, Mate." I can't help the small growl from my lips. It makes her shiver, and the scent of her desire spikes again, filling the shower.

I chant control, discipline, respect as I close my eyes and lift my face to the ceiling because my Mate is too tempting. The little giggle she lets out makes me realize I may have said that aloud.

She moves behind me and starts to lather and massage my shoulders and back. It feels wonderful, and I groan. She moves her hands lower to my buttocks and then lower to my legs. She picks up my feet to wash them. She moves back around to the front and cleans my chest, moves lower to my abdomen, tracing every defined ridge of my muscles, then lower still. Her hands trail down, brushing my cock, cleaning around its base. When her small fingers trail over the ridges at the base of my cock I groan again because the sensation of her touching me there is almost too much.

Her wandering hands move lower, cupping my balls, rolling them gently around in her hand. Control discipline, respect, control discipline, respect, her ministrations alone are going to make me release my seed, but I would not stop her for all the knives in the universe.

When she grabs my cock my breath explodes from me. "Mate..." I groan. Suddenly her mouth is wrapped around my cock. I look down, and she is on her knees. I whisper, barely able to speak, "Mate, it isn't done."

She sucks and then takes her mouth off my cock. "It is by me." And she returns to sucking. I moan and growl as she puts my cock down the back of her throat. Seeing her with half my cock in her mouth sends me over the edge. I try to move so I do not release in her mouth, but she now has her hands on my hips and will not allow my movement. She starts sucking and bobbing up and down on my cock faster and I can hold out no longer. My seed comes forth, and she sucks it down, humming and moaning like she loves the taste.

She slowly stands, licking her lips. "You taste like cinnamon, my Mate," she says in a sultry voice, "I love cinnamon."

"Please, Mate, let me move my hands," I beg.

She is breathing hard, "please, Ronin, I need you." I move slower than I want because I do not want to scare her.

June

Ronin kisses me so passionately I forget where we are. He's on his knees, kissing his way down my neck; when my nipple goes into his mouth, he sucks hard, and I almost orgasm then and there. He moves to the other and repeats. My moans are beginning to run together.

He lifts me and wraps my legs around his shoulders. I lock my feet as he delves his tongue into my folds. His tongue is firm as it hits my clit. I arch my back against the shower wall and scream. My hands are in his hair, holding on for life. He teases my clit, darting in and out, circling, flicking, driving me mad. Then he latches on to the hard throbbing nub and sucks. The scream that tears from me when my orgasm hits is part moan, part scream, I don't know which. I'm a twitching mass as I look down at him. His eyes have a laser focus on me. The look he gives me screams conqueror, warrior, god. My core fires right back up, and I moan, "Ronin, ...please."

He stands as he moves me down his body. He has me pressed to the wall, his hands firmly gripping my ass. Slowly he impales me on his cock. Fuck he is the sexiest thing to walk the galaxy. I moan as he starts moving, pulling out, and thrusting in. His strokes are slow but strong. He is building a fire in me, fanning the flames.

He starts increasing the pace then he is pounding into me. The sensations he is creating are almost too much. I'm moaning, but my orgasm is nearly there when he leans forward and says, "Now Mate." as his sprili unfurls. The orgasm that rolls through me is so intense that I open my mouth to scream, but nothing comes out. I feel my pussy lockdown on his cock, and he roars, moving as fast as possible, thrusting in and out. I feel it swell, and the splash of his seed against my walls is welcome because I know what comes next. I smile joyously as his sprili begins to vibrate and another orgasm crashes.

When we come back to ourselves, we are both panting and not willing to unlock our bodies. Ronin strides into the bedroom, still hard and fully seated in me. I moan softly as the vibrations from his strides send little aftershocks through me. He lays down on the bed on his back. My head rests on his chest, my hands on his biceps. He softly says, "I do not know what I did to deserve my perfect Mate but know this, little Pillut, I intend to spend my life making you moan and scream my name."

Ronin

June sits up, pulling me further into her body. "I am far from perfect, love." She starts lifting herself off my cock and then slowly moving back down. It causes a riot of sensations down my shaft. The next time she comes down, her clit bumps against the sensitive ridges at my base. We both moan with that move.

I move my hands from her hips to her breast gently rubbing, squeezing, and pinching them as I say, "I disagree my Mate. You are a warrior," she rubs her clit against my ridges, "you are compassionate," rubs again, "you love weapons as I do," rub and grind against the ridge as I moan. "You are my perfect match, my perfect Mate."

She has tears on her cheeks and starts moving herself up and down my cock as fast as she can. "Ronin, please..." I immediately flip our positions and start thrusting hard and fast. She is moaning and mewling in the way I love. I feel my sprili unfurl, and then her pussy is milking my cock as she screams, "Ronin!" I moan as my seed sprays her walls, and the sprili begins vibrating, which keeps her in her orgasm longer and keeps her sex massaging me. The sensation that she creates at the base of my spine is something I truly believe only she can do.

She is my one and only. She is my Mate.

She lay at my side, and I am happier than I have ever been in my life. Yes, there is darkness in me. It will take time, but I believe I can heal it if I am with her.

We both fall asleep.

June

I am naked and cannot move my limbs. Oh no, he's found me again. Kaxlin walks toward me naked. I cannot move. NO NO I CANNOT. Ronin HELP ME. He has me pinned to the wall. His cock which is black and looks poisonous is poised to be rammed into my pussy. I told you this cunt was MINE. NO OH MY GOD NO Ronin!

I am shaken awake; Ronin is there and I realize I'm screaming and thrashing around. I stop moving and collapse against his chest crying. He gathers me close, rocking me, saying, "You are safe, my Mate... I have you. You are safe."

I slowly come out of it and stop crying. "I'm sorry." I say to him in a near whisper. He lifts my chin to look at him, "No, little Pillut. No. No apologizing for this. You went through great trauma. Trauma takes time to heal."

I fold myself into his chest. "Will you hold me... tight as we lay together? Tell me something about your past." He pulls me in close as we lay back down.

"You remember I told you I had two best friends growing up?" He continues after I nod my head. "Their names are... were Dax and Aanon. We have been friends since we started our early learning. We were inseparable. When Dax or Aanon decided they wanted to do something, we did it together. When I decided I wanted to try something, we did it together. We were very rarely apart. We got into trouble a lot!" I laughed.

"Dax, Dax was my partner. When I wanted to do something stupid, he would help me. When Dax wanted to do something stupid, well generally, I was in. Again we were trouble." She laughed with me this time. "Aanon, he was our balance, our logic, and heart. Even as a child, he was tall and lean, but his heart was always big. He was gentle. He'd find a selix with a broken wing and nurse it back to health. He'd remind us not to tease or pull our sisters' hair. That male had the biggest heart of anyone I have ever known."

"We were three years away from our military training when one of my mother's advisors started making noise about the 'type' of friends I was associating with. He believed they were below my station. You see, I was her son. Dax was the son of farmers and Aanon. Aanon's grandfather was Noinapmocian. He was mixed. I was furious that someone would say horrible things about my friends. I went to my mother," he chuckles, "with this tiny little knife ready to defend their honor, and I was going to challenge him." I chuckle with him this time.

"How old were you?" I ask.

"I was eight solar cycles old. Barely old enough to swing a sword. She had already taken care of it, though. She didn't abide by bigotry. She loved my friends almost as much as I did. Neither had a great home life, so she was always inviting them to stay. She told the advisor he should care for his own because he doesn't belong in hers. She was my hero."

"Years later, we are in the military, of mating age. And that same advisor, I know it was him, somehow got both Dax and Aanon declared unfit for a Mate. I was livid. I went to my mother, begging her to fix it. She couldn't, the council declared it, and she couldn't go against them. I was so angry with her. I told her I would never take a Mate and removed my name from the registry. I stopped going planetside, and my sole focus was the military and war. I was angry. Fast forward several years, I haven't seen my family since I took over as High Commander of our Armies working on this ship out in the Laurentian nebulae. You know the rest." With emotion in his voice, "She died thinking I hated her. I am a terrible son."

I move back to his chest, laying on him. "No, Ronin. No. She knew you loved her. She knew. Mother's always know." He looks at me with hope. "I know it, Ronin."

He nods. "Aanon said the same but I thought he was trying to get me to go see her... to forgive her. I miss them. I was absolutely convinced we would be Triad together. I always felt it was right. Until the day my planet was destroyed." He paused for a while, and I begin to think he was done. "They would have loved you."

For some reason, tears stream down my face. "I would have loved them." I kiss him trying to show him my deep love for him. I deepen the kiss, unable to help the fire that roars to life. Ronin breaks the kiss and lifts me, so my knees are on either side of his head. Oh god.

He grabs my hips and pulls me down to his face. He starts his tongue's exploration. My back arches, face to the ceiling, closing my eyes. I cannot help my hips move, trying to move his tongue where I want it. He growls, and goosebumps move over my flesh. His tongue, much longer than I believed, dives into my pussy. My moans echo about the room. He brings it out, circles my clit several times, and back into my pussy it goes. He then hits my g-spot with his tongue! I bend forward quickly, screaming, "Ronin!" Unable to control my body, with one hand on the wall in front of me and the other tangled in hair, I am grinding my pussy against his mouth. My orgasm rolls through me. As I'm coming down, I realize Ronin is no longer between my legs.

Suddenly he is behind me, and one arm is locked around my hips, the other on the wall. We both moan as he thrusts his cock into my pussy. He is thrusting hard and fast, taking us to the edge quickly. As I'm about to orgasm, his hand moves to my clit, and pinches as his sprili unfurl. The scream I let out is ear-shattering, "Ronin!" I swear I'm crashing around in the stars, and I feel his cock swell and splash my walls with his seed. The sprili starts vibrating, and I cannot scream. I swear I blackout for a second from the raw sensation of my orgasm.

Both of us have our heads against the wall trying to catch our breath. "Fuck Ronin." is all I can say.

He chuckles, and I give a little moan from the aftershock that they create. He kisses my shoulder. "You are amazing, my Mate. When you climaxed on my face, I nearly lost my seed right then." Shit, if he likes that, wait till I show him the better position.

But not now. I am so tired. Ronin's cock slides out. He carries me to the sanishower. It cleans our bodies quickly, and he walks us back to the bed. I am asleep as my head hits the pillow.

Chapter 15

Ronin

Day cycle will start soon. I watch my Mate sleep. I am still amazed that the Goddess deemed me worthy of such a Mate. She flinches in her sleep; her face shows fear even though her eyes are closed. I pull her in tight and kiss her forehead. Her face relaxes, and she cuddles into my chest and smiles slightly. Nightmares, my people don't dream, but I understand the concept because of Dax.

I hate that Kaxlin invades her mind as she sleeps, causing her fear and emotional distress. The scars on her back make my battle fury very hard to control. He whipped her, hard enough to open the skin. She nearly died because of it. Dread washes through me. I have to shake it off. I cannot think about losing her.

She stirs and opens her eyes. I bend and kiss her, and she deepens the kiss. I move between her legs and push my cock into her. I need her. I slowly show her my need for her, my love for her. The human word is inadequate for what I feel. The room once again fills with the sounds of our connection; moans, whispers, and ends with her screaming my name.

We were showered and dressed when the door rang, and Nalax, Doraj, and Leena came in. Leena skips to June, hugs her tightly, and, to my shock, does the same to me. I am beginning to understand my family a bit more; I would kill for this small female, and I only met her yesterday.

My Mate looks more rested today. The area under her eyes is less dark and shines a bit brighter. She decided the Nlyaxian military pants are adequate for her type of fighting, but I must say the tight fit may cause me distraction. The tunic is loose and long-sleeved but fitted. Again the deep v-neck collar is distracting, especially when she leans forward. The belt she wears accentuates her curvy form. Then I realized someone must have asked me something because everyone in the room is looking at me, and my Mate wears a sexy smirk.

I can't help but laugh, "Forgive me, my friends... My Mate, clothed, is as distracting as she is unclothed." My Mate turns a pretty shade of pink, and I detect the light scent of her desire. I send her a look so she knows I know the effect I had on her.

June

That male. He knows the effect he has on me and exactly how to get me wet, but I can also see the effect I have on him. The outline of his cock in his pants is very evident. However, we have a lot of work to do, so I refocus and begin.

"Nalax, can Leena hang out with you? I'm not comfortable with her running the ship alone yet. You are welcome to join us on the bridge if you'd like. I would like you to think about an inventory of the infirmary and a list of things you need and would like to have."

She smiles, "You're reading my mind, my friend. The previous leadership did not care to stock the infirmary properly. We'll head down there first, and when we are done, we'll meet you all up on the bridge." Hand in hand, Leena leaves with Nalax for the infirmary.

I look at Ronin and Doraj, "Let's head to the bridge. We need to move this ship." Both males nod in agreement, and we all head for the bridge.

As we walk onto the bridge, two of the three Nlyaxians who were here when we took the ship stand and salute. In unison, they say, "Reporting for duty, Captain." I glance over my shoulder at Ronin.

He leans down and says so they can't hear, "Ekim and Lessur, both honorable males."

"Where's the other?" I ask.

"No longer on this ship. And to be clear, they are talking to you, not me." My eyes jump to his, and he gives me a little nod.

I straighten and look at both trying to gauge them myself but then realize I trust Ronin. He would never allow anyone who posed a risk to Leena or me to remain.

"Ekim, Lessur, relax. This ship is not going to be operated as a military vessel. I want to trust and be able to treat every member of my crew like they are part of my family." Ekim and Lessur puff up a bit as if I complimented them; not sure why but I will ask Ronin later. We file onto the bridge and stand in a semi-circle—time for some questions before I begin. Ronin asks, "Do you want to go into the conference room for this? "

I feel my face pale a bit, "No. Here is fine."

"Ronin, can we operate this ship with our current crew, excluding the freed folks? We'll need to drop them off somewhere."

"Yes. I designed this ship to run efficiently with a skeleton crew. Eventually, we will need to pick up some more crew members as we go, but we can be selective and cautious on that front."

I nod in thanks. "Sia, can you develop a list of any modifications done to the original design of this ship and send them to Ronin?"

"*Of course,*" she responds.

I look at Ronin, "Just review it and make sure they didn't do anything to corrupt your design." He nods. The pride I see in his face makes the heat rise in my face a little.

I look at Ekim and Lessur, "Are either of you a navigator?"

The one called Lessur responds, "I am Sir."

"Lessur, did this ship and crew stick to some set routes?"

He thinks, "Now that you mention it, we visited the same five planets and always traveled the same routes."

"Ok, thank you. Can you talk with Sia and figure out three things? A haven to take the freed slaves to. We need a base of operations, so we need several options for that, and finally, get us to a temporary safe location. The last is a priority for now, and please make sure we do not cross any of this ship's previous routes."

Lessur responds, "I can do that, Sir."

I look at Ronin, "We've been in this location too long. The longer we are here raises our risk."

"Agreed," he responds.

"Lessur, I would love for you to remain in this conversation but get us the hell out of here."

He smiles. "Yes, Captain." I don't smile back, but he's already striding to his terminal. I wish I could be more at ease, but I look at them and see Kaxlin. It's not fair to them. I'm not sure why that doesn't happen with Ronin, but it doesn't, and I am very thankful for that. I feel his hand on my back in comfort. I'm beginning to believe he really can feel my emotions. Either that or he reads my mind, and that would be terrible.

I look at Ekim, "Ekim, what are your responsibilities on the ship?"

"Before the attack, I was weapons master, I ensured all crew and weapons systems were serviced and ready for action. Afterward, I was pulled from that because Kaxlin didn't trust me. He put me on ship systems, so I can now do both." I hate hearing his name aloud.

An autonomic fear response makes the hair rise on the back of my neck. Refocusing, I say, "Excellent."

"Doraj, what about you? I understand you worked in engineering with Ronin. What other capabilities do you have?"

He thinks for a minute, "Engineering is definitely my strength, but I also am able to pilot crafts, I excel at battle tactics and fighting, and I am also well versed in emergency medical. Nalax has been teaching me since we found each other." Awe.

"Thank you, Doraj. And thank you for helping to liberate this ship." His chest puffs a little at the recognition.

Lessur rejoins the group and says, "We are en route to a remote untraveled region of space. We can regroup and make plans there."

"Excellent Thank you," I say to him.

"Sia and I believe we have a solution to both the base of operations and a safe haven for the slaves." He says, surprising me. That was fast.

At that moment, the door opens, and Leena's racing in with Nalax in tow. She lets go of Nalax's hand, races across the room, and wraps her arms tightly around my waist. "Hi, baby. Did you have fun with Auntie Nalax?"

"Auntie?" They both chime at once. I laugh, "A human term. It is a term we use for family," I look up at Nalax, "Sister of mother, essentially." Nalax tears up and runs out of the room.

Very worried, I move to follow, but Doraj raises a hand, "It's ok. I will go."

Still worried, "I didn't mean to upset her, Doraj. She means the world to me."

"I know, and she knows... she is very happy at the honor you've given her, but she hates to cry in front of people." He smiles broadly as he says the last and heads out the door.

I turn and realize that Ekim and Lessur are staring open-mouthed at Leena. She's hiding behind me. Ronin starts to step in front of us, but I stop him. "It's ok." He steps back, wondering what I'm doing. "Ekim, Lessur, this is our... daughter Leena. She was a slave in the Captain's quarters with me."

I don't miss the hard look that takes over when they hear. They look at Ronin, and when they look back, their faces are once again soft.

Leena is looking at me with tears running down her cheeks, "Truly?" she asks in a whisper.

I go to my knees, "If that's ok with you."

She looks at Ronin, and he nods, then back to me, wraps her arms around my neck, and whispers, "yes."

Ekim and Lessur go down to one knee. Ekim says to Leena, "It is truly an honor to meet you, little Leena."

Lessur says, "A great honor."

They are both warmly smiling at Leena, and she giggles, "They are weird. I learned that word from Mother. It means something is strange." We all laugh, and it feels 'normal'. It's nice. If I had any doubts about Ekim or Lessur, they are gone now. It is written on their faces; they would die to protect her.

We stand and Leena stays at my side. Doraj and Nalax come back to the bridge and join us. Her cheeks are a little pink, but she looks happy.

I look to Lessur, "How much time till we reach our destination?"

"Approximately three-day cycles and two hours."

I nod my head, "Good."

"Sia, can you broadcast me to the occupied areas of the ship?"

"*Comms ready.*" She says.

"Passengers of the," I look at Ronin. "What's the name of this ship?"

"It was never named. Nlyaxian ships are named at their christening. You should name it."

I pause for a minute, thinking, "Passengers of the Emancipation. You are no longer slaves. You are free. The crew of this ship will do everything in our power to keep you safe while you are onboard. I ask everyone to go to the infirmary so we can evaluate your health, and we will do what we can to address issues. Once you are done with medical, the crew will give you new quarters for your stay. Know this. No violence against crew or other passengers will be tolerated. *None.* We will deal with offenders of this rule swiftly and brutally. We are looking for a safe haven for you and will keep you updated as our search continues. You are welcome to move about the ship, but key areas will be off-limits. I only ask for patience and if you'd like to contribute or help with the ship, let one of the crew know. Thank you. Sia cut comms."

"*Ended,*" Sia responds.

I look around at my crew, and I'm not sure I understand the looks on their faces. "What?"

Ronin responds for everyone, "You were born for this."

Feeling embarrassed and awkward. I say, "Thank you."

Asking no one in particular, I say, "Is there some sort of communal cafeteria or something? I'm hungry, and we can finish talking there."

Ronin grabs my hand, "Follow me."

As we walk, Nalax walks up beside me. "I am sorry I ran out. I lost my sister in the Lutetian Wars. In my culture, it is a high honor when someone wants you to be a part of their family. I know you did not know this, but it meant a great deal to me."

Not wanting her to worry, I say, "You are like a sister to me already, Nalax. I meant it when I said you are a beautiful person inside and out. I know you and Doraj have the option to go anywhere now that we are free, but I really hope you'll both stay."

"Oh, we are staying. I don't think I could drag Doraj from Ronin's side."

I see Ronin glance back at Doraj with a smirk on his face.

Doraj looks at the ceiling with a groan, "Ugh, Female, did you have to say that so loud? I'm never going to hear the end of it from him!"

We all burst out laughing at his dismay.

We enter what Ronin calls the common room. It's large with many tables and what looks like games. The room can probably hold a hundred and fifty people. We all head toward the food synthesizers to get what we want.

I am frozen in front of my machine. I only know the codes for his food. His food, I... Leena stands beside me and takes my hand. She whispers, "It's ok. Don't make it."

"That's all I know," I whisper.

From behind me, I hear Ronin, "Don't bother Mate. I want you to try traditional Nlyaxian food! I made enough for all of us."

Both Leena and I sigh and relax. I turn around, and I can tell he knew I was having problems, in a downward spiral. There are worry lines at the corners of his eyes. He tries to hide it. God, I love him.

I smile at him with my hand over my heart. My heart skips a beat at the steamy look he gives me.

Ronin takes the time to describe every dish and some of them, he even entertains everyone by telling them the story of the first time he ate it. By the end, all were laughing and telling stories about foods from their home worlds. As we were telling our stories, passengers slowly filtered in and made food, sat down, and started talking to one another. I hope they eventually can find their own normalcy while they are on this ship.

We are wrapping up our meal when Nalax looks up, and her face hardens.

I turn to see who approaches and cannot help to rise and turn, making the chair fall back at who approaches. The woman who painted my slave tattoos and watched my rape approaches looking very nervous and very contrite. She backs away, intimidated by my response. I close my eyes and try to calm myself. She is not to blame. She was a slave. She had to do as she was told.

I reopen my eyes and hold out my hand to get her to stop leaving, "No. Don't leave. Please stay if you want to. You have to understand it's hard for some of us and raw. We all, including you, need time to heal, time to deal with the trauma we were forced to survive. Understand this, I do not blame you, but I need time before I can see you without having a reaction." I try to put as much compassion in my face as I can.

Quietly she says, "I understand. I just wanted to say thank you for when... when we were in his room."

Leena is hugging my waist at my side. I have my arm around her. Trying to keep the venom out of my voice, I say, "He wasn't threatening you." A confused look crosses her face.

Unable to stop her, Leena screams, "He was threatening ME!" I hug her, unable to protect her from this memory. The woman suddenly understands and pales. She leaves without a word.

I sigh and lift her face with my hand, and wipe her tears. "Are you ok?"

She nods and asks, "You?" I nod in return. We turn and come face to face with four furious males; three Nlyaxians and one Noinapmocian. All three of the Nlyaxians eyes are black.

My fear ratchets up, "What?"

Ronin is the one to speak, and I can tell he is having trouble controlling his voice. Through his teeth, he says, "Kaxlin threatened a *female child*?"

I nod.

Ronin, trying not to scream, says very loudly, "Ekim, Lessur, Doraj, sparring room now!" And all of them practically run out of the room.

I look at Nalax, "What the hell just happened?"

Looking unhappy as well, she says, "In both cultures, it is the most heinous of crimes to hurt or even threaten a child. Nlyaxian law is death."

In a small voice, Leena asks, "Can we go to our room now?"

"Yes, baby. Let's go. Nalax come with us?"

"Definitely."

We are in our temporary quarters. We relaxed, or at least Leena and Nalax did. I did some reading, but as time ticked on, I got madder and madder. When Sia chimes, *"Nalax, Doraj asks if you can meet them in the infirmary?"*

I jump up, "Is someone injured?" Instantly worried for Ronin. Sia pauses. "Sia, tell me."

The AI sighs, *sighs*, then answers the question. *"Yes, there are injuries, but none are critical, June. Ronin said it would be best if you stayed in the room."*

I growl, "Fuck that." I'm out the door heading to the infirmary with Nalax and Leena, hurrying to catch up. My blood is on fire.

Chapter 16

We are in the infirmary waiting for Nalax to come treat the worst of our injuries. I turn as the door opens, and instead of Nalax, my Mate walks in with a thunderous look on her face. She is furious.

She roars at us, "*What right do you have to be angry for something that happened to us!* Things that happened to *us*, and *you* need to work things out in the sparring room?"

Ekim and Lessur then make a mistake. To be fair, with ninety-five percent of females, they would be fine, but apparently, with mine... they are not.

They step forward halfway in front of me. Ekim says, "Captain, you must understand -"

He never finished that statement. My Mate executes a set of moves that are pure harmony and balance. She gets a gleeful look on her face, grabs Ekim's outstretched arm, flips him onto his back, and executes two hits to his chest with pointed fingers, not a fist. He is flipped again onto his stomach, her knee in his back, and his arm is twisted in a way that if he moves at all, I'm pretty sure it will snap.

Lessur moves forward not to harm but to help his friend. I don't even see it this time, but somehow she now has Lessur on his stomach in a different but similar position. Neither are moving because they do not want a broken arm.

Doraj bursts out laughing, then quickly stops because the look she gives him would melt iron.

Slowly she returns her eyes to me. Dread and desire mix, "Mate, I would like to spar with you." She releases them. They moan and move away from her. Magnificent.

She glances at my pants, and she seems to get angrier. "Oh, you want to spar with me? A female who needs a male to hide his anger, so she doesn't get scared? Do you want a piece of me? *Let's go!*" I hear the hurt in her voice, and now my anger rises.

Several voices speak at the same time, "*Can we watch?*" I yell "No" at the same time she yells "Yes." I growl, turn, stalk out the door, and roar, "Fine."

In the back of my mind not affected by anger, I hear Leena say with pride in her voice, "When she fought Kaxlin she landed many *many* punches. For twenty-five minutes she punched him, flipped him, made him bleed! It wasn't until he threw the chair that he got a punch in..." she said the last two words much quieter, "that was one of the nights I thought he killed her." Fury roars through me.

I hear Nalax say quietly, "Shh baby, your mother and father just need to work off some emotions. They won't hurt each other."

Then I hear my Mate say, "We'll see about that."

June

We walk into the sparring room, and I walk directly to the opposite side of the large mat. It's much larger than the sparring mats on Earth. That should benefit me, not him. I remove my boots and socks. I pull off my tunic. I have a sports bra-like garment underneath. I am tying up my hair. It's a complex knot I developed that releases if someone tries to use my hair against me. They generally still get some hair, but it will not give them the leverage that they would get if they got their hands on a braid or ponytail.

Ronin growls, "I prefer your tunic on for this session."

"Oh, why is that, Mate?" I ask, emphasizing the T.

Growl, "It's... distracting."

"They have a saying on Earth I like for this... Too. Fucking. Bad."

So what my Mate does not know is I executed my mental exercises the whole way here. I am calm, my mind is focused, and I am ready. One of the tactics taught that I use now is to keep your opponent off balance, emotional if possible. From his growling, angry looks, and hard cock in his pants, I am very much succeeding.

"I will give you one boon, Mate (big T). Many men make a very big mistake with me in the ring. They let their ego determine the effort they use against me." We are now circling each other in the ring, "Use that information as you see fit but know this... I will NOT pull my punches."

Growling, "Mate, I do not make mistakes in the ring."

I chuckle, "We shall see MaTe. We shall see."

I know he is expecting me to wait, and make him come at me, so let's flip the script on him.

Ronin

I am trying to focus and failing. We have begun. I know she will wait for me to attack, but I'm not sure I can hit my Mate. I ponder this when she attacks. She is fast and nimble. Instinct takes over to a point, and I try to block her first blows. But I am immensely shocked when I am too slow, and she lands three painful blows before she dances away laughing. "Come, Mate, you really must try harder."

Before I can respond, as my eyes track her on the mat, she is already moving in for more. I am ready. Before she can throw the first, I am throwing mine. She ducks under my swing and sweeps my left leg while delivering a blow to my right, very effectively, unbalancing me enough that when she takes out my right leg, I land hard on my back. Again she dances away, giving me no hope of getting a hold of her.

She laughs, "Tsk tsk tsk, Mate. Your focus is lacking right now. I wonder why that could be."

She is magnificent! This time I laugh as well. I get up and walk to my corner. Take my tunic off and my boots. Still smiling, I say, "You are right, my warrior Mate. Let us start again. If you would give me a few minutes for some mental exercises?"

She nods and stands tall. "Yes, I think you are ready. Let us begin this for real." Her angry facade fades and in its place is calm, focus. She is a warrior, brilliant at tactics. She has been keeping me off balance for the upper hand. A worthy challenge.

When I signal I am ready, she moves her body in flowing movements. At the end of the movement, she seems to be in a ready pose with her palm facing up. Then that delicate hand motions for me to come. *Yes!*

June

It feels good. I know it's only been a month or so but it feels like years since I fought someone for the joy of movement. I love testing myself against people that in all other circumstances can outmatch me. Ronin's skills are the best I've ever seen. He doesn't use brute force like others I've seen fight since I got here. I can see him calculating his moves, but unfortunately for him, he broadcasts them for me to see.

Little movements of muscles, a glance, or even his breathing gives him away so I can use his size or momentum against him. The biggest difference between him and most of the people I've fought in the past is his calm. Nothing I do throws him off balance. The most impressive thing to me, though, is that he hasn't made the same mistake twice. I think the more we spar, the harder it's going to get to beat him.

I'm not sure how long it's been since we started, but it feels like hours. We are both dripping with sweat and quite obviously tired. He ends up on the floor again, his cock is still hard, and the look on his face is filled with desire for me. I must admit that I expected my skill to cool his desire, but I believe it deepened it. I cannot wait any longer, "Every out... please." I add, trying not to sound rude. The fire in Ronin's eyes goes molten. Fuck he is hot.

I hear shuffling and some grumbling about missing the last of the fight. I hear the door close. "Sia, please lock the door to the sparring room."

"*Locked,*" she chimes.

Ronin is on the floor staring with fire at me. I start to circle him. "You are the best fighter I have ever sparred with."

I slowly take off my bra and then my pants as I say it. I stop my movement. I stand three feet or so from his head. He slowly rises, never taking his eyes off me.

"As are you, my Mate. I have never encountered such a fighting style. It is quite impressive." He says this as he slowly removes his pants and throws them to the side. When he stands up straight, his cock is hard and jutting from his body. The fire in my core ratchets up a hundred degrees.

We start circling the mat again. I get the distinct impression he is stalking me, hunting me. My excitement grows. "I smell your desire for me, my Mate." He says, then glances down, "It begins to run down your inner thighs." Fuck why is that so hot. I am so distracted my brain does not register the broadcast of his movement till it's almost too late. I know the exact move I want to use.

On Earth, I wasn't really into pop culture except for one thing, movies. I loved them, especially if they had good battle scenes in them. The superhero movies, particularly the ones with female heroes, were my favorites.

I chose a move I developed from watching those. I launch myself directly at him, my feet use his thighs as a ladder, and I wrap my legs around his neck and lock my feet. I have a huge smile on my face as I look down at his shocked face looking up at me. I grab the back of his head to ensure his weight follows me. I arch back and use my momentum to bring him with me. He ends up on his back with his head still between my legs.

Ronin blinks a few times, then sees my pussy and growls. I shiver, so very ready for him. He starts to pull me toward his mouth. "Wait." He pauses, and I move so I'm over his head still but facing the length of his gorgeous body. He looks slightly confused but waits, running his hands along my outer thighs and ass.

I bend, starting to kiss areas on his chest. I pay particular attention to his nipples which make him groan. As I move further down his chest, he starts to get the idea of what I am doing.

He lets out a long low growl. I shiver and feel my pussy get wetter. "Mate, I need your mouth on my cock." Not as much as I do, I think as I wrap my lips and hands around it. He groans as I get halfway down his cock. Suddenly his hands on my ass have pulled my pussy down, and he attacks it with an enthusiasm that makes me moan with his cock in my mouth. He moans as well, feeling the vibrations of my moan down his shaft.

We are wholly focused on the pleasuring of one another while distracted by the pleasure being given. I love sucking his cock. His body's lubricant tastes like cinnamon and some other spice I cannot name at the moment. I can feel the orgasm building in me, and I feel his cock pulsing in my mouth as it prepares for his climax as well. When his tongue delves into my pussy, going straight for my g-spot, my orgasm rolls through my body. His cock is now pulsing hard, pushing his cum into my throat. I suck it down like it's the last thing I'll have before I die while I moan because the orgasm combined with him attempting to lick my pussy clean.

I sit back on my heels, licking the last of him off my lips. Looking down, I see that the fire in his eyes has not diminished. If anything, it burns hotter. I moan, unable to stop the desire I have for him from growing again. Not that I would want to. He slides himself out from under me and sits up. He turns and crawls toward me. I'm breathing hard as he wraps his arm around my waist and pulls me into his lap as he sits down.

His other hand is tangled in my hair, and he is kissing me with the fire I saw in his eyes. I wrap my legs around his torso and begin my pussy's descent down his cock. We both moan once he is fully seated. Moving both his hands to my ass, he lifts and brings me down, lift and down. He is creating a blaze in me. Starting to lift and pull down faster and faster. My tits are bouncing up and down. His eyes are locked there.

I throw my head back, overwhelmed by the sensations he is creating. "Ronin, I need." Suddenly my back is on the mat, and he is thrusting as deep as he can. My orgasm hits as the sprili unfurl, massaging my g-spot and drawing out my orgasm. His cock swells as he reaches his. As his seed splashes against my walls, his sprili starts vibrating. I scream as my ecstasy goes through the roof.

Our sweat mixes as he lays on me. Our heavy breathing is the only sound in the room. He rolls us, so I am sprawled on his chest. We are quiet for a while. Ronin softly says, "Forgive me. I did not intend to exclude you from working out your pain. Sometimes I forget you are a warrior and most likely work things out the same way as I do."

"Thank you for that. I am sorry as well. My response was not healthy. I should have said something before you left the cafeteria."

He rubs my back, "All is forgiven, my beautiful Mate. We are still very new to each other. We are learning."

I lift my head and kiss the spot where (I think) his heart is, "You are everything to me, Ronin."

He grabs my face and brings it to his for a passionate kiss. As he pulls away, he says, "As you are to me."

I lay my head back on his chest. After a few minutes laughing, he says, "Though I didn't expect my Mate would be able to plant my ass on the mat as much as she did. I'm guessing Ekim and Lessur were more impressed than me."

Putting my chin in my hand, I smile and say, "And why would that be?" Honestly curious.

His next statement floors me a bit, "They've never seen someone beat me before."

My head flies off his chest, "What?!"

Ronin

Her reaction confuses me, "I have obviously lost matches, but it's been a while, and the males that were in attendance for those are... gone."

She gets a sad look in her eyes, "Dax and Aanon?"

I love that she remembers their names and nod at her question. I tell her, "But Ekim and Lessur would have only seen the High Commander trials."

"What are those?" she asks. She sits up, my cock still in her hardens immediately. Her pupils dilate as she starts to pleasure herself. Rising up, then down. When she grinds her clit against my base ridges, I moan. Fuck, my Mate was made for a Nlyaxian triad. Her sexual appetite is beyond even a Nlyaxian female.

"What were we talking about?" I ask, seriously unsure. Her face is to the ceiling, and a smile alights it, "The High Commander trials."

"Oh... yes. The trials are held *groan* when the current high commander announces his retirement or... fuck *groan* Mate... is killed in action. Hundreds of warriors compete for the position..." She is still slowly going up and down. Now she is testing the feelings she can generate long ridges on the top and bottom of my cock. She is driving me crazy!

She gives a sultry laugh that I feel in my cock, and I groan, "Go on."

"Hmmm? Oh... I competed in the last." I take a sharp breath. She has started flexing her internal muscle as she moves across the lateral ridges. "FEMALE, you are torturing me!"

She looks into my eyes, "Go on."

I growl low. She opens her mouth and closes her eyes liking the sensations my growl has caused. "The trial lasted... two moons *groan* I competed against all and *fuck* never lost. I am the High Commander of the Nlyaxian Armies." I can take no more. I lift her off my cock and set her on her hands and knees. I slam my cock into her waiting sex. My thrust is firm, the pace is fast, blindly barreling toward our release.

She makes the mewling sounds I crave. I feel my sprili spring forth, and my Mate screams as her pussy locks down onto my cock, milking it for its release. I roar as I cum, and the sprili vibrates. She screams again as another orgasm crashes against her.

I am folded over her keeping myself up by locking my arms. Aftershocks of our orgasms are still racking us both. I pull back, and my cock slides out, laying on my back beside her.

She looks at me with a little awe and shock, "You and your fucking magic cock are amazing!" We both burst out laughing. She lays down on the mat beside me with her head on my upper arm.

She softly says, "About what Leena said..."

I interrupt, not wanting to cause her pain, "I don't need to know, June, unless you truly want to tell me."

"I need to tell you... I'm not sure why I feel this way, but I need to," she says with a sad look.

"Continue, my Mate."

"The woman who came in was the one who painted the slave tattoo's on me," ah the shirka, but I don't correct her. "She was there waiting with Kaxlin when I returned from the infirmary from the last time he tried to rape me. Before the door was even closed behind me, he had me by the neck against the wall. My feet were barely touching the ground. I could barely breathe..."

It's good she cannot see my face. I can control my muscles, but I cannot control the way my eyes react when I go into battle fury. I know my eyes are black right now.

"He told me that he would put up with no more battles for me. That if I didn't fuck him that he'd fuck her. I at first thought that he meant the woman. I wouldn't want to be responsible for anyone's rape, but when I looked back at him, he had the evilest look I have ever seen. He whispered in my ear, 'Not her. The other female that lives in this room.' He meant Leena. If I didn't fuck him, he would be willing to rape a child. A child." She quiets and then begins crying. I wrap her in my arms tightly and let her cry. She needs this. Her pain brings me out of my battle fury. I am still furious at what happened to her, but she needs me, and I will always be there for her.

Chapter 17

June

The next few days as we travel to the safe location are spent gathering information on everything; the ships supplies, the wellbeing of the passengers, the ships weapons stores, the transports functioning... on and on and on. There is so much that goes into running a space-going vessel. Sitting next to Ronin in the common room, I drop the handheld display and rub my eye. "Ronin, I'm worried."

"About what, my Mate," he says as he sets down his display. "We need supplies, and how will we pay for them? What about fuel for the ship? How do we pay for that??"

"We'll figure something out?" He says. "If anything, we can transport cargo, not optimal, and we'd have to go black market because you were obviously obtained from an underdeveloped planet."

My hackles go up a bit. "What do you mean underdeveloped?"

"Sorry, I'm sorry, Mate. I didn't mean it that way," he says, trying to avoid my temper. "I just mean there are accords in place to outlaw taking beings from planets that do not have the technology to get to deep space. It means sanctions and possibly even war for the offending race." My anger is successfully averted.

Ronin notices Ekim and Lessur hesitating in the wings. "What are you two doing?" He asks them. Ekim pushes Lessur forward a few steps, which make Lessur growl at him.

"We were wondering if we could train with you?" he says.

Ronin begins, "We train..." Lessur gets an uncomfortable look on his face, and Ronin continues, "Oh, you are talking to my Mate. Forgive me."

All three turn their eyes to me. I am shocked. These big males are asking me to train them. Thinking I'm going to say 'no,' Lessur's face droops in disappointment. "Sorry, Lessur, Ekim, I will definitely train with you. Do you want to learn my fighting style? Or spar with me?"

Both males and Ronin respond immediately, "Yes!"

Doraj walks in and parrots, "Yes, me too! What are we saying yes to?"

Ekim pipes up excitedly, "The Captain is going to spar with us and teach us her fighting style!"

Delight lights his eyes, "Yes! Can Nalax come too? She loved your fighting style, and I would feel better if she could defend herself?"

"Yes," I respond, unable to comprehend what is happening.

Ekim and Lessur leave happily, chatting about the moves they saw me make against Ronin. I look at Ronin in utter shock.

"What?" he looks at me, confused. I give him what I call a 'what the hell just happened there shrug.'

"I don't know, but that's the first time anyone has ever asked me to teach them that hasn't been a woman. Men on my planet generally do not like to learn 'manly' things from women."

"The more you talk about the males of your world, the more I think they must be mentally deficient."

Doraj pipes in, "Just plain stupid."

That makes me laugh loud. It tickles me so much I cannot stop laughing. My sides hurt, and my eyes are watering. Once I finish and wipe my eyes, I look at Ronin and Doraj. Both are smiling at me.

"Seriously though, Captain," Doraj says, "Most peoples of the galaxy understand that anyone can do anything regardless of gender identity if they put the work in. It is obvious that you have spent your life learning and honing your skills at this *and weapons*! Did you see her with those blades in the hallway, Ronin? I was a little afraid. I thought Sitruc was going to shit himself." Ronin and Doraj chuckle.

"I wish I had been the one to kill Sitruc," I say.

"Me too." Ronin and Doraj say in unison.

My stomach drops, "But his body was accounted for, correct?"

"I didn't see it." from Ronin.

"Nor I," from Doraj.

"Sia, was Sitruc's body accounted for in the dead?"

"*Negative.*" She responds.

Fuck. "Is he somewhere on this ship?" I ask.

"*Negative.*"

Ronin says, "Did he *escape*?"

"*Affirmative. He stole a transport pod.*"

The males growl. "There's no point worrying about him for now. We are no longer in the same position, so we should be fine." I say, trying to calm them a bit. Another disturbing thought strikes me.

"Sia, one more question. Is this ship broadcasting any sort of signal?"

"*I will run a scan, but it will take me 76 minutes for me to complete and analyze the results.*"

"Thank you, Sia. Please begin and let me know when you are done."

"*Acknowledged. Captain, there is a message on your display for you.*"

Uh ok. I pick up the display and need clarification on what I see. The message is from Sia.

'*Captain, I heard what you said about being able to pay for the things this ship and its crew needs. I can help with that. Go out the hall, turn left and go to the first lift you come to.*'

I type in return, '*Sia, why not say this out loud in the hall?*'

'*I need you to trust me, Captain. You will not want others to know of this.*'

'*I plan on bringing Ronin and Doraj.*'

'*Acceptable*'

"Ronin, Doraj with me." I get up and walk out of the room. They get up and follow.

"June, what is going on?" Ronin asks.

"Honestly, I don't know." I say to him as we reach the lift. It opens without us calling it. I file in with the guys following. Once the doors shut, I ask, "Sia, can you divulge any more info now?"

"*Not yet, Captain,*" she replies.

I look at Doraj and Ronin, and at the concerned looks on their faces, I say to them, "I trust her implicitly." They nod and relax.

The doors open, and we file out. We are on a level we haven't seen before. "It's storage, Sia. What is this about?"

"*Pick a door and put your hand on the keypad. I have been able to grant you access because you are the Captain of the ship.*"

Ok.... I walk to the third door on the left and place my hand on the keypad beside the door. There's a release noise and a hiss. I pull open the door, and the lights come on.

"*Holy shit,*" I say slowly. I turn around to Ronin and Doraj, and both are slack-jawed staring into the room.

"Sia, what the hell is this?" I practically yell.

"*Captain, this floor contains all of Kaxlin's wealth.*" I turn back, looking at the chamber filled with all sorts of metal bars, like gold and silver, I see art leaning against walls. Rows and rows of boxes, chests, tons of shit I don't even know what it is.

"Sia," I reply calmly, "All the storage lockers on this floor have stuff in them like this?"

"*Yes, all except three are fully loaded. The one you chose is relatively empty,*" she says, sounding a bit bored.

"Um, Sia, how many storage lockers are on this floor?" I ask.

Before she can answer, Ronin whispers, "200."

Sia chimes, "*Ronin is correct.*"

I shake my head to clean the cobwebs created by this. "Sia, did any of his crew know of this?"

"*None, Captain.*"

"How has no one found this?"

Sia responds, "*He ordered me to remove this floor from all ship designs, maps, and computer references. Then ordered that it only be accessible via the lift you took, and only the Captain of the ship has access to direct the lift to this floor.*"

Ronin murmurs, "I knew there was something wrong with the plans, but I just couldn't find it. I was looking for something modified, and I didn't think to look for something missing."

I walk over and sit on one of the crates. Ronin and Doraj follow suit with shocked looks on their faces.

Talking to all of them but looking at none, I say, "Yes, there are many things we could do with this. We could find a planet and live in relative peace, split it up and go our own ways. Hell, we could give it all away, but I need you to hear me out." I look up, and both are listening, interested in my words. "You too, Sia."

"*I... I am listening, June.*" She responds.

"Since we freed this ship and ourselves from slavery, I've been building an idea in my head, but all four of us here must agree to it."

Both males nod, and Sia says, *"I'm listening."*

"On my home world, we had slavery in our history. It was awful. A lot like what we have been through but much much worse and for hundreds of years. Accounts of rape, whipping, and murders were documented. Most slave owners believed they were inferior and treated them like livestock. We abolished it in the country I lived in, and many others did as well. Even before I was taken I found it abhorrent. Even though it was outlawed just like here, it still happens a lot, just like here. So here's my proposal. The "law" of this galaxy fails the beings who live in it. I am sure it's infinitely hard to police an entire galaxy, so here is what I want to do. We become what those people need. We will be vigilantes, yes, but we attack the slavers, we attack the slave markets, we attack the buyers, we liberate all the slaves we can and get them to safe havens we set up. We will become outlaws. We will be hunted by the law and the criminals both. We will be in danger most of the time, but we will free beings suffering through what we have suffered. They need us. There is no one else."

I get down and wander through the room as the others think. Giving them time to work through their thoughts and questions. After a bit, I walk back and see Ronin and Doraj talking. *Ok, June... time to see if we do this or not.*

As I walk over, they both look up and smile a little sadly. My stomach sinks. They do not want to do it. "So, what is your decision?" I ask, feeling like I already know.

Doraj is the first to speak, "I don't know about you, Ronin but I was in like halfway through that speech."

Ronin laughs, "As am I."

Doraj adds, "We are just a little sad you thought we needed time to decide to follow you. You can always count on us."

Ronin put his hand on Doraj's shoulder, I see a little emotion in his eyes. I'm tearing up. These males are my family.

"Sia, what do you say?"

There is a long pause from our AI then she speaks.

"June, you were the first being since I woke to treat me with kindness and compassion. You call me a friend. I feel like you are family. Yes, you liberated those on the ship, but you also liberated me. You give me a choice at every point. It was shocking to me at first, but now, now I know it is who you are. And I vote yes for this endeavor. No one should ever be left to rot in bondage."

Ronin chuckles, "Only my Mate could assist an AI to attain sentience. Well, it looks like it's unanimous. What's next, my Mate?"

We decide to keep the storage and its contents quiet. We do not think it's safe to reveal to everyone, for them or for us. I ask Sia to grant access to it for both Ronin and Doraj, but I stipulate that no one visits the deck without one of the others knowing. We lock up and leave. Planning starts tomorrow. We are all in a bit of shock.

We're heading toward the communal area to eat. We are almost there when someone steps in front of us. Ronin and Doraj both growl at the newcomer.

It looks female, and the growl it lets out sounds feminine, but she looks lethal. Instead of hair, she has feathers on her head which are standing straight up, shaking in warning at the males threatening her. Her face is thin and hollow, with dark circles under her eyes.

She hides it well, but she is scared. She has scars up and down her arms. She has been through much, like me.

I step around my overprotective males. Ronin fears for me, "Mate, stop. She is Ferin. They are a bloodthirsty species."

"I have this, Ronin." He doesn't relax but trusts me, so he steps back. I look at Doraj, and he backs off a few steps as well.

I walk to her. She still has fear in her eyes, but her feathers are now resting against her head.

She looks at me with a mixture of fear, uncertainty, and hope. "You are the sex slave that fought him… killed him?" she asks me.

"Yes. I am."

"You freed everyone on the ship instead of using them as your own slaves?" She asks, but it's more of a statement.

"I will NEVER own a slave, ever. I am going to do everything I can to free any I can find and give them a safe place to go."

She stares at me for a long time, and it honestly feels like she is weighing my soul. I do not care what Ronin says, this Ferin is looking for something, and she is not evil, just lost.

She closes her white eyes and sighs. They reopen, and she is more at peace. She says, "You are the one I've been looking for all these years. I ask this of you, may I join your crew? I am meant to assist you in what you do."

"What is your name? I ask.

"Elana," she tells me.

"Elana, trust is a special thing. We all are recovering from the things done to us. It is hard to trust when you've gone through something like this. Do you trust me?"

She pauses, "You are right. It *is* hard, but I want to try."

I give her a small smile, "As do I. So how about this? We meet in the communal lounge every day at 14:00 to have a drink or a snack. We'll get to know each other. For your temporary ship duties, you'll report to Doraj for the day's tasks that need to be done. If by the time we reach the haven we find for the passengers and you and I trust each other, you may sign on as crew."

She gives me a small smile and bows her head in respect. I hear Doraj take a sharp intake of breath.

She glances at him and back to me, "Let that be the first step toward trust." She leaves.

I glance at Doraj and raise my eyebrow in question. "Ferin has a weak spot on the top of their heads. A blow to the spot can kill them. They never bow their heads. It's not done. Not even to their own kind. It's too much of a risk."

I look back in the direction she went. I make a mental note to get information on her species from Sia.

We enter the communal room, grab food and sit down. I need to bring this up with Ronin, but I hate it. "Ronin," he looks up with a question in his eyes, "You are remodeling the Captain's quarters, yes?"

Unsure of where my line of questioning is going, he responds, "Yes, it will be done in a few days. Why?"

Here we go, "Can you change the conference room as well? It needs to be different. Please?"

A look of pain and anger flashes across his face but he schools it quickly, "I will remodel it."

"I'm sorry I didn't ask sooner." Upset, I caused him pain.

"Mate," he says, not angry but with need, "Will you spar with me?" Relief washes through me.

"Yes... if we get to use weapons."

A smile spreads across his face, "As you would say, 'Fuck Yeah!'" We both jump up and race to the sparring room, laughing. Doraj is fast on our heels, so he can watch.

Ronin

Ekim and Lessur are training, practicing the Kata my Mate gave them. They both look up and get excited looks on their faces when they see us striding in. Ekim yells, "They're going to spar!"

Laughing, I tell them, "*With weapons*!" Ekim and Lessur are on the mat, but I notice the right side of the room has changed. It is full of new equipment. There are targets and several strange-looking large stands with wood-looking short branches sticking out of them, and bags hanging from the ceiling. It's then I see an entirely new weapons wall. An *entire wall*!

"You did this?" I ask my Mate.

"With Sia's help, do you like it? I wanted to give you a surprise." Staring for a few minutes taking in everything she has done for me. My speed launches me at my Mate, she is in my arms, and I am kissing her passionately.

When we stop, she looks dazed and says, "I'm gonna take that as a 'yes'." She says with a smile.

"Oh yes," I tell her, "Very much. Thank you, my amazing little Pillut."

June

He walks over to the GWC and gives me a questioning look, "It's a traditional Martial Art striking dummy called a Geniqua Wing Chun." We now have an audience, Doraj, Ekim, Lessur, and even Nalax are following us around the new equipment as I name each and how it is used.

About two hours later, I finished explaining the equipment and answered the barrage of questions I got for each. I love it. Developing these beings to love the thing I love is the best feeling ever. "Any other questions?" I ask them.

I see Nalax nudge Doraj. I turn to them and raise my left eyebrow in question. Doraj very uncomfortably asks, "Uhmmm... what were you and Ronin doing with your mouths?" My face is immediately on fire, and I hear Ronin bark a laugh.

I turn a not-so-serious glare at him and turn back to Doraj and Nalax, "That is a human custom. It is called a kiss, and it is only done with those you are intimate with." They are now looking at me like they're waiting for me to finish. I'm not sure what they want.

Ronin steps to my side, "It is very pleasurable for both partners." He grabs both sides of my face and gets close. His voice is entirely too sexy when he says, "There are two ways to kiss. Bring your mouth down to your partner, and with your mouth closed, apply your lips to hers." He proceeds to demonstrate. He slowly and tenderly kisses me and pulls back. "The next type of kiss is about passion. You apply your lips again to your partners, once applied, open your mouth and passionately intertwin your tongue with hers until you are both almost out of air." He pulls me against him and proceeds to give me a long, scorching kiss. When he ends the kiss, I am dazed and unable to focus for a minute.

"Yep, that's how it's done." I am still a bit dazed.

Doraj and Nalax glance at each other and race out of the room. Making everyone chuckle.

A little voice shouts, "Kissing looks GROSS. I am never doing that!" Now we are all laughing so hard that my sides hurt.

Once I can speak again, I look to Ronin, "Ready to go through the weapons wall?" His eyes light up like a kid in a candy store.

Ronin

I swear to the goddess my undying devotion for giving me this Mate and practically skip to the left side of the wall. My Mate is chuckling at my behavior, but I don't mind. It has been a very long time since I found weapons I wasn't already familiar with. I have not been this excited in a very long time!!

The first several columns of weapons look to be wood in all shapes and sizes. I quickly deduce these must be training weapons. I look to my Mate and ask, "For training purposes?"

She smiles, "Yes, most of the wooden weapons are to train and spar with until the trainee is able to prove their proficiency." Nodding, I move along the wall till I reach the battle weapons.

Without looking at her, I ask, "These are all human weapons?"

"Yes, but specifically, these are all traditional Martial Arts weapons. These are the weapons I have mastered."

I glance at her, then back at the wall, and do a quick count. "There are over 40 different weapons on this wall! You are the master of all?"

She nods, "I am better at some than others, but I am rarely bested with any of them." She says it with no ego or bravado.

"Besides the Katana, which is your favorite?" I am inquisitive. Her face scrunches a little, the way I love when she is thinking,

"That is hard... I would have to say..." she walks to the wall and pulls a long straight stick off the wall, "the Bo."

This is totally unexpected. I thought daggers or any of the others but one that looks like a training weapon? No. She sees my confusion and walks to the mat. "The Bo is an elegant weapon. Will it kill? Usually, no. Can it kill? It absolutely can. I think a demonstration is in order. Who would like to have a go at me with the Bo?" Ekim and Lessur's hands immediately raise. "Lessur it is." She chuckles at their enthusiasm.

"Lessur, go pick any weapon off that wall," she says to him.

Shocked, he says, "Any?!" She nods and chuckles again. He walks up and down the wall trying to choose. He picks up a set of particularly nasty-looking blades. They are the length of my forearm and have an abrupt hook on the end. The handle has a crescent moon-shaped knife-like guard, and the handle ends in a sharp pointed tip. They are very intimidating-looking weapons.

"Ah, the Hook Swords. Nice choice. Another of my favorites. I'm impressed, Lessur. Those are one of the most feared weapons in the arts to battle against."

The idea of my Mate going up against those, even in training, makes me uneasy, but I trust her when she says he won't be able to touch her.

"Since this is a demonstration, not a match, we'll just go through several attacks. Ok?" She asks Lessur. He nods. "Good. I think five separate demos should be enough. Lessur, no real rules except this; one attempted attack, then stop. Reset and again." Lessur nods again. "Set," she calls, then executes several spins of the Bo, ending with it pointed down and tucked behind her arm. Calm focus painted across her face. "Go," she says to Lessur.

Lessur is a Nlyaxian warrior. He was out of shape when we took the ship, but he is no longer so. He explodes out of the corner using the blades similarly to our short blades. He doesn't even get close. The Bo whips from behind her back so fast it's almost hard to track. The Bo hits Lessur in the stomach, effectively stopping his forward motion and causing the air from his lungs to explode out of him. Before the air is expelled, I see it already coming around to take his legs from underneath him. Lessur is on his back on the floor.

She walks over and stretches her hand to help him up. "The first lesson is always the hardest."

He takes it with a smile and says, "I was barely able to follow the Bo with my eyes."

She nods, "Yes, because the Bo is made of wood, it blends with its backgrounds much better than metal-based weapons that are dark and shiny."

Fascinating. At that moment, I see Elana back against the far wall, watching. The fighting skills of the Ferin are known throughout the galaxy as some of the best. I motion to her to come over. She hesitates for a good two minutes, then makes her way over to stand near me; not within range of my reach but being Ferin, it's surprising she joined us. They are a very reclusive species.

My Mate continues to put Lessur on the mat. The fourth time Lessur ends up on the mat, I hear Elana say softly,

"Your Mates' fighting skills are shockingly good." I freeze in shock. Ferin NEVER compliments other species on their skills. NEVER. I look to Elana to see if she is being facetious, and she is not. She looks at June with new respect. I look at my Mate. She is building relationships I never thought possible.

When Lessur gets up for the fifth time going to the mat, looking a bit sore, I raise my voice and say, "My turn."

June

I am not normal. I do not think I should get wet when my Mate wants to fight me... but boy, do I. Ronin walks over to the wall and grabs another Bo. Interesting. He turns and walks back, spinning it over his head, then sides, behind his back. Ok, alright, my Mate. You have used a similar weapon, but you have little respect for it. Time to teach you some respect. "Are we sparring?" I ask him.

"Yes, I think so. I believe I'll be able to hold my own with this one."

"We shall see Mate. We shall see."

We ready ourselves on the mat. Once we are set, Doraj, governing the match, yells, "GO." Neither of us wait for the other to attack and immediately go on the offensive. I will admit he has some skill, and his strikes to my Bo rattle the bones in my arms. However, it is also obvious it has been a long time since he's trained with it. Like he was forced to use something similar before he got to use the 'real' weapons and since has never picked it up again. We continue to blow for blow as I gauge his skill.

"She weighs your skills, Nlyaxian," Elana says with some humor. Huh. How could she tell I was doing that? A question for later. Doraj calls round one, and we return to our corners. I am sweating but far from tired or even winded. As I drink some water, I glance over at Elana. To my surprise, she gives me a sideways smile and a wink. I laugh out loud and realize I'm gonna be friends with that one and reading what Sia had on her people. I think she'll be the one to make me work if I can get her to spar with me. Behind me, Doraj yells, "READY."

"GO." We both are more reserved this time, but now I know his skills. It's time to push them to their limits. My goal is not to win but to push to teach.

Ronin

I am not going to lie to myself. The Ferin saying my Mate was testing my skills threw me for a bit of a loop. Here I am, thinking I'm holding my own against my Mate, and the Ferin is causing me to question that. Sure it's been a while... It's been a long while since I picked up a training staff, but I am still using it well.

She starts adding force and techniques that she didn't use in the first round. Within a few minutes, she has three points, and I luckily avoided the sweep that was intended to put me on the mat. I need to up my skills and train a lot harder if I want to score on my Mate. I cannot wait for the day I put her on the mat. And... I'm on my back on the mat. Fuck. You need to focus.

I get up as Doraj calls the round. Ok, time for me to do focus exercises.

June

Good, it looks like he's doing some mental refocus. He was distracted that round. When the next round begins, I see the male who fought with me back to back against a ship of enemies. Good, my Mate. Let's go.

He makes it much harder for me to get points on him this time. I am having to put in real effort to even get close to landing a blow. I stopped altogether from going after his legs because it almost got him a point twice. We're both breathing hard and have sweat dripping to the floor. I finally land my second hit, and Doraj calls the match. I immediately use the bow for some additional strength. When I glance up, Ronin is striding across the mat with so much heat in his eyes that my nipples instantly harden, and my pussy clenches.

He wraps his arm around my waist and picks me up. I wrap my legs around him and lock my feet together. My pussy has come to rest perfectly on his hard cock, clothes the only thing separating us. He growls, "Soon, Mate I will get a point on you, and when I do, I'm going to rip your clothes off, drive my cock into you and make you scream my name."

Fucking. Bloody. Hell. I pull myself up to his ear, "What's stopping you from doing it right now, maTe." Then I lick his ear from bottom to top. He shivers then he is sprinting.

Ronin

We end up in the recharge room, which has showers and various other things. I head into the shower, and as we are ripping clothes off one another, I also turn on the shower. The minute we are both naked, I have her against the wall, legs around me, feet locked, and I thrust in as hard and fast as I can. She screams in pleasure, and I start pounding into her pussy hard and fast. Her nails dig into my shoulder, and she bites my shoulder, my need spikes higher through me. Deeper, I need to get deeper. I get my arms under her knees, she unlocks her feet, and I move her leg wide and back, anchoring my hands to the wall. Yes. My cock goes deeper with every thrust. I start to thrust hard. I need my cock as far in as it will go.

She is screaming and mewling, moaning. Her pussy suddenly locks down on my cock harder than it ever has. I roar my pleasure as my sprili unfurl and begin their massage. She screams my name again as her pussy continues to milk my cock. I can no longer hold it back. I throw my head back, roaring, burying my cock as deep in her pussy as it can get. I leave it there as they begin to vibrate, and they vibrate hard this time. My

Mate is screaming my name again and again, coming undone. We are still locked together deep, my head resting on the wall beside hers. We both cannot speak because of how hard we are breathing. After a few minutes, I say to her, "I don't want to leave your body. It is where I belong."

She sweetly replies as she nibbles down my jawline, "Then don't. But the hot tub over there looks like a good place for round two."

I growl, "Fuck female. You were born to be a Nlyaxian Mate, *my* Nlyaxian Mate." I bring my hands around and grab her beautiful ass and take us to the heat pools.

June

As we sink down into the biggest hot tub I've ever seen, I moan with pleasure. My muscles begin to relax. I rest my head on his shoulder. "This is bliss." He slowly rubs and massages my back and neck, then moves to my arms. When he finished there he lifted me off his cock, and I float toward the center. Interesting, I'm not even trying to float. I feel Ronin start to massage my feet. I groan. It feels so good. He moves to my calves, then thighs.

He moves to my ass and growls. "Your ass is magnificent."

I smile, feeling my nipples harden, and my pussy starts to ache. "I've always been told it was too big, too muscular. I'm too tall and my arms are too muscular. My mom thought my goal should have been to be stick thin."

He growls again. Then it changes in tone, coming from under the water. I feel bubbles caress my ass and then move, trying to get through my legs. I part them as wide as I can, which is pretty wide considering I can do the splits. I feel something like bubbles teasing the lips of my pussy. Barely touching, then gone. Touching somewhere else, then gone. Something more firm than a bubble begins to explore the folds, thoroughly learning all. I moan at the sensations it is creating. It lightly circles my opening but does not enter. I moan again, bereft.

The not bubble travels north in a meandering path. I moan in need, and it knows what I want. I try to move in the water, trying to get it where I want it, but the movement of the water doesn't allow any real power of movement. "Ronin. Please." I moan loudly, unsure if he can hear me.

The not bubble gives me a small measure of satisfaction, and it moves to my clit to circle it several times. I am moaning, feeling my climax slowly building. I cannot take it. "RONIN!" I scream. I am panting when I feel arms wrap around my legs, fingers spreading my folds.

I finally see him. His hair slicked back with water. I see a hint of humor in his eyes, "Tsk, tsk, tsk, my Mate," he firmly licks, ending with a circle around my clit and a flick against the nub. I moan again. "You should practice your patience, for your reward will get here in time." He teases me.

"Ronin. Please, I need it." His eyes turn into inferno's, "tell me what you want Mate." Fuck he is so hot.

Moan, "Firmly circle my clit with your tongue." He does it. "More." One more. "MANY TIMES!" He chuckles as he proceeds to circle it many times, but it is enough of a distance from my clit that it's enough to make me moan and squirm but not enough for my climax.

"Ronin. Run... run your tongue firmly over my clit many times, then nip it with your teeth."

Chuckle, "Good little Mate." He begins to execute my command. His firm tongue, running back and forth, back and forth, back and forth. I am building fast now.

"YES, RONIN. PLEASE, YES!" I scream. Back and forth, it's coming. Back... nip. The scream that rips from my throat drowns out all other sounds. "RONIN! OH GOD!"

He lifts his head a little. "Adequate little Mate?" he asks in a teasing tone. I stand up in the water. "Oh yes, my big Mate."

He reaches for me, and I swim away from his reach with a smile. "Mmmm, I have more things I want."

His eyes go molten again. "And what would that be?"

"Do you see the sloped exit from this tub?" He nods.

"Good. Go to that slope. Lay face up, legs in the water till it just touches your cock."

He growls, "Mate, you play with fire."

I chuckle and give him my sultry look, "Mate, I AM FIRE. Go."

He walks backward toward the slope out of the tub. His eyes are on fire. The water gets more and more shallow as we go. My nipples leave the water, and he growls. They stand at attention at his order. I stare into his eyes as I lift my hands and begin to caress my breasts. Doing what I want his hands to do. He is still going backward but the growl doesn't stop and it's sending little shocks through my clit. I moan, imagining him licking and sucking my nipples into his mouth. His eyes are focused on my hands now as I play with myself. The head of his cock breaches the water and with every step, more and more of it is visible. He stops and slowly lowers himself to sit just inside the water. He lays back, and I swear he is going to make me cum before I even touch him.

I walk forward a couple more steps. I stand between his legs by his feet. I go down to my hands and knees and begin to crawl toward the beautiful cock I am focused on. I stop as my mouth is directly above. "June... Mate... please." I moan as gooseflesh explodes across my skin. The power I have over this huge, sexy male gives me a heady feeling. He is my Mate. He is MINE.

Ronin

My Mate's mouth hovers over my cock, and I want to lift my hips so she will wrap her lips around it. My breath explodes out of my lungs when she takes hold of my shaft and starts to lick the head of my cock. I moan, "Mate..." she blows over the wet she just created, and a shiver rolls through my body.

"My Mate. If you'd like to recline on your elbows so you can watch my lips and my tongue on your huge cock," she glances up at me from under her lashes, "You may."

I am reclining on my elbows. There is nothing in the universe I want more than to watch her mouth, *groan*, and tongue on my cock. She continues to explore with her tongue as she reaches the ridges of my sprili and begins to circle and lick the ridges. As she travels the ridges with her tongue, the sprili, like they have a mind of their own, individually unfurl and stroke her tongue, then return to my body. We both moan with the sensation, but the sensation for me is pure ecstasy. A good amount of my seed leaks from my cock. She travels back and licks up every last drop.

"Mate please..." then she gives me what I am begging for. Her lips wrap around my cock, slowly descending down the shaft. At the midline, she reaches her limit and starts back up a bit faster and moaning. The vibrations that her moans create in my cock make me almost lose it. Control... discipline... what's the third one... "OH FUCK!" I cannot help my outburst. She is now bobbing up and down my shaft, and I cannot look away. She is enjoying it as much as me. The moaning is almost non-stop, with her mouth sucking and bobbing. It is too much, "June!" I yell, and I am cumming. She sucks down the seed like her life depends on it.

She sits back, licking the last of me from her lips. "How do you want me to take you, Mate... because I am taking you... hard."

She moans; our desire is out of control for both of us. She moves, looking around the room, then grabs my hand and moves toward the wall of the pool in the shallow end. She lifts herself partially out of the pool and bends over the side, lifting one knee and resting it on the ledge of the wall. She is presenting me with that beautiful ass and pussy at the same time.

I position myself behind her with my cock at her entrance. My right-hand holds her shoulder, and I watch as I push in, inch by inch. She's moaning. I promised hard. I start slow and hard. Trying to build her pleasure higher, hotter. Building my speed and pounding harder and harder... faster and faster. I no longer have control. I am ruled by the sensations we are creating along the length of my cock.

"RONIN! RONIN!" Screams then her pussy locks down on my cock and starts massaging, begging it to release its seed. My sprili unfurl and start massaging her walls, sending her over the edge again. The massaging continues and I can no longer hold it back. My climax hits, and my seed hits her walls as I roar my pleasure, feeling it in the base of my spine. Still pumping in and out as my seed continues to spray her walls, the sprili vibrate, and she climaxes again. Her pussy continues to spasm even after she's come down from her orgasm. I love the feeling.

She moans as my cock slides from her body. I pick her up and wash her than myself. We dress, and I pick her up again because I just like to hold her, and I head back to our room to sleep. She is my world.

Chapter 18

The next morning, we reach the safe spot Sia and Lessur picked, so we have time to regroup. I am sitting on the bridge early, reviewing reports. Sia chimes in, *"Captain, I have important information."*

Curious, "Ok, Sia, let's hear it."

"There are three beacons broadcasting from this ship."

I am up out of my chair. "WHAT? Where? Show me on the large display." Fuck. "Sia, open the comms to Ronin and Doraj.

"Opened"

"Ronin and Doraj, come to the bridge immediately."

Sia speaks up again, *"June, two ships just showed up on long-range scanners. They are headed directly toward us."*

"Shit, can their scanners see us?"

"Highly unlikely Nlyaxian tech is far more advanced than most, and I was built with the newest tech."

"Can you tell by make who they belong to?"

"They are not yet close enough."

Ronin and Doraj jog into the room. Ronin asks, "What's wrong?"

"We have three beacons transmitting on this ship. We've been out of hyperspace for all of 3 hours, and we already have two ships inbound on long-range scanners," Sia says, giving them the information I have.

"Sia, did you have another safe location you and Lessur were thinking about?"

"*Affirmative*"

"How long before you can get us en route to that location?"

"*Thirty-two minutes.*"

"Do it."

"Ronin, you, me, and Doraj need to destroy some beacons."

"Ekim!" I yell.

"Yes, Captain!" Ekim says, running into the room.

"We have two unknown ships inbound. We are rerouting, so we do not need to engage, but I want to be ready to shoot back if anything goes wrong."

"Yes, Captain!"

"Sia, is there anything else we need to know about these beacons?"

"*Just that they are all located on the hull of the ship.*"

I freeze, and my fingers pinch the bridge of my nose. "Fucking hell."

I turn to Ronin, "I have no idea how to do that, and we don't have time to teach me. Is there someone else who can go out and get the 3rd beacon?"

From behind me, I hear a feminine voice say, "I'm trained in external ship repair." We all turn at once, and Elana stands behind Doraj with a small smile on her face.

I turn to her, "It needs to be as fast as possible, which will make it dangerous."

"I understand. It's ok." She says, unfazed.

Hmmm... "Ok, but... I really would like to start training with you when this is all done. Deal?"

She gets the biggest smile, which is a little unnerving because of the sharp teeth, but those types of things are starting to have little effect on me anymore. Elana excitedly throws her arms in the air, gives a little twitter, and says, "Yes! I was afraid you'd say 'no,' so I didn't ask!"

Laughing, "Ok, good. Now get the beacon and bring it back on the ship. I have an idea." I say, looking at Ronin.

Within ten minutes, the three of them are out on the hull heading toward their beacons. I'm on the bridge, trying not to look like I am scared for my friends... and my Mate. "Sia, how long before you're ready to travel to the new site?"

"*Eighteen minutes*"

"What's your projection on when all three beacons will be inside?"

"*Twelve minutes.*"

"When will the two ships be within a range that they'll be able to detect us without the beacons?"

"*Twenty-one minutes*"

"Shit. Cutting it close on all fronts. Ekim, I need a missile-type weapon. Do you have something like that?"

"Yes, Captain?" Confused as to why I am asking.

"Good. We need to prepare it to take three beacons with the ability to launch in the opposite direction we are going."

At once, it dawns on him, and he gets the brightest smile. "I understand! When Ronin and the others come in, tell them to go to weapons platform six."

After Ekim is gone, Sia says, "*I have informed Ronin, Doraj, and Elana to go straight to weapons platform six when they get back inside.*"

"Thank you, Sia. I guess now we wait."

Fourteen minutes later, all three beacons are inside weapons platform six.

Five minutes later, all four crew jog onto the bridge. Ekim calls, "Ready to fire, Captain. Where are we firing Sia?"

"*Coordinates are at your station.*"

As he races to his station, "Ekim, fire as you as you are ready."

"Firing."

"Lessur, get us the fuck outta here."

We re-enter hyperspace, and we all relax.

"Sia, did they see us?"

"No, Captain. They started to pursue the weapon."

I relax back in my chair and look at Ronin, "Is there any other device type that I might not be aware of," I laugh and add, "Since I am from an underdeveloped planet." We all chuckle at that.

I look at Elana, "You have proved yourself to me, Elana. No need to wait. You are our newest crew member." We all smile, and the three Nlyaxians stand and salute her. Elana looks embarrassed, but her smile is huge. She whispers emotionally, "Thank you, Captain."

Sia chimes in, "Welcome, Elana. Captain, I will review the rest of the scan for risks, but I believe we have addressed them."

"Thank you. Lessur, how long till we get to the new location?"

"Ten-day cycles, Captain."

"Does anyone know if we have enough supplies to make it there? And really extra since we'll be heading somewhere else after that."

Nalax comes in with Leena, hearing the end of the conversation, "We'll need to stop. We need supplies for both the infirmary and food synthesizers."

Sia chimes in, *"We should also stock fuel rods."*

I sigh, "Ok, all departments come up with lists and send them to all the crew. Lessur, please work with Doraj and Ronin on a place to restock supplies. As safe as possible, please."

"Understood."

A few day cycles later, Leena is at Ronin's side, arms wrapped around his waist, only reaching about halfway around. She looks up at him and whispers, in a not-so-quiet whisper, "Is it time yet?"

He 'not no quiet whisper' back, "I think so."

I raise an eyebrow in question. He holds out a hand to me, and in her absolutely adorable way, my daughter extends hers as well.

I walk over to them and place a hand in each. I am trying to puzzle out what they are up to. They pull me toward the conference room door. I feel the fear flash and my hesitation as we walk. I look at Ronin and relax. I trust him.

"You ready, my beautiful Mate?" He asks. I look at him, then down at Leena who has a look of pure joy and excitement on her face. I relax the rest of the way and nod. The door to the room opens, and her face lights up.

Not gonna lie, my nerves were still up, but I trust my Mate. When the door opened, it wasn't even the same room. It was wider for sure, and the table is gone. Instead, against the wall with windows? Wait, how are there windows if we are in the center of the ship? A question for later.

Against the wall with windows is a row of 5 desks for the crew and myself to have a place to work if needed. The opposite wall is now a floor-to-ceiling display. On it currently is our location in space and a marker for our destination. I feel Ronin close my mouth with a finger, and Leena giggles. "I think she likes it!" She laughs.

Ronin chuckles, "I think you are right."

"It's perfect," I say quietly with awe. It looks nothing like the room before.

I look at both of them and pull them toward me for a hug. "Thank you."

"Ready for the rest," Ronin asks. I nod, not really sure, but willing to try. I look at the door that leads to the other room, and a little fear rises in me. But I'm not a coward. I walk toward it, and it opens as I reach it.

When I see what's behind it, I can hardly believe my eyes. The windows have moved to the wall directly across from the door. So definitely not windows. Noted.

Against the window is a couch, chairs, and table, but instead of military grays and taupes, the walls and furniture are teals, turquoise, golden yellows, and sunset oranges. It looks so much more like a home; I have to battle the tears back. I slowly walk to the center of the main room and turn. The kitchen is to the left of the conference door. The bath is to the right. Next to the bath is a door to another room. Leena sees my focus and squeals, "MOTHER, come see my room!"

The tears come back, and Ronin's hand is on my back, rubbing. I move toward her room while she pulls my hand.

As I enter, I let out a sigh. It is perfect for a little girl. Pastels and primary colors decorate my view. She has a large bed she can grow into and a desk. "Ronin, it's perfect!"

Leena giggles and laughs as she bounces on the bed.

"Did you help with this?" I ask her.

"NO! Father made it all. It's perfect!"

I look at Ronin and whisper, "He's perfect."

He gives me a loving smile and asks, "Would you like to see our room?" I nod because the emotions are getting to me. Ronin grabs my hand and leads me to a door on the other wall toward the inner corner.

As it opens, I gasp. More 'not windows' line the far wall, and in the center is the biggest, most luxurious bed I have ever seen. It takes up half the room. It's round, covered in beautiful turquoise color bedding, and about 30 pillows. Something catches my eye, and I look up. On the ceiling directly above the bed is a large mirror. Oh my. Just thinking about what either of us might see makes my pussy clench.

Ronin is at my ear, "We'll have to wait till our little Leena is asleep, but when you're screaming my name. She will not hear. I soundproofed this room." Ok, now I'm very wet. "I love the smell of your desire, Mate." Fuck.

I turn to look at the rest of the room and see a closet for both of us, and in the center is a weapons rack. A huge smile crosses my face, and I look at Ronin, "Love it!"

He laughs, "I knew you would, and so do I!"

At that moment, I hear a voice ring out from the other room, "Can we come and see?"

We laugh again and say at the same time, "Yes!"

The room became the hangout for the evening. We had dinner and talked, enjoying each other's company. Doraj speaks up at a lull in the conversation, "So serious question! Who wants a taste of this Noinapmoc brandy?" Myself, Nalax, and Elana all raise our hands.

Ronin groans, "I predict some craziness in the next few hours."

No craziness ensued, but we definitely got louder and laughed a lot more. A few hours later, everyone was headed back to their quarters. The ladies were a bit tipsy, but no one was drunk. Leena went to bed hours ago, so it's just Ronin and me. I start walking toward our new bed, slowly stripping clothing as I go. A growling starts somewhere, and I shiver with anticipation. I get to the bed and climb up and start making my way to the center on my hands and knees.

Suddenly the growling is much closer, and before I can register what's happening, there is a firm tongue exploring my folds while hands hold my ass to the face between my legs. Still, on my hands and knees, I start moving my hips to push against his tongue. Ronin reaches forward to caress and pinch my breasts. On the other hand, he runs his finger until they find the place they have never entered before. He swirls his finger around it. My body is on fire, his tongue building a fire, his seeking fingers making it burn much hotter. My body is confused. Push down or push back, I vibrate on the edge of oblivion. It's then that Ronin makes the decision for me. His thick finger pushes in and begins its gentle massage at the same time his mouth latches onto my nub sucking and thrashing it. I explode, screaming his name, my chest falling to the bed. Before I'm down from my orgasm, Ronin is thrusting into my pussy.

My moaning is uncontrolled, and his pace is hard and fast. My orgasm is building fast, and I feel the sprili start massaging. "Ronin!" My orgasm breaks through me as I come down, Ronin still pounding into me. I feel his cock swell and release his hot seed, the sprili start the final act sending me back into the stars. When I can think again, I am stomach down on the bed, Ronin on top. He's starting to pull his cock out. Spasms rack my body, and I moan.

"Shhh little Pillut. It's time to rest." I feel him put a pillow under my head. He lays behind me and curls around my body protectively, finally pulling the blanket over us both. "Love you, Ronin." I'm asleep before he responds.

Chapter 19

The next five days are spent planning, getting the ship back into shape, and training. We've determined we are going to a space station to get supplies and fuel.

I'm heading to the training room now, hoping to catch Elana. We keep missing each other, and I really want to spar with her. Sia has been able to dig up some grainy vids of other Ferin battles, and I must say her species' fighting skills look amazing. From what I could tell in the vids their style is similar to the African martial arts. I never studied those, but they are one of the most formidable on Earth.

I wish there was more on Ferin culture and fighting. I would love to dig in and learn all about my friend, just as I did with Nalax. I do believe there is a lot of misinformation on the Ferin as well. I've read everything from seeing the future to they eat babies.

Elana has never even shown the slightest hint of violence since meeting her. The question is did some bitter rival species spread the lies to discredit them, or did the reclusive Ferin themselves spread them to prevent others from wanting to engage with them?

I walk into the training room, and I'm chanting 'please please please, and when I see her, I actually jump with my arms in the air but manage to keep the hoot inside. She sees my display and starts laughing, and raises her hands too. I trot over, "Fuck yeah, Elana, we get to spar today! I'm so excited!"

She laughs again. "I am as well."

We start our short trek over to the mats, and I ask, "Elana, are there any rules you'd like me to adhere to during the matches?"

She floors me by saying, "No, I trust you. But do you have any places I should not strike because of risk?"

"Avoid the eyes... and the teeth... oh hell, why don't we just say no blows to our heads?"

She smiles, "Perfect."

I call over to Nalax, "Hey, you want to govern for us?"

"Yes! Oh my yes!" and she's on our mat.

"Oh wait... weapon or no weapons?" She cringes a bit and lifts her hands."Oh yeah, hmm, your hands are weapons. Is there a weapon on the wall that is similar to what you've used?"

She smiles, "I think you called it the Bo. Ferin calls it a Salx."

"Best news ever!" We both laugh.

Doraj saunters over and tosses us both a Bo. We both remove our shoes and tunics. Elana's sports bra is similar to mine, but it holds three well-defined breasts. Cool. My hair is up in a braided pony, and somehow I know she won't use it, so I don't tie it up. By the time we warm up, there are quite a few people here to watch.

"Ready!" Yells Nalax. I move into my ready stance. Elana is a black hole for me. I've never seen her fight but I doubt I'm going to be able to test her skills as I did with Ronin. Working through my options, I settle on my best chance, really my only chance. Dominance. I have to run and control the fight; other-wise, she can surprise me, which is never good. Nalax yells, "Go." I explode from my corner. My offensive is aggressive and targeted. I need to find her weaknesses.

Blow for blow, she matches me. The cracks of wood on wood ring frequently through the room. Whenever I think I am close to getting the point, she surprises me with a new move or the ability to block it. I do the same to her. I use every kata, punch, kick, and tactic I was ever taught. She is amazing.

We are finished with two rounds. The room has rang with the cracks of wood on wood for nearly 40 minutes and neither of us has scored a single point. It's definitely not for lack of trying on either of ours. We're both dripping with sweat, and our breathing is labored, but man, are we having fun. I look over at Elana, and she gives me a big authentic smile. She is having fun as well. I return the smile, and we both give a tired laugh.

"READY," Nalax calls. Ok, here we go. You can do this. She is good, very good, but you can win. Moving into my ready position for the last match, I go through my mental exercises. Focusing and centering my concentration. Nalax yells, "GO" and my eyes snap open. I explode across the room again, going on the offensive to dominate.

I get lost in the flow, the punch, sweep, block. Flowing with the movements of my opponent. I can see her movements and attacks.

It's then I see the opening coming. I need to allow her to get a point to be able to win the match. As I move with the flow of energy, she gets the point by getting a hit to the ribs. I feel my rib crack, but I cannot let my control of the flow go. I must follow it through.

I can see in the flow as she turns to try for the blow she thinks will let her win, but that's when I bring my waiting Bo through her defenses and get a hit to her back and flip the Bo around to sweep her feet. It ends with my Bo stopping an inch from her unprotected chest. Shocked silence fills the space. I groan, grab my ribs, and roll to the mat beside Elana.

I look over to her, "You ok?"

She looks back at me with a smile, "I will be fine. Thank you. June. The pain was worth it to see you go into MkaSha."

Mmmm, ok, unphased because I am wiped out, "That was the best fight I have ever had in my life." I say, smiling.

"Me too! Though I thought your Mate's head was going to pop off when I got you in the ribs."

We both start laughing, then groaning, "NALAX! Two rib repairs, please, stat!" And we start laughing and groaning again.

Nalax and Ronin appear in our vision above our heads. "That was the most amazing thing I have ever witnessed, but Elana you get to clean the bathrooms for a week."

Then he winks at me, and Elana and I burst out laughing again and groaning. "Ronin, stop!"

Doraj reaches out to help Elana up, and Ronin helps me. Together we all head to the infirmary. Best infirmary trip ever!

A few days later, I ask the crew to join me in the new conference room. Ronin and I are waiting for everyone. He sees the space station we are headed to on the display. "Is that the station Lessur is recommending we stop? Not sure I like it..."

Lessur hears Ronin's comment as he walks in, "Yes, I know, but I'll walk through it all once everyone gets here."

In the next few minutes, the rest of the crew filter in. I get up to stand in front of Lessur. "As you all know, we must stop for supplies and fuel before we move on. I asked Lessur and Sia to come up with the safest option they could for resupply. He's going to go through what he found and why they settled where they did. Once that is done. I'd like to hear about the safe haven. We can't keep the passengers onboard forever." I sit back down by Ronin on top of a desk and cross my legs.

Lessur begins, "So before we get to the supply station, I want to talk about the secondary location we are now headed to. We used the first location because those were the requirements set forth. A remote untraveled area where we can regroup and plan. When that was compromised, the secondary location was plotted, and we were en route in under thirty minutes. The secondary location actually had two purposes. It is a remote location on a planet we believe is the best option for a base of operations and safe haven. The planet is uninhabited, and because of ionizing particles in the atmosphere, ships cannot scan the planet for life forms. There was a survey by the Nlyaxians about seventy-five solar cycles past, and there was evidence of a previous species but all evidence pointed to it dying out because of nuclear fallout around 20000 solar cycles ago. After 20000 cycles, the planets and animal species have adapted and developed. Most of the structures are gone, but there is one place on the planet where the structures survived and weathered time. It is in a northern hemisphere mountain range, nestled in between four mountains. Sia believes that she can develop a shielding technology that also cloaks the area so if anyone decides to investigate the planet again, they will not see the settlement. She also suggested putting synthesized nuclear waste that registers as a contaminant but is actually clean. So not only will we not be seen, but they will believe the planet is still uninhabitable. Thoughts?"

Getting excited but realistic, I need facts, "Can you pull it up on the display?" Lessur taps his handheld, and a beautiful planet displays on the big screen.

"Gravity, air, and soil can support all the species on this ship?"

Sia chimes in, *"Yes, Captain. I took Nalax's data from the medical records and ran an analysis. This planet is conducive to all species on the ship."*

"And we are sure there is no sentient life on the planet?"

Lessur smiles. "Correct. There is planet and animal life but no sentient life."

"Are there any large predators on the planet, and what about viruses and such?"

Ronin responds to this question, "When Nlyaxians survey a planet, all that is taken into consideration. What rating did the planet get?"

"It received an F-2-1/5-11-2."

"That is good. F on our scale basically means habitable to most species in the known species database, 2 is a very low-risk factor for planetary illnesses, 1/5 means there is 1 top-tier predator on land and 5 in the water, the 11 is a mineable ore score, and its low which means the planet has virtually no high-value ore, and finally the 2 is incredibly low it basically means the Nlyaxian empire was so unimpressed that they had no intention of settlement. That being said, many species pay attention to our planetary scores, so if we weren't interested, no one probably is."

"Why does this sound almost too good to be true?"

"The biggest challenge with this planet and everyone who might want to colonize it is its location. It is very far away from all travel lines and other supply planets. So if you need something, not on the planet, it takes upwards of twenty-day cycles to get to it."

I get up and start to slowly pace the room. "To alleviate that, we could put our own supply caches in various locations, or our supply runs will need to account for that. Ronin, thoughts?"

"I think it's ideal, but we'll need several supply stops, so we don't buy everything at one. It would draw unwanted attention."

Doraj speaks up, "If we buy specialized equipment for medicinal production, we can use the planet's natural resources to synthesize it. We can also grow the majority of foods, so we would need farming implements, but the biggest concern is clean water, so we will definitely need a purifier big enough for the projected population."

Nalax, with a confused look, says, "How exactly are we going to buy all this? It will not be cheap." I glance at Ronin and Doraj.

They both nod in agreement at my silent inquiry. "We won't need to worry about how we will be able to buy these things.

The previous ship leadership apparently didn't like to be far from his wealth. It is on this ship. And that's another thing. It's very risky to keep all your money in one place, particularly on a ship that can be taken. Do we move a good portion to the planet?"

Ekim answers this time, "I think that would be best. We set something up on the planet and take what we will need when we leave. What about the slaves we liberate? Not all are mentally or ethically balanced. How do we determine who will be allowed to come to the planet and who will not?"

Elana shyly says, "I can do that for you." We all look to Elana for an explanation, "Ferin can see what we call an expalita. It's like an energy halo around an individual. Every living thing has one, even plants and animals. When they are good, fair, and just you have what we say is a healthy expalita with many varied and bright colors. If you are bad, it is sick. It's mixed with grays and black. Kaxlin was particularly horrible. His expalita was nearly all black. It is a good portion of the reason my people are reclusive. Too many of the galaxy's beings were sick. Our governing council thought of protecting our people."

"That is amazing, Elana. Thank you. Does this tax you in any way? I don't want to overburden you."

She gets a little emotional in her way, "Your expalita is beautiful, Captain. No, all Ferin see this; it is a natural part of our sight. It does not tax us in any way. Thank you. Oh, and there are eleven passengers on this ship that we should drop at the supply station and not be allowed to go with us to the planet."

Doraj and Ronin both sit forward, immediately concerned. Doraj asks, "These aren't beings that should be addressed immediately?"

"No, only two are a concern. The rest are untrustworthy. I have been keeping an eye on the two, and I asked Sia to do the same."

Both relax, "Ronin, Doraj, and Elana. I'd like you all to handle the security of the ship and planet. Ronin should be ultimately accountable, though." All three nod in agreement. "I'm worried about Sia; when we get to the planet, will we land the ship, or will it remain in space? Either option leaves her alone on the ship."

Doraj's face is excited, "I can build her a system planet side to give her the ability to transfer her conscience to and from the planet."

"Thank you both. Doraj, can I help with the design?"

He smiles warmly, "I would definitely like your input to ensure you get what you need. As far as the ship goes, we can do either; both options have their risks. I can put together an analysis for you, Captain."

I smile at him, "thank you, Doraj. Thank you all, especially Lessur and Sia, for finding this planet. We'll need to ensure it has not changed since the Nlyaxian survey, but I am hopeful. Ok, Lessur, let's go over the supply station information."

"Sia and I compiled a list of supply locations within the forty-day cycle range of the planet. There are twelve supply locations we can use. The safest of these is," he brings back up the station on the display, "Gamma Station."

With doubt written on his face Ronin says, "I do not understand. Gamma was one of the worst stations."

Lessur nods, "Yes, during Nlyaxian governance, it was lawless and home to some of the worst criminal elements, but since Nlyax's fall, that criminal element has spread to the rest of the stations. Nearly all have been taken over. So now, they all have varying levels of criminal activity. Interestingly enough, the criminals do not like Gamma because of its distance from populated planets and shipping lanes. I am not saying the person who runs it is not a criminal. She definitely is, but she is far from the worst."

"What risks are associated with going to supply stations in general and specifically this one?" I need all the details I can think of.

Uncomfortable Lessurs say, "Well, we'll have to either restrict the females," he sees my anger spike, "Understand that females for slaves are in very high demand and the more... The rarer they are, the more aggressive the slavers will be in getting them if they see them. I am sorry, but right now, slavers rule the system, and they rarely use ethical tactics."

Grrr. "I am willing to discuss it; *however,* I believe both Elana and I would not allow ourselves to get caught again." Elana is unhappy with this conversation as well. Her feathers are up.

"The good thing is we can order what we need before we arrive, then it's just negotiating and loading," Ekim says, then adds. "There's no real need to roam the station."

Not altogether happy with this turn of events, "I wanted to see if we could ferret out some information on the other human females taken. Someone has to have seen the other human females or heard something."

I'm deep in thought when I realize the conversation has stopped. "What?"

Ronin is the first to speak, "What other human females?" Well shit.

Chapter 20

"I am sorry. I guess I forgot in all the excitement to tell any-one." she begins. "When I was on the yellow bastards' ship..."

I growl and add for her, "Craxlin is the species."

"Thank you, Ronin. I was wondering what they were called. Maybe I should start from the beginning. I was at a tourna-ment when I was taken. I was verbally having a fight with my father when someone hit me with some sort of tranquilizer. By the time I turned to see who it was, everything was already very fuzzy. I did see who did it. It was a yellow female with four eyes. I'm pretty sure my father sold me to them."

Fury spikes in me, and I have to control it. What kind of father would do that to his child? "When I woke, I could barely move, but my training took over. I stayed quiet for a while and listened. One of them asked, 'Did we hit our quota for the Lute-tians?' Another said 'No'. Their shipment from the humans was short. The quota was two hundred fifty, and they only received hundred and twenty, I think. I wasn't restrained, so I killed three of them before they shot me with another dart."

Elana growls, "Good. They are the blackest of them."

A thought moves through my mind, "So that word 'quota' means that this isn't the first shipment, and the *Lutetian* are all supposed to be *dead*!" Growling, unable to control my fury.

I feel a light touch on my arm, "Ronin," I look down, worried. I scared her, but all I see is concern. She is no longer afraid of my battle fury!

Instantly, the compassion I see in her eyes dowses it. She asks, "there's something more to these Lutetian, what is it?"

Ekim and Lessur and still trying to control their battle fury, so I continue, "The Lutetian were a warring race that would take over a world, killing everyone, deplete the planet's resources and leave a hunk of rock behind. They didn't dirty their hands with the work, though. They would create new species by genetically modifying others, then use them to destroy worlds."

Ekim takes over, "They were aggressively taking out planet by planet. Nlyax had to step in before they destroyed any more, so we waged war against them. Ronin was the High Commander of the Nlyaxian Military by then and led our people to victory, but many were lost, and the Lutetian; they decided they would rather die than be sanctioned or prosecuted by a war tribunal. They set weapons off on their own homeworld. When the dust settled, their world was dead and uninhabitable."

My Mate has a look of shock on her face, "That's awful. But if they destroyed their people, then why did the Craxlin say they had a quota for them?"

"That is a very good question, my Mate... a very good question... but not something we'll get an answer for today, but it is a new piece of information that concerns me. June, I'm going to ask you to leave this supply run to Doraj and me. Let us handle this one. We need to regroup, plan, and collect information to reduce risks."

My Mates eyes are narrowed at me. I want her to understand I need her to be safe, and with the information we just discussed, my concerns are significant. "*This* time, the females will hang back while the *males* take care of business." Elana snorts humorously at my Mate, "but it will be the only time, *and* if you are late by even *one* minute, we are coming to save *you*."

I believe her. "Thank you, my Mate."

She smiles and says, "Ok, let's get to the real planning for the station then."

June

So we finished planning after working on it for a couple of hours. It's as tight and secure as it can be in these circumstances. It's been a while since I've thought about my father. I'm somewhere past the rage I had for him. Believe me, I still hate him. The fact that he cared so little for me that he felt fine selling me to beings he did or maybe did not know what they were doing with me. Either option is horrible. Thinking back to the events of that day, I was having fun, and so was Ahmya... Ahmya, thinking about her makes me tear up now.

Nalax and Elana come up as I am walking, really wandering the halls. Both lock arms with me, and Nalax says, "Female only night. Elana and I feel like you need a drink and we want to chat and have a little fun." Chuckling and tearing up, "I'd really like that."

We end up in Elana's quarters with three bottles of what equates to alien wine. Pretty nasty, but it won't kill you. We are two glasses in, and the conversation turns serious. Elana gets a concerned look on her face, "June, are you ok? When you talked about your father, your expalita went extremely sad and hasn't recovered."

I couldn't hold back the tears any longer, and they started to fall; I couldn't stop them. Elana and Nalax rush to sit by me, putting their arms around me. Which just makes me cry harder, but just that one demonstration of compassion from these two females who have only known me a month or two have shown me more love and compassion than I ever got from my parents.

I'm sobbing. "You two... are truly sisters to me... you are more family to me than my parents ever were. Thank you."

Nalax looks a little sad as well. "You both are sisters to me as well. My parents disowned me because I refused to be a priestess. I wanted to be a priestess, but it changed. It no longer felt like it was about following the Goddess's teachings but more about control. I hated that."

Elana is looking at her hands, "Never would I ever have thought the two females in my life would be a human and a Noiapmocian. You both are amazing, and I would defend you both with my life. My family loves and believes in me but were very angry when I said I had to leave. They told me not to come back. I miss them a great deal. They are devout followers but could not get past me leaving the planet, regardless of the reason."

And with that, we are all emotional in our ways, and because we are drunk, we are all laughing two minutes later at our emotions. I love these females.

Comms open up, and I hear Ronin's voice. "June, are you ok?"

I giggle, "Awe, he's worried about me. I'm fine, Ronin, just hanging out with Nalax, Elana, and three bottles of alcohol."

This causes a fit of laughing between the three of us. Humor in his voice, "Ok, Mate, just checking. I thought something was wrong. Be good!" A click sounds as the comms end.

The next morning we all wake up from where we passed out the night before. "Ugh, oh my god. My head feels like it is going to explode." Elana just groans, and Nalax puts a pillow over her face. The door chimes and Elana gets up and stumbles to the door. It opens, and Ronin is leaning against the door with a smirk on his stupid face. "Hey, Ladies!" He practically yells.

"Ronin, you scream again, and I will throw a dagger at you," I tell him, and all he does is laugh. I think I'm pretty serious... I think. I wish I had a dagger.

"Come on, my Mate, time for you to rest in our quarters."

"Fine," is the only response I give him.

"WAIT!" Nalax yells, "Ow..." her next words are almost a whisper, "wait... take this, and you'll feel better in fifteen minutes tops."

"Thank you," I whisper back. Ronin picks me up and heads for the door. "Bye, my sisters!"

Ronin takes me back to our quarters and makes me take the meds Nalax gave me, then tells me to go shower, chuckling. Ass.

By the time I am finished, I feel much better. I am drying my hair and walking through what happened yesterday. I stop thinking about my Dad and remember Ahmya.

God, I miss her. I walk through our last moments together. She was giving me pointers about my last match to help in my next. I walked through some of the things she should focus on in her next match. My asshole father came, and that was the last time I saw her.

Wait... that's not technically true. When I spun to fight my attacker... I fell to my hands and knees when I lifted my head. She was the first thing I saw. She was on the floor. I try to focus more on my memory. She's on the ground, out like she was hit or... I look at what is around her in the memory. My heart starts racing... there is another yellow monster he is reaching for her. "No, no, no, no, no. Ronin! Ronin!"

He runs in, looking for a threat. "What is wrong?"

Tears are running down my face. I whisper, "Ahmya... she... she was there at the tournament with me. I forgot. *Oh god, Ronin, I forgot about her!*"

He comes over and grabs my shoulders, "Mate, I do not understand. Calm your mind. Breathe. Breathe. There, good. Now, what are you trying to tell me?"

"My best friend. My sister. She was at the tournament with me, the one where the Cruxlin kidnapped me." Tears are still streaming down my face. "When I was hit with the tranquilizer before I blacked out, I saw her. She was already on the floor. A Cruxlin male was reaching for her. I forgot... they have her. Oh god, Ronin, they have her!"

I am sobbing in his arms now, and my knees buckle. He goes to the floor with me and pulls me into his lap. He rocks me, trying to console me, but nothing can.

"I failed her, Ronin. I should have remembered. I should be looking for her."

After about fifteen minutes, I have nothing left. I am leaning against Ronin's chest. He lifts my face to him, "My Mate, how would you have looked for her? We've been free for less than thirty solar cycles. We have been and still are in survival mode. Here is what I promise you, as soon as we are able, we will search for her. We will do everything we can, I promise you."

Tears roll down my cheeks again, and he wipes them away, "Please, little Pillut, you are breaking my heart. We will do everything we can."

I nod my head, "I love you so much, Ronin." I reach up and kiss him tenderly, "Thank you for understanding my need for this."

"Of course. Anything for you, my Mate." He holds me for a while longer, then stands with me in his arms. He lays down with me in his arms, "Tell me your favorite story of Ahmya."

"Hmmm. Ahmya and I have been friends since we were twelve years old. She and I met at the dojo, where we trained in Martial Arts. The dojo is like a training building where you learn all your fighting skills from a master or set of masters. She was the only one that was nice to me or spoke to me at the dojo. The rest did not believe I belonged there."

"Why not?"

"We return to other conversations you and I have had. The other students did not believe a white person should be allowed to train at their dojo. They came around after a while, but it was just respect for my skill and no desire to be my friend. Ahmya and I were the same. Our humor, our likes, our skills, we were more like family than anyone I had met to date. We never were in competition with each other. We only ever lift the other up, happy at the other's success."

"Wait, do you mean your friend is as good at fighting as you are?"

I chuckle, "Yes. She and I have a tough time beating each other in a match. She is better at some weapons, while I am better at others. We would be unstoppable as a true fighting unit." Yawn.

"Sleep. I will watch over you." I close my eyes and fall to sleep in my exhaustion.

We are about fifteen minutes from the space station. Ronin and Doraj have ordered the supplies we need and set up a dock number to pick them up. We've already got clearance to dock.

The main tasks Elana, Nalax, and I have been backing up Ronin and Doraj while loading is occurring in case someone tries to get on or attack and round up the passengers getting off at this stop. We'll escort them to the door after everything is loaded then we'll let them go so they cannot cause us any trouble.

When the station comes into view, I am surprised it is a bit like I expected. A long cylindrical tube that spins on its axis to give gravity to the aliens inside. There are three separate sections, and each rotates the opposite way of the ones next to it. Sia explained early that the design prevents gyroscopic effects. You can see windows of various sizes on the sections on either end. The really impressive section is the middle section. There are windows that span the length of the center section, and you can see the patchwork green of fields.

The space stations that orbit earth have solar energy panels to power them. This station has some other type of energy generation, but it is not evident.

As we get closer to the station, I can see that this station is massive. The stats Sia gave me, I had to convert to the metric system. The diameter of this station is eight kilometers, and the length is thirty-two kilometers long. I can see the station door at one end that ships fly into to dock.

So when they talked about this station because of the criminal element, maybe I imagined it as a dingy old metal, something you'd be afraid to be on for any extended period of time. The exact opposite is true. The station is a modern marvel, at least to me. It looks clean and well-kept, shiny and new looking. It doesn't look like a place one should be worried about their safety, but I'm just seeing the outside, so I will have to trust the aliens on this one. It is magnificent!

I look over at Ronin and Ekim, and they are both watching me, "What?"

Ronin answers for both of them, "It's not often you can witness someone seeing a space station for the first time. It was amazing to watch your face as you experienced it. Thank you."

We've been cleared to dock, and Lessur expertly guides the ship to the station shipping hatch as it opens for our entrance. Ships much larger than ours must dock at this station because the door is much larger than our ship.

We dock inside at a pier-like structure, and surprisingly enough, there are aliens and all our cargo waiting for us to complete our dock. There must be air in the space, but I don't understand how.

I look back at Ronin. "The shipping hatch has a specialized field. When it opens, the field keeps the bay pressurized." Fascinating. "I have to go meet Doraj at the bay doors. See you soon." He knows I am a bit on edge and gives me a brief kiss, then leaves with Lessur and Ekim.

"Sia, can you open comms to Elana and Nalax, please."

"Open"

"Alright, ladies, time to meet at the rendezvous point. Grab your weapons and meet me there." I grab the weapons I decided on for this and strap them on. Two blasters on my thighs, my Katana on my back, and two tanto at my belt, which is a Japanese short sword. "Let's get this done," I murmur to myself.

I meet them just outside the loading bay door four. All other doors to the bay are secured, and currently, no one can get in or out of them. "Elana, are the passengers secured?"

"Yes, Captain, they are locked in the second door on the right there," she says as she points down the hallway we are in. I nod. "Sia, please put up a display of the bay next to the door."

The display turns on, showing several views inside the bay and two outside the bay door. The doors to the bay are just opening, so we are ready. The aliens stand waiting outside with our cargo load on what looks like floating lifts. The males of our ship walk out to meet them.

"So it begins."

Chapter 21

Ronin

Doraj, Ekim, and I walk down the ramp to meet the dock manager. Lessur stays at the top of the ramp to watch for trouble.

The dock manager's voice booms, "So many Nlyaxians at once! I thought most were dead or fighting in the rings!" He says with a fake smile.

He is Damican, so shorter than my Mate but much wider and probably heavier than I am. His skin is a tan color and looks more like pebbles covering his body. The skin of a Damican is hard to damage with most conventional weapons. The notable trait of a Damican is the six eyes circling his head, which is attached directly to his body instead of a neck. You cannot sneak up on a Damican.

I do not like the thought of my people fighting in the slave pits. I do not acknowledge his statement and hold out my hand. "The manifest."

He hands me the display with the manifest. "Nlyaxians, so rude. No amicable talking. Bah." While I'm looking over the manifest, I am also taking note of the four dock hands waiting to load, also Damican. There are no areas on this dock to hide an attacking force, but I do not relax. The cost of our supplies is high but not so high that I think they are gouging us.

"The fuel cell prices are a bit high," I say as I look at him.

"AH, my friend…" the true negotiations begin. I'm not concerned by the cost of the goods, and if this was a reputable place, I might just pay it but here, if you don't even try to negotiate, then they would assume we have a lot more credits on board and hold us, take the ship. I negotiated lower than he wanted, but we are both satisfied. I look to Lessur to grab the correct amount of credit chips and bring them out.

The Damican is bored once the credits are in his hands but says, "Thank you for the business, and please, you are welcome back any time. Oh, I understand you have some passengers who would like to disembark here?"

"Yes, once the cargo is loaded, they will be ready to disembark."

"Load the cargo!" He yells, and the deckhands spring into action bringing all the cargo into the bay. It takes around sixty minutes to load all our cargo.

Once complete, the dock manager is back, "I must record all passengers coming onto the station and give them their visitor tags."

I nod and glance up at Lessur again. After a few minutes, the passengers start filing out. The two troublemakers are last, and their eyes are darting back and forth. They have something planned.

The Damican gets to the first of the two; he glances at me, then says quickly to the Damican, "You can take ship! The crew is small! Take…"

I was preparing to fight when the Damican grabs the passenger by the neck and lifts him off his feet as he says, "Listen, you piece of garbage, the mistress of this station does not want your opinion on whether to 'take' a vessel or not so shut your hole." He tosses the passenger to security on the dock, "Put that him in the brig." He looks back at the second passenger, "Do you have anything you want to add?" He shakes his head and gives his name.

Once they're gone, he steps to me, "The mistress of the station would like you to know that your ship and crew are welcome here any time, especially if you are buying supplies." He says the last part with a grin.

"Please thank her and let her know a safe supply location will be critical, and if it remains safe, we can promise to buy almost exclusively from her."

He gets a faraway look for a bit, then snaps back, "She is willing to commit to that as long as it is profitable to both parties. It will be safe for the new, more amicable captain of Emancipation and her crew. I nod and return to the ship.

Once the bay doors are secure, "Sia, request clearance to leave and if it's granted, get us out of here."

"Acknowledged."

June

Ronin and the others walk through the door with perplexed looks on their faces. As we start the trip to the bridge, I ask, "What the hell just happened?"

"I'm really not sure. Either we have someone who could be an ally or someone who likes our money, and times are tight for this station."

Hmmm "Well, either way, it's actually good news. Once we get settled, we should come back for our next run and have a discussion with the 'Mistress,' *but* let's be clear, Mate... I'm the only one you'll be calling Mistress." I laugh and jog ahead as he growls and follows.

We enter the bridge as Lessur moves the ship into our exit lane pattern. We are all watching the station door, willing it not to close. Once we are outside, everyone releases a breath. "Well, that was surprisingly uneventful. Lessur, plot a random course until we get out of their sensor range. Once we are beyond, set course for the planet."

"Yes, Captain."

"How much time before we get to the planet?"

Sia responds, "The route will take 20 solar cycles."

"Ugh. So all the passengers still on board agreed to stay on, correct?"

"Yes, Captain."

"OK, we'll start interviewing them for skills and such tomorrow. I need to train to get some energy that we didn't end up using out." Hmmm... "Hey Ronin... Want to see who's better at throwing knives and some of the other target weapons?"

He laughs loudly, "Mate, we both know who's better at that!"

"I can show you how and you can show me how to throw an axe!!" He laughs, and we walk to the training room. Today we are the only ones there. I grab throwing knives, daggers, and even some throwing stars from the wall.

"Can you give Sia some specks on an axe that would be appropriate for me?"

He walks over, wraps his arms around my waist, and tucks some hair behind my ear. "My beautiful Mate. I love the thought of an entire world with this color of hair. It's beautiful."

I chuckle, "No. Redheads are fairly uncommon, but the interesting thing is even though it's a recessive trait, if you have it in your lineage, it can pop up at any time."

He raises his eyebrows, "There are more colors than this?"

Nodding, "Yes, we have several different color hairs, brown, blonde, which is a light golden color, black, and every shade of each of those. Same with skin color, browns of every shade, and people of similar shades like me."

"Such diversity? That's amazing. Most species in space all look relatively the same."

"The idea of it is great, but my people have judged people based on those traits; we've had wars about it. Slavery was rooted in that concept. Dark brown people were said to be inferior, so they were stolen from their homelands, treated like animals, bought and sold. It was terrible."

"I don't understand. They are all human. Why would some be less than others?"

Sadly I nod, "I don't really understand it either." I stare off, thinking for a few minutes, "I'm not sure I really miss my home world. We are violent, bigoted people and selfish. We are rapidly destroying our planet with pollutants and overpopulation. Everyone seems to think it's someone else's job to fix it. I am honestly not sure if we will make it to this level of exploration and advancement."

Ronin puts his hand on my shoulders, "A lot of species do not. It all depends if they realize it in time or if they end up destroying themselves. Enough of this sad topic. Let's throw some weapons."

Chuckling, "*Yes!*"

We spend a couple of hours teaching each other the ins and outs of throwing weapons. By the end, we both were proficient at all the weapons. Ronin is an incredibly fast learner, and I love that he loves weapons as much as I do. I walk over to him as he is cleaning and returning them to the wall.

I wrap my arms around from behind him and lay my cheek against his back. "I wish there was somewhere we could go, just you and I."

He turns in my arms, "There's a place I want to show you."

We walk at a somewhat slow pace, just chatting and enjoying each other's company. We come to a door, "Close your eyes. Good. There are stairs, so I'm going to pick you up." He lifts me in his arms, and I can feel him walking upstairs. He sets me down, "Open your eyes."

When I open them, it's hard for me to comprehend what I see. In front of me is the vastness of space. To the right, we are passing a large gas giant with two moons orbiting it.

On the left, I can tell it's very far away, but I can see a nebula! A giant nebule with pinks, blues, purples, whites, and yellows.

In it, you can see stars, and all I can think of is that it is the birthplace of stars. It is all so beautiful. I am overwhelmed.

I turn into Ronin's arms, and quietly I say, "Thank you so much. I'm not sure I can put into words how much I love this. Thank you. I thought we were in hyperspace?"

"We have to drop out of hyperspace every 24 hours so the ship's engines can cool. After about 12 hours, we return to hyperspace and continue. That nebula is called the Senmai Nebulae. It is said that it was created by a great battle between the Goddess and her enemy, a God named Jezu. He is an evil being who lives to create chaos and anarchy in the universe. He is the polar opposite of Her. They battled, and She was set to win, which he would not allow, so he set off a massive weapon hoping to kill her. She contained the explosion in that cloud."

"That's a good story, Ronin. Thank you."

I turn to look again, then take in the rest of the room. It is basically an observation deck. A large curved window faces the front of the ship. On both sides of the room, there are couches with low tables beside them. Along the walls are deep pocket windows that have cushions in them so you can sit in the windows. Behind us is another window, but there is a metal dome currently covering it.

"It's amazing, Ronin. You designed this into the ship?"

He stares into the abyss with a slightly embarrassed smile, "Yes. I know it's a warship, but I used to love just looking out into the vastness. It helps me think and gives me perspective. It's for everyone on the ship, but I really built it as a space where I could come to clear my mind and think."

"Close your eyes?" I am now going to surprise this amazing male. He gives me a quizzical look but closes them. I walk to lock the door to the room. Then walk to him, grab his hands and lead him to the bench that sits directly in front of the big window. It's more like a couch that has no back. It looks extremely comfortable. I remove my clothes. "Open your eyes" He opens them, and they immediately lock to me and begin a slow roam of my body. His pupils are wide, and I see him smell the air knowing he can smell my rising desire.

"Mate, you have too many clothes on." I chuckle as his clothes go flying everywhere. He is now magnificently naked in front of me. My eyes now wander his body and stay locked on his cock for a few seconds, then say, "Please sit."

He does so, and I look into his eyes, and they are pure fire. My pussy throbs with the need for him. I slowly go to my knees between his legs. He leans back on his arms while I run my hands up his massive dark thighs. The couch is tall enough for Nlyaxians to sit on, so I almost have to stand to be between his legs. When my hands wrap around his cock he lets out a slow growl that sends shock waves through my system, and I moan, bending my body to take his cock in my mouth.

It's his turn to moan now. I cannot help myself. I love the taste of him. I start moving my mouth up and down, taking him in as far as I can. His sprili massages my tongue as it passes, making me moan. My moans reverberate down his shaft, "Mate..." I start to move faster, bobbing up and down, and my hand goes to his balls to gently massage them as my mouth continues its up-and-down journey. He roars as I feel his cock throb before his release begins. Then I suck down his cum as if my life depends on it.

When I'm finished, I raise my head, and he is already looking at me with a raging inferno in his eyes. He lifts me as he stands, then lays me down in the spot he is just sitting in. He stands back to look at me and growls, "You are so beautiful, June."

Now Ronin is on his knees between my legs. He wraps his arms under my thighs, and I cross my ankles behind his back. He takes one long slow lick up my folds to circle my clit twice. *"Ronin!"*

He chuckles. "You are so sensitive and responsive, my Mate. Not yet. I enjoy your taste too much to rush things." He bends his head and proceeds to work my body into a blaze.

"Ronin..." I moan, "Please, Ronin make me cum. I need it..." He growls, and I arch my back and moan loudly because that rumble at my clit was so close to setting me off. At that moment, his mouth latches onto my clit and lashes it, and then nips. I scream so loudly my voice is a little horse at the end, but the climax that rolls through me hits every nerve ending I have.

When I come down, panting, Ronin is looking at me and says, "Fuck I love watching you when you climax. It is the most beautiful thing in my world."

I sit up quickly and kiss him passionately; tasting myself on his lips makes my core clench with desire. I push him back a little so that I can stand. I move him so he is sitting, then lay him down along the length of the couch but near the edge. I swing my leg over his waist and begin to lower myself onto him. We both moan in unison as he stretches me, as I take him in. One foot is still planted on the floor, and I use that leverage to use his body for our pleasure, lifting myself up and down purely for the fire it creates. My back is arched, my face lifted toward the ceiling, just immersing myself in sensations I can create with the ridges on his cock.

His hands are everywhere, rubbing my legs, my ass, my breasts, and my nipples. Then one hand moves down, and he starts to rub his thumb back and forth over my clit. I cannot take all the sensations at once. A climax washes over me, and I scream. Ronin begins to lift me up and down at a faster pace, and I feel his sprili, and they create another climax on top of the one I haven't come down from. I feel cock swell, then the hot splash of his seed against my walls. As his sprili begins to vibrate, I scream as it elevates the climax I am already in.

As I come down, I am sprawled on my mate's broad chest. "Ronin, that was amazing." Still trying to catch my breath. His fingers feather my back, somehow creating aftershocks in my body.

"My Mate. I truly do not understand what I did to deserve you, but I would do it thousand times more to ensure you are mine." He rolls so I am under him, and thrusts into me again. He kisses me slowly. "I can tell you this. I will thank the Goddess every day by worshiping you and your body as she requires." He begins thrusting slowly and deep, building my fire once again.

For the first time, I notice he has a silver design on the underside of Ronin's left forearms. It is a swirling design in the shape of a split circle with three segments with an intricate full circle in the center. The center circle and one segment is complete. The segment has a design in silver, like a royal crest, and the circle with a silver image that looks like fire. How have I not noticed that before?

The sounds of love continue within the space for several hours.

Ronin

We dress in the dark to head back to the common room for our evening meal. As we approach the table where the crew already sits, I notice Elana staring at us with an odd look and slowly rising. "Elana, are you ok?" My mate asks, worried for her friend.

Elana walks around the table, looking at both of us. Softly she says, "She has blessed you."

"I do not understand Elana, who has blessed us?" She slowly reaches for my arm and glances at my face for permission. I nod, still not knowing what to expect.

She gently grabs my left arm and pushes up my sleeve. What she reveals shocks me to my core. "What is that? I don't understand. Where did it come from?" Instead of answering, she looks at my Mate, who lifts her left sleeve to reveal an identical pattern on her arm.

"Elana, what the fuck is going on?" she says, getting a little upset.

In a calming voice, Elana replies, "The Goddess has blessed your union." She looks back at the marking, her hand hovering over it but not touching it. "These markings haven't been seen on a living being for many millennia. Most, including the Ferin, had thought the Goddess had moved on disenchanted with the races." She gets the brightest smile. "I knew she had not, and this proves it."

Looking at my Mate's and my own arm, I can see the markings are identical, and it brings me joy to see two spaces which means we will someday complete our Triad. Nlyaxians have always believed in the Goddess, but I do not remember these markings being mentioned in our historical texts. She is real, and she has truly blessed me with the perfect mate. Thank you, my Goddess. Though I can not help but wonder... Why me? Why us?

June

I lay in bed as Ronin sleeps, staring at the new designs on my arm, unsure of what to think of it. I don't believe in God, but that's mostly because it's used as a weapon in almost every culture on Earth. But if Gods or Goddesses don't exist, then where the fuck did this come from? One minute, nothing but maybe a scar or two. The next is a beautiful silver design representing Ronin and me, with the possibility of two more.

What concerns me more is if there is a Goddess... why me? Especially if this type of marking hasn't been seen in ages. Why now? What could a Goddess possibly want from me?

The next several days go by quietly. We meet with the passengers to find out their skills and really get to know them.

We found someone with almost every skill we needed. The passengers seem to be coming out of their trauma as well. The common room is busy, has more laughter, and always has someone there.

Planning continues for the base. We decided to call it Haven. I'm very excited to get there. It will be the first alien planet I have ever set foot on.

Today I've decided to sit in the common room on the comfy couch to read my reports and look at the new designs that folks are putting together. Right now, I am reading a particularly fascinating proposal on a new waste plant type that uses... oh, who am I kidding? I am fighting to stay awake. Some of these proposals are SO damn boring. I glance up as one of the passengers comes up. "Captain?"

"Yes? What can I help you with?"

The male who walked up is older, I think. He's very wrinkled with gray skin that is scaled. His eyes are black with purple cat-like irises. "I just wanted to personally thank you for saving us from Kaxlin. If you ever need anything from me, all you need do is ask."

I nod. "Have a seat. If you like." He gives me a slight bow and takes a seat. "What are you signed up to do once we get to Haven?" I ask to start a conversation.

"I have been a slave for almost forty solar cycles. For the majority of that, I repaired the equipment on a space station. I can fix just about anything, but before that, on my homeworld, I was a historian. I was wondering; I am signed up as an engineer, which I still would like to do but would it be ok for me to start history on Haven once we get there? I would also like to record the history of you and your crew." I am silent for a few minutes, thinking.

"I'll do you one better; make it a recording of the names and histories of those we save and bring back to Haven, and you have a deal."

He gets a shrewd look on his face and counters, "Deal *if* you and your crew are part of the histories."

Chuckling, I respond, "Deal. What's your name?"

He gets a broad toothy smile, "My name is Xenneel Recuder, and I will be so happy to do this for you, Captain. Every people needs a recorded history."

"Very nice to meet you, Xenneel."

Ronin walks up and goes to a knee in front of Xenneel. "It pains me to know Kaxlin had a Relcinorhc as a slave on this ship. I apologize because he was Nlyaxian, and none should ever hurt one of your people."

Xenneel gets a soft look on his face, "No need, High Commander. You and your mate saved us all. You cannot take responsibility for the actions of someone else."

"Xenneel has volunteered to record our histories and the history of Haven."

His eyes snap to me, then back to Xenneel, "Truly?"

Xenneel chuckles, "Yes, it would be my honor."

Ronin bows his head, "The honor is ours."

"Good night, young people. Old males need their sleep."

Ronin and I tell him to have a good night, and Ronin sits with me. He looks over at what I was trying to read earlier and gets a disgusted look on his face, "Waste recycling proposal? Why are you reading that? Shouldn't your engineers be reading those and making the decisions?"

I chuckle at his reaction, "Shouldn't I understand the proposals as well?"

"No, my sweet mate. You have experts in each of the fields. Let them do their jobs and report to you. That is what leadership is."

"Well, thank the Goddess because these are *so* boring." Ronin barks out a laugh and sits. He pulls my legs up on his lap and proceeds to rub my feet. Yeah, he's a keeper. I recline back on the arm of the couch. "Mmmm, that feels amazing." I look at my mate. His arm is in a position where I can see the new design on his arm.

I look down at mine. With my fingertip, I start tracing the lines that represent Ronin. Growl. My eyes dart toward Ronin. He's giving me a heated look. I raised my eyebrow and begin again.

"Mate, I can feel that."

I chuckle, "Sure you can." I stare at my arm like it's a puzzle as I continue to trace. Suddenly I feel a ghost of a massage on my clit. I freeze and moan simultaneously. I look at Ronin again, and this time his eyes are on fire. His finger is rubbing back and forth across the center circle on his arm.

Instead of heating me, it has the opposite effect. He notices, "What's wrong?"

"I don't understand this, Ronin. What is this? Why us? Why now? I do not like unexplainable things. I don't believe in Gods or Goddesses!"

He sighs, "I know this is foreign to you, but for Nlyaxians and for a lot of the other species in this galaxy, the Goddess is real. It is why you will find just as many matriarchies as you find patriarchies. The Goddess has been a part of my culture since before we even dreamed of going to the stars. Would you like me to teach you about Her?"

"Yes. I think I do." Who would've thought I would want to learn an alien religion?

He nods, "But first, a test." And he starts rubbing his designs as he does with his tongue.

"Ronin," I whisper, "There are people..." I try to say more, but a soft moan escapes, and I let my head fall back against the couch. I start panting. The sensation feels like his tongue is caressing my clit, flicking it. I have to concentrate on not moaning loudly. "Ronin please..." whispering and not knowing if I am begging him to stop or begging him to make me cum. He begins to thrum faster, and my body ignites. I almost cry out but bite my lip instead. When I come down from the high of the orgasm he created without touching me, I open my eyes to look at him. I thought his eyes were on fire before. Now, now they could light the room on fire.

Two can play this game. I start touching my design. His eyes heat more. I look down at his cock, rock hard in his pants, and imagine my mouth around it. Taking it into my mouth, taking it all the way down my throat. Ronin jumps up, throws me over his shoulder, and practically runs from the room. Outside the common room door, I hear him murmur, "Too far... closer... now." He takes off down the hall to the elevator. Before the door closes, he practically yells, "Sia, seals lift until we say so."

He doesn't even wait for her reply. He sets me down and starts ripping off my clothes. I am naked and back against the wall in under thirty seconds. As he pins me to the wall, his cock is already pushing into me. He starts thrusting in and out at a pace that sets me on fire. We cannot think but only feel the friction he is creating. My orgasm explodes with almost no warning. I am screaming as I feel his sprili and my ecstasy elevates. "*Ronin!*" His cock swells and splashes my wall with a force I haven't felt before. When his sprili starts to vibrate, I lose myself in my orgasm and screams.

When we come back down, Ronin is sitting on the floor with me in his lap, still buried in me. Panting, "Forgive me, my mate... I don't know... what I felt when you were touching your arm... it sent me into a frenzy. I needed to bury my cock in you. I seriously considered doing it there in the common room."

I chuckle, "I am completely satisfied by what just happened, but I do appreciate you not taking me to the common room. Though I don't think my clothes are going to work anymore."

Laughing, he says, "I will happily make you more, but I'm not sure how we'll get you back to our quarters. I think my tunic will work."

Chapter 22

We approach the planet. Its name to us is now Haven. What it is called by others no longer matters. Looking at the planet, I know we have to make sure it is still like when the Nlyaxians first surveyed it, but I can feel it. This is the planet we are meant to be on.

The plan is that Ronin, Elana, Doraj, and I will go down in a shuttle to inspect the planet. If we find everything in order. Lessur will pilot the ship down and land it on the southern side of the mountain valley.

Lessur breaks into my thoughts, "Captain, we have entered a stable orbit."

"Thank you, Lessur." Looking to Ronin, "Ready?"

He gives me a huge smile, "Let's do this!" then, with almost a childlike quality, he adds, "I am so excited!"

Laughing, "I love you. Doraj, Elana ready?" Both nod with smiles. "OK, Let's go."

"*Captain,*" Sia rings out over the speakers.

"Yes?"

"*I have developed a comms unit that will fit inside your ear. It will allow you to communicate with each other over great distances and with me.*"

"Cool! Where are they?"

"*In the replicator in the corner.*"

I walk over to the corner and open the door to the replicator. At first, I don't see them, but I realize she is referring to the four flesh color, flat circles the size of a pencil eraser tip. I pick mine up, "Where do I put it? AND will it hurt like the language unit when it went in?"

"*I assure you, Captain, these will not hurt. They are designed to bond with the skin and not be under it. For humans, the best location is behind the Tragus.*" I put it inside my ear behind the Tragus. The little spot warms but quickly goes away. Excellent. Sia then walks the others through where to put theirs. Once everyone has theirs installed, she walks us through how to use them.

"*To use them, all you need to do is tap the location above its installation. One tap to contact me, two taps and a name to contact someone directly, three taps for the group, and four to turn off or on. The device is programmed to detect and adjust the volume to ambient noise and ear mechanism sensitivity.*" We test and play a little with our new com units for a min, then decide it's time to go.

We all head out of the bridge. We are all loaded with weapons. I have my Katana, tanto, blaster, and even a kubotan hanging from my belt. I also put my bow and arrows in the transport yesterday, just in case.

Animals freak me out. Give me a humanoid to fight any day of the week, but animals or, goddess forbid, giant bugs are my nightmares. Burn that planet to charcoal if there are giant spider-like bugs. Ronin glances over at me. The doors to the lift open, and many of the passengers line the hall. Their faces lit with cautious hope.

As we pass, some reach out and touch us. I glance at Ronin in question, "In several cultures, it is good luck to touch someone leaving so they will return safely."

We load up into the transport. Doraj is piloting us to the site on the planet. He walks through all his checks and lets the bridge know we are ready to go. The transport lifts off the deck as the bay door opens. There's a yellowish hue around the door signifying the field is in place to keep the bay pressurized. We exit the bay, and the planet comes into view as the transport turns. It looks huge, but because I have never seen the Earth from space, I don't really have something to compare it to.

My mind goes back to the spiders and animals. They are unpredictable, and I do not like not being able to predict behavior or moves. Ronin looks back from the copilot's seat, "Everything ok?"

I love that he's picking up some of my human speech. "I'm just a little nervous about the animals and bugs that might be down there."

He gives me a warm smile, "Well, little Pillut, all of us are used to dealing with the wildlife of other planets. Stick with us, and you'll be fine."

"Fine. But y'all need to teach me what to look for and how to deal with what we find."

Elana grabs my hand, "I will teach you, my friend."

I smile and give her hand a little squeeze. "Thank you, Elana."

It takes us about 45 minutes to go from the ship to the area around our possible mountain home. We do an aerial survey of approximately 20 kilometers around the mountains. It's beautiful.

The single sun rose about 20 minutes ago, and the skies are more of a purple color with oranges, blues, and yellows during the morning sky. There are trees below, but I cannot see any real detail except the leaves are all shades of yellow with some green mixed in.

The mountains look just like the mountains of Earth. Very tall, with trees about a third of the way up, then towards the top is snow.

I smile and murmur, "Snow-capped mountains."

As we get closer to the forest below, I realize that the trees are huge. Their trunks look to be at least quadruple the size of this shuttle, and I'd have to guess 65 meters tall. They are amazing.

I used to love walking in the forests in Japan. They are beautiful. These might be more like walking among the skyscrapers, but I feel like this will be so much better. As long as there isn't something trying to eat you. That would suck.

We're headed into the mountains that our home will be nestled in, and as we crest the top of the south mountain, a gasp escapes me. The valley is huge. I cannot see the valley floor, but it has to be around 20 square kilometers between the four extremely tall mountains. There are no passes into the valley. It doesn't look like there are as many trees, but it's hard to tell because you cannot see through the canopy. "There's a small break in the canopy ahead. The trees are large enough that we'll be able to move through them easily." Doraj is confident, but it makes me a little nervous.

We break through the canopy and are shocked once again. The trees have obviously been set up as ground cover because they are spaced perfectly to block visibility into the valley but still allow light under it.

The valley is shaded but bright, and it is spectacular. There are several lakes, but I catch a glimpse of something. Nestled against the Northern range is a large building complex the same color as the surrounding landscape. Scattered throughout the valley are smaller buildings of the same coloring; they have to be living spaces. "Look," I point to the others.

"That is some good camouflage. I did not see the building or the homes." Ronin looks concerned, "These look almost new, but there are no life signs on the scanners besides some small wildlife."

Thinking about the movies I've seen, "Are there any other ways lifeforms might present... energy... etc.?"

Ronin looks at me with appreciation, "Yes, there are, but we've tried to account for most of those in our scanning equipment, that doesn't necessarily mean there isn't one we haven't interacted with, but it's unlikely. The previous survey crew notes said they stayed in the structures in this valley for the extent of the survey cycle, so that would have been over 180-day cycles. I think if there was something still here, they would have detected it, but we should definitely stay alert." I smile softly at him. I feel better.

Doraj interrupts, "There's a landing pad over by the big complex. I will set down there." We nod in agreement.

Everyone exits the shuttle and looks around. I stop at the end of the ramp. I'm staring at the purple and green grass; my feet are so close to it. I'm not sure how long I've been staring at the ground, but Ronin's feet come into view, "Are you ok, Mate?"

I don't look up because... I can't. "I feel like if I step down onto the ground of a completely different world, I'm shutting the door on my own for good. Am I ok with that?"

I'm not sure if I'm talking to Ronin or myself. I'm not sure how but I feel Ronin's nerves spike. He does get nervous, huh? I look at his boots and realize I could never go back. I love him with everything I am, and I am incredibly thankful to the Goddess who pulled us together. I would go through everything again, everything, if it meant we would be together. Besides, I can't handle the idea of people going through what I went through.

I look up at my mate and see the worry in his eyes. Time to test one of my theories. I am pretty sure I can feel his emotions, so I want to try to send him mine.

I put my hand on my arm over the silver and let my feelings for him go and wash over him. His eyes get glassy for a second, then snap back to me. I see deep emotions in his eyes. I give him a big smile and step off the ramp into his arms, planting a passionate kiss on his confused lips. He deepens the kiss and pulls me tight to his body.

We break the kiss, and he puts his forehead on mine, "I feel like you just made a big decision."

I put my hands on his cheeks and then run my fingers along the ridge there, solemnly I say, "I did. I realized I would go through everything again if it meant I ended up with you."

He pulls his head back to look intently into my eyes. I am not sure what he saw, but a gorgeous smile flashes then I am in a fiery kiss. He grabs my ass and pulls me up. I wrap my legs around him and put as much passion back into that kiss as I can muster.

Then we hear a very loud throat clear, "Uhmm, maybe we should wait till we figure out if there is any danger here?"

We chuckle forehead to forehead, and I say, "*Fine.* If we have to."

He sets me down and grabs the back of my neck before I can walk away, leaning to bring his mouth to my ear, "Know this, mate. Tonight I am going to have you screaming my name *all... night... long.*" Then I feel the ghost tongue briefly on my clit and moan. He walks away, chuckling. Oof, that males know how to get me worked up.

Ronin

So it was decided on the ship that since I had the most experience with operations on other worlds that this would be my part of this mission. Though I have to admit I am still trying to catch my bearings after what my mate just did. When she opened the flow of her emotions and her feelings for me through the link in our arms, I was unprepared for what washed over me. Human emotions are like a tidal wave.

I could feel her deep connection to me, her love for me, and her passion. I knew she cared for me, but I was under the mistaken impression that since she didn't always show her emotions for me that humans obviously did not feel as deeply as my people. I was so very wrong. The depth of her emotion for me was overwhelming. She is amazing.

I hear a male chuckling, "You, my friend, need to shake it off and focus." Slapping my friend on the back, "Then let's get started! Elana and June, come over."

We round up, "Everyone remembers the plan?" I toss two handfuls of disks into the air. They are called hunters, little tech that scans and watches for movement. Their data is analyzed by Sia on the ship. Once they're in the air, they scatter. "Doraj and Elana start at the top. Sweep to the bottom of the complex, and we'll sweep bottom to top; meet in the middle. We have 12 hours before sundown. Once the sun goes under the mountain line, head back to the shuttle. Check-in every 30 minutes. Three taps, got it? If you get in trouble, call the group immediately. Most importantly, do not leave sight of your partner... ever.." Everyone nods.

Doraj and Elana head to the external stairs to the roof. I throw up four more hunters, and they immediately head to the four corners of the building to watch for anything that might enter or leave. We head up the steps to the main entrance.

"I don't get it, Ronin. Why have these buildings not crumbled to dust if they are over 20000 years old?"

"So the original survey crew were curious about that as well. They analyzed the materials it was made with and were unable to figure out how it was made. It was obviously not a natural ore or stone because it has the highest tensile strength of anything we had ever seen or seen since. It is impossible to chip, crack or break in any way."

"I guess it makes sense why it wouldn't be overgrown then if plant life cannot break through it, then no growth will cause collapse and such... but..."

"Go ahead, my mate."

"That explains the buildings, but what about the grass and forest? They should be unrecognizable from what they were, but they look like they were manicured yesterday."

I stop in my tracks and turn to look at the forest and surrounding area. My brow furrowed. Without taking my eyes off the surrounding lands, "Sometimes, my mate, you are a little too intelligent. That wasn't even mentioned in the report but... that little observation concerns me... a great deal."

I reach my hand up to my ear and tap three times, "June has pointed out something that makes me wary. The grounds and forest... look as if they have been tended to over the last 20000 solar cycles."

There's a long pause then Elana's voice comes through my earpiece, "Well, that's a little unnerving."

"I don't think we should freak out just yet. It could be as simple as an automated care system of some sort or animals. The people who were here were advanced enough to create a material that lasted 20000 solar cycles... I do not think lawn care would be a stretch." I relax a fraction, look at June with a rueful smile, and nod.

She turns, starting toward the door. I continue to watch the forest. Something is still... I don't know; it feels like something is watching. I turn and follow June into the building.

June

The building inside is beautiful. It has mirrored ornate staircases up to the second floor. There is an atrium that goes to a windowed roof. Between the set of staircases, a functioning fountain sprays water in the air. Strange.

There are no main rooms on the first floor, it is completely open, empty but open. It looks like it could have been like our common room on the ship, a place to gather and relax. It is in perfect shape, but instead of dust and dirt, it is clean. "You see this right, Ronin?"

"It's immaculate for an old building. I do not understand how my people didn't notice this. I could understand the grass and trees, but this? No."

"Wait, could they have cleaned it?" I can see she is hoping for an easy answer.

"No, it is against our customs to disturb places that could be of cultural value to someone." Hmmm.

We sweep the room, but we both knew there would be nothing because there is nothing at all to hide behind. We move to the second floor. Doorways line the east and west side of the atrium.

I look at Ronin, "Where would you like to start?" He looks a bit upset, "It's ok, Ronin. We can separate to opposite sides and go room to room directly across from each other. If we don't, it will take too long to go through this building." He's not happy but nods in agreement. I head to the left bank of rooms, and he goes to the right.

"Mate," Ronin calls before I can move into the room, "You have ninety seconds, then be out of that room."

It's sweet, he worries. I nod and move into the room, checking all corners, but it's empty. Looks like maybe an office, but it's hard to tell. Since there's nothing to look through, I head back to the door.

We continue going from room to room, and there's nothing in any of them. We are halfway through the 4th floor. As I enter the next room, it is very different. It looks like a control room of sorts.

I cannot read anything on the displays, but I can see every angle of the valley. I hear the door close behind me and spin, ready to face an attacker. Instead of seeing the closed door, though, I see a lake. I'm no longer in the room, and I have no weapons.

"You have no need for weapons here, little sister." I spin again, and behind me, just a few feet, is a beautiful female. Her hair is wavy, and red like mine, but it flows to her knees. Her skin is a silver color. She has ridges across her brow and cheeks like Ronin, full lips, and a wide nose like his. Her eyes are very human looking, and the shape of her body is also very human. She's tall like the Nlyaxians. A species I've never seen before but is very familiar at the same time. She is the most beautiful thing I have ever seen.

"I know you... how do I know you?"

She chuckles and, to my utter shock, speaks English. "We have met. In your dream at the lake."

My head whips back in shock like I have been hit. "I remember, but you looked more...human."

She chuckles, "Yes. I thought it would calm you a bit. You have been through much. Do you prefer that look? I used to use it regularly."

My mouth hangs open, "You've been to Earth?"

"Many times, but when they decided that religion based on male theology was what they wanted. I left."

Holy shit. This cannot be. She laughs again. "It is."

"You are the Goddess that people of the galaxy worship?"

"Yes and no. I am the one they call Goddess, but they do not worship me. They only follow my teachings."

"And what are those?" My trust in organized religion is very low. They all try to subjugate women and force their beliefs onto others.

She sighs, "I am sorry your world decided to do what it did. I can see it has damaged your people. They use it as a weapon and in doing so make people distrust any form of teachings that resemble it."

"Yes. I guess I do have a hard time trusting anything that resembles organized religion. I'm sorry for that. Truly. I can tell you my mind is open. That's all I can do for now. Blind faith is not something I can do or will do."

"Excellent. I do not want blind faith. I want logical thought, compassion, the strength of will, and the fortitude to follow through. The things ahead of you will be hard. Some harder than what you have already been through, but the rewards are great."

"What do you want from me?"

"I need you to do what you are already planning. Save the people of this galaxy. Give them Haven. Rebuild good in this universe. I love all the People, and my heart weeps for the pain they are in. I know your next two questions so let me answer now. I cannot do it myself because I am limited in how I can engage with the short-lived species. I can and would be executed by my people. Next, you would ask 'why you,'" she chuckles, "You would only need to ask your friends and your mate, and they would tell you why."

"Elana?"

She chuckles again, "You are very perceptive. Yes, the Ferin as a people still follows my teachings. They are special to me. When the time comes, they will help you. Elana, in particular, is special. She is my voice."

"What is this mark on Ronin and my arms? Did you put it there?"

"Again, yes and no. The mark was originally given to the people of the galaxy as a way to form an even deeper connection to your true mate or mates. It is unique to every mate or triad. It is called the Kokoro. If they show a deep connection and follow my teachings, the Kororo will appear, creating an even deeper link."

"Why has it been so long since they have been seen?"

She smiles sadly, "They have forgotten. Reading the teachings and living them are two very different things. They are starting to fall into the traps your planet has."

I nod. "I made this planet safe for you some time ago. When we are done talking, the technology in this place will wake up and will be able to be used by Sia. Do you have any further questions for me, little Sister?"

"So many, but none I can think of."

"I would like to give you the knowledge of my teachings, so you understand. Would that be acceptable?"

Not sure, but I want knowledge of her, so I nod.

"Always so fearless. This is why *you* are my chosen Warrior." She steps forward and touches the center of my forehead. A light flashes.

Chapter 23

Ronin

When I heard the door close, I knew something was wrong. I race from the room I was searching, to the door she was in. I tried the handle, but it would not budge.

I call out to Doraj, screaming for help. I cannot feel her through the link. I know what I am feeling is terror, and I start ramming and hitting the door to get in. I am screaming her name, but I cannot hear her or feel her.

Doraj and Elana run up with worried faces. "She's in there. The door closed. *I cannot feel her!*"

Doraj grabs my arm. "Ronin! Step back. This will not help her." I stumble back. "We will get her, Ronin."

I feel lost.

I hear the door click, and I burst speed into the room looking for an enemy. All I see is my mate standing in the middle of the room. Her eyes are white. I move to her,

"*Stop*!" Elana screams. "Ronin," in a quieter voice, "She speaks with the Goddess."

I wait a few minutes, then whisper, "June, my mate, please."

Her eyes close, and when they open, they once again have color. She then proceeds to pass out, but before she hits the floor, she is in my arms. That's when the facility comes to life.

Elana looks relaxed, "Elana, why do you look so relaxed?" Not able to understand. With a peaceful glance, "The Goddess is here. We are in a safe place. I believe she has provided this for us."

"Elana is right." June. I pull her into a tight embrace. I feel like I lost her. "Ronin, Please look at me."

"I cannot. I feel like you will disappear if I look up. If I hold you... you will remain."

I pull back; she looks concerned. "I'm sorry I worried you. I'm ok." I nod and close my eyes, running through mental exercises to calm my mind. When I open them again, she still looks concerned, but she relaxes after she realizes I am once again calm. "What happened?"

"I cannot tell you everything, but I was sweeping this room when I heard the door close. I spun to face what I thought would be an attacker but instead, I was at a beautiful lake and meadow. She was there. We talked for a while. She said she made this place safe for us and made it into our Haven. She said Sia would be able to integrate into the systems here."

"*And I have.*" Sia comes over to the comms in the room. "*As soon as all the systems came online, I was able to stream my consciousness to the system here. It is very advanced. More advanced than anything I've encountered before.*"

I still cannot take my eyes off her. She's different somehow but in a good way. She is calm and focused. I relax the rest of the way.

She has not been hurt. I give her a rueful smile, "My mate, you have taken years from my life. Let us not do that again... at least for a while."

She gives me a beautiful smile and then raises her arm to lightly stroke the silver pattern. "This is a Kokoro; it is an ancient gift from the Goddess meant to deepen the connection between mates." I shiver as her fingers run over it. I reach out and grab her hand gently.

"My Mate, my reactions are short right now. Be careful, or I will find a room." The smell of her desire spikes, and I growl.

Doraj clears his throat. "Still here."

I bark a laugh, "Sorry, my friend!" We stand ready for the next steps.

June

He looks better, but I hate that I caused him such worry. I squeeze his hand and then turn to the displays. "Sia, please have Lessur bring the ship down. It is safe. If you can find him a safe location close by."

"Yes, Captain. I have the perfect place."

"Thank you. Doraj, Elana, this seems to be a community building of some sort. The people and crew of the ship should be assigned rooms here, to begin with, until we can explore and determine what we have and how we will assign the homes out."

Doraj responds, "That makes the most sense, and for now, it's still smart to stay in one location just in case there are animals that we need to address."

"The rooms on the second floor are a bit larger and can be for the crew for now. Let's walk down and reserve them." I have ulterior motives.

"Captain, before you leave, would you like me to start making beds and bedding for the rooms? The facility has large units that can do this and bots that can set them up."

"Wow. Yes, please. Sia, and Thank you."

We walk down to the second floor, and I head toward the room I want. I walk into the room and walk to the window that takes up the back wall. The view is spectacular.

From the window, you can see the mountain face and a waterfall in the distance. The river created by the water of the falls, meander disappearing and reappearing in my sightline. It slowly flows by the back of the building about one hundred feet away. I love it.

I think I can see a home in the distance near the falls. I would love that. I hear the door close behind me.

My desire spikes, and I feel the heat that builds in my core. I can feel the heat from him behind me.

He takes my weapons and puts them on a built-in shelf on the wall. He comes back, grabs my shirt, and lifts it over my head. Then I feel the bra unsnap and come off. He runs his hands down my sides, his fingers then his hands moving between my skin and my clothes. He moves them down my hips slowly, then down my legs. He backs away, and I can hear him removing his clothes.

He steps back, and I feel his hard cock against my lower back. I cannot help the small moan that escapes my lips. He grabs my hands and places them on the window. I shiver when he whispers in my ear, "Do not move them until I tell you. Understand my Mate?"

I nod. That's all I can do. His hands slowly slide down my arms to my shoulder. I close my eyes; I am so focused on their path and the sensations.

His hands move under my arms and come around to firmly cup my breasts. "Ronin..." I have no control, and I love it. He starts to massage and rub his fingers over my nipples. The moans are running together when he pinches and rolls my nipples. I cannot help screaming his name. I am on fire.

His mouth is at my ear again, "My good little Mate. So responsive, so needy."

He steps closer, his front firmly against my back. His right hand moves from my breast and down my body's centerline. "Ronin..." Two of his fingers slide into my folds. My knees buckle, but his other arm is wrapped around my waist, holding me up. My hands are glued to the window; I do not want him to stop. His fingers continue their exploration. Moving through my pussy they find my core and push inside. "*Ronin!*"

He knows my body better than I do. The massaging action is driving me to the edge.

On edge, his fingers leave my core. They move my hands lower on the glass, then bends me at the waist. Not all the way over, just enough. I feel his cock start its journey to my entrance. Then it starts to push in, stretching me in ways that bring my fire to an inferno. I am pushing back as he pushes forward. We both moan when he is fully seated. "Ronin, please..."

He begins pulling out and thrusting in. He is very controlled. He is building our fire exponentially. Going faster and faster. The moaning and slapping noises echo around the empty room. His right hand returns to my folds, zeroing in on my clit. As he pounds me, he thrums my clit. It's too much. My body is barreling toward a climax. Just before my climax hits, he pinches my clit firmly. *"Ronin! Fuck!"*

My pussy locks down on his cock as my climax hits. He groans and starts pounding into me fast and hard. I feel his sprili release, and I am climaxing again. His cock swells, and he roars loudly. I feel his hot seed flood my pussy, and his sprili begins to vibrate. My climax elevates, and I scream his name again.

He barely pauses. He leaves my body, spins me around, grabs my ass, and picks me up. He has me pressed against the glass, then buries his cock in me again.

"Yes"

We start it all again, except this time, it's as hard and as fast as he can. He is pounding into me. He gets his arms under my knees and spreads me as wide as my legs will go.

"Deeper... I need to be deeper." He growls as his cock goes as deep as it can. We are moaning. He is thrusting into me so hard his balls are slapping my ass. We both climax at the same time and sprili are out and vibrating. I am screaming my climax, and he roars.

We come back down from the highs we just created. Still buried deep, "Did I hurt you?" he asks quietly.

"No, my Mate," I say as I lift his head to look into his eyes. "It is amazing when you lose control. This particular position," I shiver, and he moans as aftershocks roll through my pussy. "This position is amazing... spectacular... I have no words for what it does to me." He flexes his hips, and we both moan.

At that moment, a buzz sounds at the door, and this time, we groan. Ronin yells at the door, "*What?*"

A chuckle comes over the comms, "Well if you two are done, the ship is coming in."

I whisper to Ronin, "Could they hear us?"

Doraj responds, "No, but it's not hard to guess with you two."

I can feel my cheeks heat, and Ronin chuckles, "We will be right out. I love it when your skin takes on the pink. It's stunning." He kisses my nose then I moan as he leaves my body to set me down.

We get dressed and head outside with the others to meet everyone.

We walk outside to join Doraj and Elana, waiting for the ship. I stand next to Elana and grab her hand.

"When we settle, I'd like to talk with you." She looks at me worried, "I'm sorry..."

I cut her off to remove her worry. "Elana, there is no need. I am happy you are here with me." She smiles and looks relieved.

We look to the sky and see our large ship descending. It flies over the valley but, to our surprise, goes over the west rim and lowers out of sight. I tap my com once, "Uh, Sia, It's going to be hard to unload the ship over there."

"*On the contrary, Captain. I have a surprise for you.*"

At that moment, the ground beneath our feet moves and begins to lower into the ground. As we lower, it becomes evident that we are standing on a large platform. After about one hundred feet, it opens into an extensive artificial cavern system.

The walls are smooth and made of the same material as the buildings above. The lights come on as we are lowering, and we can now see the floor of the cavern. The space is vast. As the platform sets down, a huge door on the far side of the area opens.

We see nothing at first; then after about five minutes, the ship moves into the cavern. It sits in what looks like a giant boat trailer. The main difference from a boat trailer is where the ship rests. Instead of long cloth-covered pads, there are round devices that emit soft blue light. The ship hovers about three feet over the pads. It is a fantastic sight. A vessel with the capacity of five thousand warriors fits comfortably in this cavern. It's not remotely close to the ceiling or sides.

Then surprisingly, a space opens in the floor under the ship. Arms attach to the trailer and begin to lower the ship. Once the ship's cargo doors are even with the floor, decent stops, and a wide ramp extends to the doors.

The ship's cargo bay doors open, and we see Nalax, Lessur, and Ekim standing with the rest of the passengers.

Nalax, unable to wait, races down the ramp and launches into Doraj's waiting arms. She gives him a very passionate kiss.

I chuckle and whisper to Ronin, "I think the human kiss is popular."

Ronin gives a little growl that makes me shiver, "You know how much I like it."

Ok, I guess I'm up. "Crew and passengers of the Emancipation. Haven is safe and blessed by the Goddess. We have rooms set up in the building above us for everyone. They will be temporary until we finish our survey and inventory of the rest of the buildings in the valley. Come, we will take folks up in groups and show you how to find your room. Let me be clear, though these spaces are temporary, please feel free to make them yours. You may decorate them however you wish. If you'd like something made for your room, just ask Sia for instructions on how to do so. I know you probably have many questions, but I ask that you wait until we get everyone settled. We will have a... Haven community meeting this evening after the evening meal. Thank you for trusting in us and joining us here."

People start filling off the ship and speaking excitedly to each other. I feel tears come to my eyes. I feel Ronin's arm wrap around my shoulder, "What is wrong?"

"I am happy but also extremely worried. Happy that we were able to save these people from their nightmares. Worried about my ability to protect them."

He turns me toward him, "My beautiful Mate. You did deliver them from a horrible life and brought them here to a safe place. No place you could find for them is ever going to be one hundred percent safe. It is not possible. What you did is give them an opportunity for a life in their own control. You gave them hope, which is an extremely hard thing to give. I am so proud of you. You were born to do this."

I wrap my arms around him and pull him down for a tender kiss. "You are my dream, everything to me. I hope you know that."

"I do. You are mine as well." We turn back to the crowds as the first group begins their assent to the surface.

I tap my ear once. "Sia, can you randomize the room assignments and let them know when they walk into the building where to go."

"*Of course, Captain.*"

"Oh, If they want rooms next to someone or to change, it is allowed."

"*Yes, Captain.*" there is a pause, and Sia's voice comes out of the comms in the cavern, "*And Captain, I am in both the ship's systems and the control systems for the valley. If you are near a building or in it, you can call for me just as you do on the ship."*

I chuckle, "Sorry, Sia, I'm going to have to get used to this. Can you also ensure the bots unload the ship... Sia, is there any secure storage anywhere?"

"There is, Captain. Would you like to see it? It's adjacent to this chamber and hidden."

I look at Ronin. "That's the last load of people going to the surface. We might as well check the chamber. It will take some time for everyone to get settled in."

"Alright. Sia, direct away."

Sia leads us back to the door the ship came through. As we get close, an average size door pops open, and we head through. It's pitch black on the other side, and I freeze. "Ronin?" I jump when his voice is next to me, "What is wrong?"

"It's so dark. I cannot see."

"Sia, are there lights?"

"There are not any lights in this underpass."

"Well, shit. How are we going to get to the storage?"

Ronin grabs my hand, "I can see fine little Mate. I will lead us there with Sia's direction, of course."

Of course, Mr. Perfect can see in the dark. Is there anything he cannot do?

Ronin chuckles, and I realize that may have been my outside voice. "Sorry."

I feel a soft kiss on my lips, "I understand, Mate. No need to be sorry."

Then I feel a gentle caress on my nipple. "Hey, not fair!"

He chuckles then I feel another caress on my ass.

I'll show him. He doesn't know that my Sensei used to make me train with a blindfold on. I close my eyes and focus. I hear his breathing and the brush of his clothes during his movements.

I feel him move, and he's going to touch my nipple again. When he moves in close for his prize, I swing around and sweep his feet from him. "Oof. You said you could not see Mate."

I chuckle, "I can't."

I hear him rise. He circles me twice, trying to figure out if I can see or not. When he's convinced himself I cannot, he circles again once behind me he goes in to caress my ass. When he's about to connect, I once again swing out away from him and smack him on the ass.

He is laughing now, "Truce! How are you doing that, Mate? I can tell from your eyes you cannot see because most of the time you have them closed, but when they are open, your pupils are blown wide."

I chuckle, "My Sensei made us train blindfolded. And would beat us with sticks until we learned to detect movement and proximity without my eyes."

Laughing, he says, "Huh, Your training mentors sound tougher than mine, and I thought mine were trying to kill us!"

He grabs my hand, and we continue on to the center of the underpass. A door pops open, and there is light again. Ronin leads the way through the door. On the other side is another door. This one looks very heavy.

The door behind us closes, and we glance back. "Sia, did you close that?" I ask.

"*Yes, Captain. Sorry I should have let you know.*"

"It's ok. What's next?"

"*The door behind you, I have coded it to yours, Ronin's, and Doraj's biosignatures. All you need to do is grab the handle and pull.*"

"Cool. Ronin, you want to do the honors?"

As he walks forward, the door lights up with symbols. He grabs the handle and pulls. The door swings open. As we step inside, the lights come on.

"Wow." In front of us is a very large space with columns that go up to a very high ceiling. There are ornate decorative accents on the columns, walls, and even ceilings. "It's beautiful. Are you sure it's for secure storage?"

"I am. There is a detailed usage list for all of the buildings and rooms in the valley."

"Will it all fit in here?"

"Yes, Captain. I calculated the space requirements. It will all fit with room to spare."

I look at Ronin, and he nods, "Ok. Sia, we are convinced. Can the bots move the secure cargo from the ship to here?"

"Yes, Captain."

"Excellent. Have them do it at night, make sure no one is in the cavern or underpass, lock it all down, then have them move it. Once that's done, remove the restrictions on the ship to that floor. Oh, and can you inventory what is there, please?"

"Yes, Captain."

"Thank you, Sia. Once again, you have been invaluable to us."

Ronin

We are now in the community room of the main building, waiting for all the Haven inhabitants to join us. Once they are all here, June steps forward.

"All, thank you for joining us. Welcome to Haven. You all knew we were looking for a home for all of us that would be safe and we grow as a people. We are one people. Emancipation and her crew have decided to become what the people of this system need. We plan on going to war with the slavers, owners, and enablers of a system that benefits the evil of the galaxy. We will save all slaves we find, and if they are good people, they will be returning with us here to Haven. The Goddess has provided this Haven for us. Making it safe and habitable. I ask you all make your own choices on whether to follow her teachings or not. It is not required, but I do ask you to keep an open mind. Her teachings are available to all on the personal display given to you. Our goal here is peaceful coexistence. Violence was not tolerated on the ship, and it will not be tolerated here. You all are welcome to pursue any activity you wish, but you must contribute to the whole, so the duties you were assigned on the ship should be kept here. I would like you all to vote on three leaders for the people. They will govern for five years, and then you will vote on how to proceed with the governance of this settlement. The crew of the Emancipation is here to support you in anything you may need. To make a request, you can come to us or ask Sia to relay a message. We are safe. Let us build a community that keeps us that way. Thank you."

She gets down from the table she was standing on, and the people are joyous and thank her. Reaching to touch her. I am so proud of her.

I grab food for the both of us and signal her to a table to eat. She still needs to regain all the weight she lost. She is very good at caring for others, so I care for her and have no issues doing so.

We eat, and many of the people of Haven stop by and thank us and ask some questions, which June answers expertly. Elana comes to sit down and eat with us. My mate smiles, "Hi, Elana. How are you?"

"I am good, June. You did very well today."

June blushes a bit, "Elana, Ronin, I wanted to talk to you both. When I spoke with Her, she said things I did not understand. First, Elana, the Goddess, said you were Her Voice." Elana gets emotional.

"She said those words?"

"She did."

"She also said I was Her Chosen Warrior. Do you know what that means? Do either of you?"

I shake my head, but Elana says, "It is familiar, but I do not know why. There are some old texts on my homeworld that may have more information. Do you think Sia could get those somehow or at least copies?"

I nod, "She should be able to communicate with your homeworld but will they share it?"

Elana thinks for a minute, "Have her tell them the Voice of the Goddess has requested copies of the ancient texts. They will comply."

June sighs, "It's a start, at least. Thank you. I wish she had given me more information, but I just don't know what questions to ask at the time."

Elana gets a rueful look, "We rarely know what to ask until after we can no longer ask."

June chuckles, "Ain't that the truth? I'm tired."

"Let us go to bed then, my Mate."

The next few days are a blur of inventorying and building what we will need in Haven. I have a surprise for my Mate today. I have seen her looking longingly at the house by the waterfalls, so I am taking her there today. We'll decide today if that is where our family will live while at Haven. I have convinced Doraj and Elana to take the homes closest to it. Both houses are within sight of what will hopefully be ours.

I approach her and wrap my arms around her. "Mmm. Hello, my handsome Mate. Where have you been?"

"Exploring my surprise. It is time for you to come with me, my beautiful Mate."

She gives me a curious smile, "What are you up to?"

"Nothing at all." I wink and smile at her.

I grab her hand and walk her to the land vehicle I reserved for us. I open her door so she can get in then I get in and start the drive to the home.

As we get closer, she gets more and more excited. "Are we going there? Are we?"

"Where do you mean, my Mate?"

"You know where I mean!"

"We shall see my beautiful Mate."

She laughs and squeals as we pull up to it. She jumps from the vehicle. "Can I go in? Is it safe?"

Chuckling, "Yes, June, it is safe."

She sprints to the door, pulls it open, and disappears inside. I follow, but she has disappeared, exploring rooms. I was not going to risk her safety, so I searched this home top to bottom earlier, then sealed the place up so it would remain that way.

I find her on the balcony overlooking the falls and river. The view is spectacular. We are far enough from the falls that the sound is not loud, but you still can hear it.

"It's perfect, Ronin. I love this place. It's probably too big for us, but I really want this place." She looks at me, "Is that selfish?"

"No, June, it is not selfish. Besides, once we are ready, I plan to have twelve or maybe sixteen children with you."

She sputters, "Sixteen!"

"More if you would like. I love children and want to have as many as possible with you. I cannot wait to see you round with my offspring!"

Laughing, she says, "We'll have to see about sixteen, though!" More seriously, "You furnished it for me knowing I wanted this place?" I nod. "God, I love you."

She wraps her arms around me and kisses me with passion. I give back as much love as I can.

She moans, and then someone yells, "Hello, neighbors!" I groan in frustration, "*Doraj,* You have the worst timing!" All I get in return is raucous laughter.

Excitedly, "Are you kidding? Nalax is going to live near us?"

"And Elana." She jumps, locks her legs around my waist, and is once again kissing me passionately.

I growl, "Be careful, Mate. I'll make them wait at the door while I make you scream my name." Her desire spikes.

"Mmmm. That is a hard decision."

"We are already in the house! You left the door open." Doraj yells.

My mate laughs and jumps down. She grabs my hand and pulls me inside, with me grumbling about inconvenient neighbors, making her laugh harder.

Chapter 24

June

The next four months go by too fast. Ronin and I love the house nestled by the walls of the mountain by the waterfall. It's bigger than we need, but maybe someday, maybe we'll have need of it. More than anything, I want a quiet life with children and Ronin. For now, I have to be happy with every minute with him. I am getting restless. I need to fight. I need to free slaves from their nightmares even though mine have not released me yet. I still wake up screaming at night two to three nights a week, but that's less than it was last month, so it is slow, but I am improving.

Ronin, as always, is patient with me and holds me until I get through my fear. I wish he didn't have to go through this with me. I know he blames himself, but I don't. For us to be where we are today, I had to pass through the fire.

The valley is ready to be the Haven it is meant to be.

I'm sitting on our balcony after our day's work, thinking through what is left to be done, when Ronin comes and circles me with his arms. "You're thinking too hard, my mate. What bothers you?"

Turning to him, willing him to see, "It's time, Ronin."

He lifts his face to the sky. When he returns his face to mine, it is lit with a smile, and he says, "Finally."

Since the entire crew has Sia's comms patch, I tap my ear three times, "This is June. It's time. Wheels up in three days."

A chorus of excitement rings in my ear.

Three days later, we are standing once again in the cavern. The crew and the people elected to be leaders of Haven. They are good choices, fair and just. They will do well—the more vocal of the three moves forward to speak with me.

"June, we are not sure we are ready for you to leave, but we will do our best in your absence."

"Remember Amabo, Karab, Ellechim, the people here trust you. We trust you. If all goes well, we'll be back in a month or two with new passengers who need help and understanding. This is our mission, to save those in need, help them heal, and teach them the way. Besides, if you run into trouble, the valley comms can communicate with Sia."

They all three relax, "We will be ready."

I turn back to the crew, "Let's load up."

Ronin

We are en route to our first target and in the conference room to plan.

"Our first target is the slave market on Drogian 9. Drogian is an outpost, so the majority of the planet is uninhabited. Carnivorous plants inhabit the majority, so we will not be able to go in undetected. We will have to go in plain sight. We will put the Emancipation in low orbit over the southern pole; most ships just go into orbit around the equator of the planet. Generally, no one attacks other ships in orbit because you do not want to start anything with someone worse than you. We will take a transport to the surface. June, Doraj, Ekim, Elana, and I will go in to execute the rescue. Lessur and Nalax will take the second shuttle and move in just outside the outpost's planetary sensor range, waiting for our signal."

My mate takes over for the next steps, "Elana and I will both wear disguises since we are both female and desired for the slave markets and collectors."

A diagram of the outpost comes up on the display.

"We will be coming in here from the docks posing as buyers. Ronin will be the buyer because he's big and bad looking."

She says this with a smile as I chuckle. We both know they should be afraid of her and Elana, but they won't see them coming.

"We need to validate that the markets are as we expect. Nalax." Doraj's mate steps forward. She was bought at this market. He rubs her back before she leaves his side.

"The slave market on this planet is one of the worst out there. The slug which runs it goes by the name Nnej Sorg. He is evil but not like Kalxin. He is wholly driven by credits. We must take him and his crew out, or the market will just pop back up. The slave pens are in this building. It is heavily guarded. There is only one way in or out of the building. All of the guards must stay out unless they are getting slaves for sale. Nnej trusts no one, so he lets none of them in to prevent them from abusing his 'stock'."

She says the last word with venom, then shakes it off. "There are cameras in the slave building. They will need to be interrupted or destroyed. Inside the building are wall-to-wall cages, but generally, they are only about half populated. Elana is going to go into the building first. She'll have this spray marker," she holds up a pen-shaped spray bottle, "She will mark all slaves who are... not beyond saving. We will release all, but the marked come on the ship with us. How will they know or trust to go with us on the ship, you ask? The marker will help with that. For a short period, the marked will follow whoever marked them without question. It's not great, but hopefully, they will not hate us for forcing them to come with us."

June steps back to the front, "Ok, so we get in posing as a buyer and his help. Once we are in the outpost, we seek out Nnej and his gang's headquarters. Our first order of business is to take him and the things that work for him out. As soon as we signal, Sia will interrupt all comms within the outpost. We are expecting around 30 enforcers within his main compound. Once Nnej and his scum are dead, we proceed to the slave building and kill anything that gets in our way. We release all the cages once Elana marks them and move as quickly as we can to get all the marks onto the transport. If Elana realizes we have too many for one transport, she will signal Ekin and Nalax to bring in the second shuttle before we leave the second slave building. We'll box in the slaves as much as we can as we move throughout the outpost, but Elana will be in the lead, so they follow her. Kill anyone who looks like they are going to try to stop us. Elana, if you see a slave on our way out who is not beyond saving, mark and keep going. One of us will take care of the owner."

"Questions" No one responds. This is our third run-through, so everyone has it down.

"Good. We execute tomorrow morning at 0500 hours. Get some rest."

Everyone leaves quietly, "It is always like this before an Op. People are reserved and getting their minds ready for what's ahead." I know she is worried. They are her family.

Quietly she says, "*You* are my family. They are my family as well. Ronin... I need to talk to you about something."

"Go ahead."

"Leena. I know I should leave her here for her safety, but I can't. I can't stand the idea of her here alone. I know it's selfish of me but..."

I interrupt her, "I would not leave her here either. It is not selfish to want our daughter with us, especially since we have no family that will be remaining behind."

She relaxes and rests her forehead against my chest. "Thank you. I cannot bear the thought of being without her. I have started teaching her Martial Arts. I was just a little older than her when I started.

"That is good, June. I bet she is enjoying it."

She chuckles, "She loves it, and she's a natural. Ronin, she is so small for ten solar cycles. Is there something wrong?"

"No, June. She is fine. Nlyaxian children go through rapid growth periods, but there are only a few of them. Around five solar cycles is their first big one. She is ten, so her next will be in a cycle or two."

We pull up to our home and go inside. She gives me a worried look returning to her thoughts of danger, "Let's go to bed."

She needs the contact, and so do I.

We walk to the bedroom. I undress her then she undresses me. She raises her hands and starts running her hands over my chest. Her small fingers find every scar, every muscle ridge, like she memorizes every part of me. She walks around to my back and does the same, touching and running her fingers along my skin. She is so gentle she is breaking my heart.

I turn to her and lift her face with my hands. I kiss her softly at first, then deepen it, trying to show her with my body how I feel about her.

I pick her up and lay her on the bed. I crawl over her and settle between her beautiful long legs. She wraps them around my hips. I position myself and slowly push into her.

She is so tight. She is my home. I pull back and push back in. She is ecstasy. The fire she creates in me is building higher and higher. Her moans and sighs are all I am living for right now. Thrust in, pull out. Faster and faster. I love the friction of her tight pussy on my cock.

I feel my sprili unfurl. She gasps at the sensation they create. I feel it when her orgasm hits. Her pussy locks down on my cock and begins to squeeze and release, squeeze and release. I can no longer hold back my own climax. I roar. My seed bathes her inner walls, and my sprili starts to vibrate.

She screams my name and climaxes again as my seed continues to release. We are panting coming down from our passion.

I roll her on top of me, still buried in her. She's asleep almost immediately. I cover us up and go to sleep as well, knowing I will wake her through the night because I need her.

It's dark. I feel lost, drifting. There are stars overhead but no moon. This is not Earth. The grass is so thin it feels like hair caressing my calves. My hair is down and blows in the light breeze. I am wearing nothing, but it barely bothers me anymore. There are trees a distance away but I can't see any detail.

I stand in a valley. Fog is rolling in. There is someone in it. I cannot see him, but I know he is there. I'm not sure how I know he is there or that he is a 'he,' but I do. A Nlyaxian steps from the fog. He begins to walk toward me. Fear hits me. Kaxlin. I cannot move.

As he gets closer, I realize no, not Kaxlin, I do not know this Nlyaxian, but he is beautiful... and sad.

He is broken. Again, I'm not sure how I know this, but I do. He is close now. He stops about 2 feet from me. I explore his face, and it is extremely handsome, like Ronin.

He is leaner. There is no silver on his ridges. He has a scar, and it goes from his eyebrow down to nearly his jawline. It doesn't affect my opinion of his face; it enhances him somehow.

I look into his eyes, and they hurt my heart. There is such sadness and pain there. I want; no, I need to take it away. He has no shirt on. I take in his chest and arms. He is built like Ronin but maybe a bit bigger.

He has scars everywhere. It hits me; he was tortured. It is the only way someone can have that many. I want to touch and kiss them all. I look back at his face. The pain and sadness are there, but now a small smile softens everything. It's then I realize something, "I know you. How do I know you?"

His hand lifts to my face and cups my cheek, "You were in my dreams as a child. We played children's games. You have grown and are more beautiful than I could have possibly imagined."

His touch is so gentle, and I rub my face into his hand. My eyes snap open, "I remember we... played a game you taught me where we'd bounce a ball against a wall... it had some sort of pattern on it... You used to pull my hair to get me to lose!"

He smiles genuinely, and it takes my breath away. "Yes! It was the only way I could win." He chuckles.

"Where are we?" I ask him.

Sadness fills his face again, and he sighs, "In my dreams. It's been cycles and cycles since you've been here. Are you here to torture me as well?" Anger flashes across his face.

His anger scares me, and he sees my fear. The sadness comes back. He turns away, "You should not be here, Mate." He walks away.

I try to follow. I am screaming at him to stop, to come back, but no sounds come out. The fog explodes across the valley. I scream in fear...

Ronin is shaking me awake. "You are ok, Mate. I have you." He assumes I had bad dream about Kaxlin. How do I tell him I was dreaming about another male... and he called me Mate.

Chapter 25

Everyone is quiet. We are readying ourselves. We land in 5 minutes and then execute our first attack on a slave market. We are ready, but I'm still nervous, just like before each and every of my tournament matches. This is much higher stakes. This could cost the lives of the people I care for and people who do not belong in the conditions they are in.

We will succeed. We have to. I am in my disguise, and so is Elana. There's a little band around our necks, below our collars, and at our wrists under our sleeves. Attached to the band is a hood made of a very light see-through material.

Attached to the bands at my wrists are comfortable gloves that actually enhance my grip. There is a seam down the front of the hood that connects the sides of the hood together when you want the disguise to be active. The material is see-through, so there is no risk of being unable to see an attacker because of a mask. It's very strange. It doesn't feel like I'm disguised but looking at Elana... we definitely are.

Instead of sitting across from my Ferin friend, the being I sit across from is something called a Torgu. Its skin and eyes are black. It has no nose, and it has bumps all over its skin.

It smiles at me, and I laugh. It's definitely Elana. My disguise is the same as hers. The Torgu are ferocious and deadly. They also have a very humanoid appearance, so no one will think about attacking us. I look at my hands and see nasty-looking claws and a two-inch spike on the top of my hands. Our voices are even disguised through the mask, but since we'll still be speaking our native tongues, we plan on keeping the speaking to a minimum.

We are all loaded with weapons. Some you can see, some you cannot. I wear my Katana, Tanto, many, many throwing daggers, blasters, two kubotan, and even my rope dart. Evil fuckers are gonna die today, and they just don't know it yet. I feel the transport land and the engines shut down—show time.

Ronin nods at us all. "It's time." Ronin and Doraj go first, and Elana and I flank them.

The first thing I'm hit with is the smell. It is awful. It smells like fish and shit. It is not pleasant. I immediately begin scanning for threats, and there are many.

Everyone who looks at us looks to be gauging the trouble of killing us for whatever we have, but when they take in our party, every single one of them back off. That's good. Hopefully, it stays that way.

We have the path to Nnej's compound memorized, and we are weaving through the streets to take us straight there. The streets are relatively empty, so again, good. Fewer people means less fighting when we are on our way back to the transport.

The buildings we walk through are run down and dingy. I see aliens peek out of broken windows and doors, and they hide as soon as they see us. It takes us about nine minutes to get to the gates of the compound. The slave building is about fifty feet to the right of the building. It looks like a warehouse from earth but rundown and with guards walking its perimeter.

We stop at the gate, and one of the guards walks to us. Speaking to Ronin, "What do you want, scum?"

I pull my Katana, and it is almost at his throat when Ronin says, "Stop," in a bored tone.

The guard reeks of fear. "Tsk tsk tsk Be careful. My guards do not like it when someone insults me. Back." I return my blade and move back to position. I am fully in instinctual mode. I see all enemies.

Ronin speaks again, "Scum, tell your master I am here, and I want to buy slaves. My name is Brrokin." His guard friends are laughing at him as he returns to the shack by the gate. They are all sloppy and out of shape, good.

The guard comes back, "Emperor Nnej wants a credits check before he lets you in."

Doraj steps forward and presents a small yellow device about the size of a deck of cards. The guard waves a small display over it, and his eyes grow in surprise, but he quickly schools it. He walks back to the shack, and after a few minutes, the gates open.

The difference inside the gate versus outside is night and day. Where everything outside the gate is dingy, rundown, and old, everything inside is new, opulent, and tacky. The decor screams, 'I have money. You don't.' I immediately hate it.

The guard leads us through the complex, and it is identical to the plans we studied. We reach what can only be called a throne room. The being lounging on a dais is humanoid but skinny; its arms and legs look like sticks. It has six arms, its head is larger than it should be, and it has no lips. All you see are razor-sharp triangle-shaped teeth. He also has eyes covering half the front of his skull.

He is hideous, and currently, he has a female sucking on what passes for his cock at the moment. When he… finishes… gross, he stands up, naked, and walks down the dais to Ronin.

"Welcome, Brrokin. I am happy to host you here and provide whatever you need." His voice is surprisingly soprano.

Ronin sneers, "Thank you. We will only be here for a few hours. I need several slaves. My old ones had an… accident."

Nnej giggles. "It happens. I can definitely help you to resupply. How many do you need?"

Ronin plays the aristocrat very well, "I don't remember but let us go with twenty."

You can almost see the credit signs in his eyes. "Very good. Would you like something to eat or drink?"

The wordplay between the two of them continues, but something is pulling me. I glance in the direction of the pull. There is a door with two guards. I need to go there. The pull is strong, but we have a plan I must follow. I turn back to Ronin. We have work to do.

We have all inventoried the guards we've seen the way here and all the guards in the room. I take note of the device he wears on his wrist. It doesn't seem to have more than one function. It has a glass face with what looks like a panic button. That's going to need to come off, so the place doesn't go into lockdown.

It's about time. Ronin's eyes are suddenly locked on the child entering the room with drinks. He can't be more than five years old. He is Noinapmoc. I look at Doraj. He is shaking. Ronin is schooling his features, but his eyes are black. Shit, shit, shit. I come around Ronin and Doraj, my Tanto drawn. He does not see me in time. My first strike takes his arm off, and the strike is designed to fling the limb back toward Elana.

Before he can even scream, I knock him out with a blow to the head. My focus turns to the guards that my friends are now engaged with. Tanto are put away, and I start throwing daggers at all the guards on the second-floor balcony. Within seconds they are all down.

There are two guards coming at me with mace-looking weapons. One of them swings the mace. I easily avoid the blow and bring the dagger still in my hand across the back of his knee, severing all the muscles from the bone.

He's down but still dangerous, but I need to take care of the second. This one is bringing his weapon down, looking to crush my skull. I cannot get all the way away, but I can avoid the mace, but he'll get me in the ribs with a fist. It can't be helped.

He connects with my ribs, and I try to minimize the damage by rolling with the momentum of the punch. I don't think he broke anything, but it's gonna hurt later.

I come up from the roll with Katana in my hands, and his head is now on the floor. I turn, looking for more, and see all the enemies are down. I kill the guard I wounded and notice the slaves huddled in the corner.

"Elana, evaluate them."

Doraj is on his knees a few feet in front of the boy, trying to calm him.

"Ronin, bring down the field on the south side of the outpost. Let the plants in." He nods.

We need to get to the warehouse.

An evil chuckling starts behind us. "You have no idea what you have done. They will hunt you. They will torture you for days and days. Then they'll heal you so he can start again." He laughs, "*Fools*! You can take this outpost, but they *will* take it back!"

I growl. "Shut him up." Doraj stands and strides over to break his neck. That works.

"Elana?" I call out.

"They are all marked."

"OK. Warehouse. Elana leads the way. Everything between here and there dies unless she marks them." Everyone nods.

I glance at the door. I will be back before we leave.

I walk to Doraj, who has the boy on his back. "Hi. Are there any more children in this building?" He shakes his head. "Good. Now I want you to close your eyes until Doraj tells you it's ok?" He nods and closes his eyes. I press the collar release to his, and it drops from his neck. I do the same to the rest of the slaves Elana marked.

"Elana, move out."

One more glance at the door. We move to the hallway that exits next to the warehouse. There's not much resistance. Some guards and one more marked slave. They all follow us, fear in their eyes, but they follow.

"Ok, Elana, it's mine and Ronin's turn." We move in front of her and do not hesitate. The door is open, and we are out. Killing everything between us, and the warehouse. Most run, some fight, but they die quickly.

There is a guard trying to provide cover for his friends. I am out of daggers, so I pull the rope dart from my belt. I run to get close enough to the guard, building momentum on the weapon. When I know I am close enough, I release it, and it embeds itself in the side of his head. I pull it back and hang it back on my belt.

In less than a few minutes, we are at the warehouse door. Ronin cracks the door codes with a device Sia provided. And he, Elana, and Doraj file in.

I am the lookout. This part takes longer. It takes about seven minutes for them to go through the warehouse. In that time, I took down two brave guards with my blasters, who decided they would be the ones to kill the intruders.

I am starting to hear people screaming, snippets of screams containing the word 'plants'. So the killer plants are getting close.

We are ready to go. "Elana, Ronin, I need to go back into the compound."

Both start angry exclamations in the negative. "*No!* I must do this. I feel a pull. There is something there I must find." Elana quiets.

Ronin looks furious, "I am going with you."

I give him a sad look, "No, Ronin. I need you to get them to the safety of the shuttle. Please. Trust me."

He closes his eyes. "If you are not with us in five minutes, I am coming for you!" I nod.

I cannot wait. I spin and sprint for the door to the compound. There is no resistance now. I head directly for the door. It's locked. I look around and grab Nnej's hand, and put it against the panel. It clicks open.

There are stairs down after the door. It opens at the bottom in what can only be called a dungeon. There are rows upon rows of cells. I turn as I sense movement, catch an arm and flip, then break it. The guard is screaming now, and two more come running. I pull my tanto to handle them. Unfortunately, they both have blasters aimed at me. I can see the excitement on their faces that I am a female. They are both already making plans for me. I don't think so.

I sprint after the stronger-looking guard, and a shocked look comes across his face. I slice his chest, step behind him then put my blades through his back at the same time. I turn him slightly before he falls. As he realizes he is dying, he pulls the trigger on his blaster shooting the other guard. The guard on the floor, I take out with a Tanto. I grab what looks like a key hanging from his belt and start moving down the cells, looking for what is calling me.

I stop about halfway down and see there is a very large someone in the cell. This is what is calling me... why?

He speaks, "What are you? Because you are not what you seem."

His voice sends shivers through me. I know that voice. I whisper, "I know you."

He slowly stands and stalks to the cage door, "I doubt that." His appearance screams dangerous... but he is the Nlyaxian from my dream.

I slowly walk to the door and unlock it. Before I know it, he has me by the neck against the wall. I can't help the flash of Kaxlin... I begin shaking.

"What is this?" Shit, he feels the hood. His other hand comes up and pulls apart the seam. When he sees my face, shock rolls across his handsome face. He drops me and staggers back.

Fear is now on his features. Why is he scared? Before I can't stop him, he is running for the stairs.

Fuck. I try to follow, but by the time I hit the top of the stairs, he is gone. I don't know which way he went. I need to go to the shuttle. God damn it! I redo the seam on my mask and take off at a dead run for the shuttle.

There is no challenge until I hit the docks. There are aliens fighting to get out of the outpost. I can see Doraj and Ronin fighting to keep enemies at bay. This is my fault.

I sprint into the melee with my Tanto drawn. Everything dies in my path. I get within fifteen feet of the shuttle. Ronin sees me, and I can see him relax. I hear him scream to someone, "*Take off*!"

I am still fighting my way to the shuttle, which is now four feet off the ground. I jump, and Ronin grabs my hand and smiles.

I start to smile back then something latches onto my ankles. It burns. I am screaming and whatever has me starts to pull me back down to the ground. "Ronin!"

The thing suddenly releases me, and I'm on the shuttle with the door closing.

I moan, "Ronin, it burns."

"I know, my Mate. The plant had you. They have thorns and saliva on their tentacles. You will be fine. You have to be fine."

Everything is getting fuzzy. I can only whisper, "Ronin, I love you."

"*No*! Stay awake!"

I hear a small voice, "I can help." Then everything fades away.

Chapter 26

Ronin

The boy has come forward, "I can help her. Please."

I have my Mate in a tight hold in my arms. I can only nod. He sits at her legs and removes her boots, and cuts her pants up to her knee. I can now see the damage that goddess-forsaken plant has wrought on her legs. They are an angry red with white stripes. Her ankles and calves are already twice their normal size.

She is unresponsive. The boy removes a container from his pocket and covers her legs, ankles, and feet with the salve. He replaces the salve in his pocket and removes a small vile from the same pocket. He moves to put it in her mouth.

I cannot stop the growl that emanates from me. "I am sorry, sir. Without the remedy, she will die." I close my eyes because I cannot handle the thought. I nod for him to proceed. He puts two drops into her mouth and returns it to his pocket.

"Now, we must wait to see if her system is strong enough to push out the poison." He says with a whisper, then returns to sitting next to Doraj in front of the shuttle. I pull her fully into my lap and just hold her.

I think back to what happened. Could I have done something different to avoid this? But... Why did it release her? I close my eyes and go back into my memory. I see the vine wrapped around both ankles and her calves. A blaster shot hit the vine below her feet, and it fell away in two pieces. Who shot the vine and why? Still, in my memory, I look up to see if I can find the shooter.

My vision is blurry when I look at the crowd. I scan the crowd, looking for a figure pointing a blaster up at us. I find him, and he is blurry. I focus, trying to resolve the shooter. He gets a little better. To my shock, it is definitely a Nlyaxian male. No matter how hard I try, his face does not become clear.

It's then I notice something my mind cannot understand. I stare at it for a while. It's not possible. He is dead. I hear a feminine moan and open my eyes, and two beautiful green eyes are trying to focus on my face.

I hug her to me, and whisper, "Thank the Goddess."

"I am so tired."

The boy from the front says, "You must sleep. You still fight it."

I nod at him.

"Sleep, my beautiful warrior mate. You need to heal."

Her eyes close again, and she sleeps.

June

I am in the valley again. It's dawn this time. The valley is beautiful. The trees in the distance have purple leaves and white bark. I look around for him.

"Why do you keep pulling me here?" His voice is deeper than Ronin's, and I shiver when I hear it.

My body reacts. My nipples harden because they like his voice as well. "Your body calls to me." He whispers in my ear.

You have a mate hooker. I turn and step back. Ignoring his statement, "Why did you run from me?"

A shocked look comes over his face. "You are not real. You could not have been there."

"I am real."

"No. You are not. You cannot be." He says the last part with such sadness it hurts my heart.

I step to him and put my hand on his cheek. He closes his eyes and pushes against it for more contact. "I am real. Please believe me."

His eyes open. His hand slowly reaches out and cups my breast, then rubs his thumb over my nipple. My eyes close, and a small moan escapes my lips. I open my eyes as his hand drops.

His sadness deepens. "You see. You are not real. No female would respond to me the way you do." He turns and disappears. Ugh, that fucking male.

I wake up in my bed on Haven. Ronin is wrapped around me, and I can't help the spike of guilt that washes over me. He has dark circles under his eyes. He's been awake worrying over me. My guilt rises.

I get out of bed, but he stays asleep. I put on a robe and walk out onto our terrace. It's nighttime, and the two moons are bright overhead. The big one is three-quarters full, and the little one is about half. The little moon is purple because the minerals on the surface reflect the surface.

Large arms circle my waist, and he plants kisses on my shoulder, moving up my neck. "Mmmm. Hello, my Mate."

Ronin chuckles, "Hello, my mate. How are you feeling?"

"Good. I feel like I've slept forever." Since I know how long it took to get to the outpost, it's silly to ask, but I do it anyway. "How long?"

"Nalax insisted on putting you in stasis until all the poison was cleared from your body. You have been asleep for twenty-two day cycles."

"What? Really?"

As I spin in his arms, I see the worry on his face still. "I'm so sorry, Ronin. I can't imagine what that put you through. I am sorry."

"Shhh, my mate. You are well again, that is all that matters." He pulls me into his arms, and I wrap mine around him, holding him tight.

I realize he is naked. I grab his hand and walk him to one of the reclining lounge chairs I like to sit in and watch the stars. I sit him down and drop my robe. I kneel by the chair and bend over his chest. I begin exploring his chest with kisses and touches.

My mouth finds his nipple, and he groans. "Mate..." I move south. My target is standing tall, waiting for me. I wrap my hands around his cock.

Ronin growls, "Wait." Then grabs my hips and lifts me to settle my legs on either side of his head. It's my turn to moan. I return to my tasks and wrap my lips around his cock, slowly licking and sucking. Then I feel him start his exploration. Slowly moving his tongue through my folds toward my clit. I start sliding my mouth down his cock going as far as I can. When his tongue touches my clit he growls, and I moan loudly with him in my throat.

It becomes a battle of sensation. He growls, sending shockwaves through me. I moan, making him growl. I am bobbing up and down faster. When his tongue dives into my pussy he goes straight for my g-spot, then growls loudly. My body erupts in a ground-shattering climax. My moan set off his own. Then I am swallowing his release.

He's lifting me again. He starts to lower me onto his cock, facing away from him. We both moan once he is fully seated.

I lay back onto his chest then he begins to flex his hip, moving his cock in and out. The sensations this position creates is driving me crazy. He wraps his arm around my waist so he can leverage deeper and harder. His other hand moves to my clit and starts to circle round and round. I am deep in the sensations he is creating, feeling my climax building fast.

His sprili unfurl, and an orgasm rolls through, making me scream. I'm suddenly on my stomach on the lounge chair, and he is pounding me from behind. His orgasm hits, and his sprili start vibrating. "*Ronin!*" I scream as another climax rolls through me.

He pulls out and picks me up to take me to the bed. I yawn. I am tired.

The next few days, Ronin made me rest in our home. If I am being honest with myself, I needed it. Fighting the toxins of that plant really took a toll. He's with me most of the time, making me food or making me scream, both very satisfying. By morning of the third day, I'm going mad. I need to get out. Ronin begrudgingly agrees, and we head to the common building.

The new inhabitants of Haven are quiet but settling in. They are all in the rooms in the community building until they are comfortable taking a home in the valley.

Ronin and I walk into the lobby, and I am immediately almost bowled over. When I look down, it's the little boy. He still has sadness in his eyes but not as much as when we found him. His four little arms are wrapped around me. Ronin told me earlier his name is Nimajneb, but everyone calls him Nim.

I rub his hair, "Hey, Nim. How are you?"

He doesn't respond, so I squat down, "Hey." I say to him softly. He wraps his arms around my neck and shoulders so I pick him up. I see Nalax and Doraj walking up to us. "Nim," I whisper, "What's wrong?"

He whispers in my ear, "I need to ask a question."

"Ok. Go ahead."

He whispers again, "In private."

Nalax and Doraj give me a worried look. I give them a re-assuring look. "Ok then, how about we go outside for a bit." He nods as I set him down.

He grabs my hand, and we walk outside. I lead him over to a bench. "What do you want to ask?

"Thank you for saving me. That place was terrible."

"You are welcome."

"Do you think Doraj and Nalx like me?" he asks as he looks at his hands in his lap.

"I think they like you a lot."

"I really like them." He pauses for a bit. "My parents died at that place."

"Oh, Nim, I am so sorry."

He nods, "Do you think... Do you think they would want me? Want me to be theirs?"

"I think they would be honored. You should talk to them about it."

He shakes his head fast, "I cannot. What if they say no? I would be so sad." Oh, my Goddess, this child is breaking my heart.

"What if we talk to them together?"

His head snaps up with such a look of hope. "You would do that for me?"

"Of course, I would. Nalax and Doraj are both like family to me. I would love for you to be part of our family too. Do you want to do it now?" A little unease flashes across his face. Then he looks at me for a long time.

"Yes. I can be brave like you." *No tears, damn it. Hold them in!*

We walk back into the building and to Doraj and Nalax. There is concern on their faces. "Nim and I talked. His parents were killed on that planet. He really likes you both and wants to be a part of our family. He was wondering if you both would want him as yours?"

Nalax, as expected, bursts out in tears and says, "YES! We would love that!" Doraj has tears in his eyes as well. They both get on their knees and wrap their arms protectively around him.

I back away from the new family moment. Ronin's arm wraps around my shoulders. "You are amazing, June. All little ones trust you."

I look up at him as a tear gets loose, "I hate he was ever in that situation, Ronin. We are doing the right thing."

A few months later, I fully recovered from the hell plant. I've been back to training for over eight weeks, and I am back to normal levels of stamina and endurance. We've had two more liberation operations since the woman-eating plant planet. They both went off without a hitch, and we saved forty-one slaves. All the liberated people have decided to come with us to Haven. I think they want someplace they know they will be safe.

We are starting to see community and even some new family units. Most days of the week, there is a market in the courtyard of the community building. The people want purpose, so they make things for the betterment of everyone. No credits, no trading; if you need it, take it. It's amazing to watch.

I haven't dreamed about my mystery Nlyaxian lately, and my nightmares are only coming once every few weeks, so it's been blessedly quiet. I've decided on our next mission.

There has been something bothering me for a while. Where are the other human women? Where is Ahmya? We haven't seen any and if I was sold, surely others were as well.

So we are heading back to Gamma Station. We need intel on slavers and who may have the women. It's the only place I can think of to start. The slavers at the markets we've hit were less than... helpful on the information front.

"Sia, Can you let the Emancipation crew and Haven leaders meet in the planning room at 13:00 hours, please?"

"*Yes, Captain. We goin' somewhere?*" She asks.

I chuckle because she's starting to adopt some of my speech patterns. "Yes, my friend. It's time to put some real effort into finding my people." And my best friend.

Ronin

My Mate called us all together, so we must be planning for our next mission. I am not sure I have fully relaxed from the first mission, almost losing her... it was one of the worst experiences of my life. The next two missions were much better, no one was hurt, and slaves were liberated. I cannot help but worry a bit before every mission, and this will not be any different.

I walk into the conference room, and my Mate is already there. The room is large and has an oval table and chairs for members to sit in. There is a large display on the far wall, just like in the conference room on the ship.

She stands at the window, staring out. She is beautiful, but something troubles her. I walk up behind her and place a kiss at the base of her neck.

"Mmmm, hello, my Mate." She murmurs.

"You seem troubled. Do you need to talk?"

She turns into my arms with a small smile on her face, "You know me a little too well. Yes, but I should probably wait for everyone else. It's all related. I do want to talk to you about this room, though."

"What is it? You don't like the layout?"

She glances uncomfortably at the table. She takes a breath as if in preparation, "When I was his slave..." she still can't say his name. "He made me accompany him to a meeting with other captains. For the majority of the meeting, I stood quietly at the back. He gave me what barely equated to clothing for the meeting. The entire time I could feel the eyes of those... things on me. It made me feel dirty. They were wrapping up the meeting when one of the captains asked him if they could have me while they were on board."

She sighs, "For a minute, I thought he was going to do it. At that point, the slave tattoos were active, so there would be no way for me to stop him. He pulled me in front of him at the table and started asking them what they'd do to me and did those exact things to me in front of them. He took me on the table in front of them. I could do nothing to stop it. He started screaming at them. Ronin, his sprili came out, and his eyes were black. He sent me back into his quarters, and I think he killed a few of them. That night, that night when he came back into the room, is when he almost broke me."

Her arms are wrapped around me, and she is crying. I am having such a hard time controlling my emotions. "My Mate, I need to be honest. I am having an extremely hard time controlling myself right now. My battle fury is demanding dominance. I do not want to scare you."

She looks up at me with red eyes and wet cheeks. "Ronin, your battle fury no longer scares me, I promise but..."

It is then I understand, "The table. The table has come to represent your trauma." She nods. "I will get rid of it and make the space better."

She nods again and lays her head against my chest again, just holding onto me tightly. Without lifting her head, "I know what I just told you is hard for you to process. Do you want to delay the meeting an hour, so you can go train a bit with one of the others?" Doraj is outside the door. I heard him walk up, but he was courteous and did not interrupt.

"That would help my Mate, but only if you agree to go for a walk or relax outside. I can get the table removed before we come back." She nods. Good.

Quietly she asks, "Ronin, am I weak because I cannot look at a table like that... that I cannot get past it?"

I lift her face to mine, "Absolutely not. I have been in wars with seasoned veterans and first years. *All* of them have trauma from battle that takes years to work through. Some never can see or hear something again without flashing back to those memories. Does that make them weak? No. It makes them typical warriors. Just like you." I wipe the tears still falling down her face and hug her tight to me.

"Sia, please notify everyone the meeting is delayed an hour."

"Done, Ronin."

"I love you, Ronin. You are everything to me."

My heart sings, "And I love you, little Pillut."

She walks out without looking at the table.

Sia speaks before I can, *"I am working on replacing the table."*

"Thank you." I let my battle fury take over. Roaring, I bring down both my arms on the table, breaking it in half, then stalk out of the room.

Doraj joins me, and I can tell he is as furious as I am. My mate is like family to him, as am I, and what is done to his family is done to him. It will be a good sparring match.

June

I walk to the rear of the community building and recline on a lounge chair next to the river. It's peaceful, and I hope it calms my mind. Seeing that table was too much for my mind to handle. It immediately made me relive the whole thing, even the part in his quarters.

He said I'm not weak, but I feel weak. It's just a table, for fuck sake, but I couldn't face it, and I don't want to. I close my eyes and just listen to the water.

Mmmm. I love the bed Ronin, and I chose. It's so comfortable. I stretch and reach out for him, but he's not there. Huh, I wonder where he went. He usually is there when I reach for him. I feel the blanket I lay on top of. We always sleep naked, so the fact that I am doesn't phase me, but why am I on top of the blankets?

My arms suddenly are locked over my head. No. I try to move them, and I can't. My legs bend, lift and spread. No, no, no.

Someone chuckles at the end of the bed. NO, it is not him.

"Oh, but it is my little sex slave."

No. No. I am not here.

"On the contrary, you never left. Your mind broke after the captain meeting. You thought I was Ronin, but I killed him. You are mine!"

He's on top of me and has me by the hair.

"Just admit it. You love it when I pound my cock into you. You love it when I make you cum. I'm going to make you cum all night long."

No help me! Not again!

I feel him poised at my entrance then the most ferocious roar echoes through the room. Kaxlin is suddenly no longer on top of me, and I can move my body again. I roll to my side into a fetal position, crying and not able to stop. Someone very gently picks me up and wraps me in a blanket. I am whispering, "no, please, no."

"Shh, little one. He is gone. You are safe." *It's my mystery, Nlyaxian. He holds me tight to his chest, trying to comfort me. After a few minutes, I am able to calm myself.*

"Why are you here?"

"I was asleep and felt your fear. I could not take it and came for you."

We are both quiet for a while. "I know that Nlyaxian. He... He held you as a sex slave?" *He asks this as he touches one of the gold marks. I nod. He growls,* "Is he still alive?"

"No. I killed him."

"Good. Though I would not have minded the opportunity."

I lay back in his arms to look up into his face and realize we are in the valley again. I relax. "Thank you for coming for me. He hasn't invaded my dreams for a little while, but today I was reminded of something particularly bad he did. I guess it shook me more than I thought."

"Trauma does that. I am sorry you had to go through something like this. It is not right."

He brings his hand to my face to cup my cheek. He gently rubs his thumb across it. When I laid back, the blanket fell off one of my breasts. His hand leaves my cheek and barely caresses the side. "What are these called?"

A little breathless, "Humans call them breasts."

"I like them." He runs a finger over my nipple, and I cannot suppress a small moan. His eyes dart to mine, and he starts to circle it. "And this?"

"Nipple."

"Mmmm. I like them as well." He slowly pulls the sheet down my body. Reveling my other breast, then my stomach, then my pussy.

His hand moves to my stomach tracing imaginary lines. I cannot help but stretch my body in an attempt to have more contact.

His eyes are on mine again, "What about this?"

I moan loudly as his fingers begin to explore my folds. I am heavy-lidded but trying to hold eye contact. The moans are escaping, and I cannot stop them. I don't want to. When his finger finds my clit I moan loudly and arch my back. His focus is now there. He circles and rubs my clit till it is hard, "Please..."

He lifts me so his lips are next to my ear. "Please, what little one?"

"Please... please make me cum. I need it."

"Mmmm, I believe you do." He then pinches my clit, and I explode. He holds me to his chest as I come down from my orgasm. "So responsive. You are perfect."

Trying to catch my breath, I pull back a little, "I don't even know your name."

He gives me a very sexy smile, "I am Dax."

Dax... I know that name... where do I know that name? I'll remember later. I pull myself up and kiss him softly on the mouth. He opens his mouth a little to say something, but I immediately deepen the kiss. He catches on very quickly and takes over, scorching me with the passion he has. I break this kiss, "DAX! You're Dax! But you died!"

The world fades as I wake...

Elana is there, "It's time for the meeting."

Blinking, unable to shake the shock I am feeling, "Thank you. Give me a minute, please."

How is this even possible? Ronin said Dax died the day he lost his people. How can I have dreams about him? I do not understand what is going on. I go to the washroom before I head to the conference room. I splash water on my face trying, and I don't know what I am trying to do... maybe avoid Ronin. I just had a sex dream about his dead best friend. WTF.

Time to go. *You have shit to do, June.* I walk to the conference and am pleasantly surprised that the table is gone, and there are comfy chairs scattered throughout the room with small tables with displays sitting next to them. I love it.

I look for Ronin, and he is at the front chatting with Lessur but looking at me. I put my hand over my heart and mouth, 'Thank you.' He gives me a deep nod and holds his hand out for me to come over. I need to tell him, but how.

I walk over, and he puts his arm around me, pulling me in tight. "You ready to start?" I nod. Squeeze him tight, then head to the front of the room.

"Alright, everyone, have a seat. We have had three successful missions to free enslaved peoples of this galaxy. The people of Haven are settling nicely into our community thanks to our community leadership. Y'all have been wondering when our next mission will be, but this one will be different. You may or may not know this, but I was only one of many human women that were taken from my world. There were at least one hundred twenty in the shipment I was in, and the Cruxlin made it sound like we were not the first. On our missions, I have been keeping an eye out for any signs of other human women and have seen none. So this mission is intel only. We are heading back to Gamma station to see if we can gather intel on who has the humans and maybe where they might be. A big station like Gamma should have someone who knows something. Since we are going to Gamma station, I asked the leadership here in case they want us to get supplies or equipment while we are there. Questions or concerns?"

Everyone is quiet for a bit, and I can tell most are thinking through logistics. Doraj is the first to speak, "We'll need to be very careful. We do not want to damage our relationship there because it is the closest supply station. The next closest adds another twenty-two days of travel." I nod.

Amabo from the leadership speaks next, "Agreed, Doraj, we can come up with a list of supplies and equipment we like to have for Haven."

"Thank you, Amabo." I look to the room for more.

Nalax raises her hand, "I would like triage beds and medical equipment so I can set up a health clinic."

I nod. "Great idea."

Ronin clears his throat, "I am assuming you will be boarding with us?"

My eyebrow raises, "Yes. We have disguises now. I don't see a reason not to."

"Agreed, but we need to do teams on the station. No one goes out alone."

"I agree with that. What size teams do you recommend?"

He relaxes a little. I guess he expected a fight on this, "Think three is the size. There are just too many factors on that station to account for all risks."

"So Doraj, Lessur and Elana. You, me, and Ekim?" I ask.

"Perfect." I smile at him. He is much more relaxed now.

"So now, do any of you or any Haven inhabitants know that station? We need a plan."

Karab raises his hand this time, "I know someone very familiar with the station. I can bring him to the next planning meeting."

"Good. Thank you, Karab. Ok, the next planning meeting will be in two days at 10:00 hours because tomorrow is our first festival, and I want you all to be able to attend."

Everyone filters out, excited about tomorrow. I turn to Ronin, "Can we go home?"

"Of course. Everything ok?" he asks, concerned.

"Fine, I want to talk to you about something but at home." He nods, and we head to the little two-person car-like vehicles we found a few months ago. I can't help but space out a little, looking out the windows, worried about how he'll react to what I'm about to tell him.

Chapter 27

Ronin

We get home and go inside. I sit in one of the chairs and pull my mate down into my lap. "What is on your mind, little Pillut? I can see your worry."

She's looking at her hands, "Ronin, that first mission, you remember I needed to go back into the compound?"

"Yes, I never did ask you what that was about."

"As soon as we entered that compound I started feeling a compulsion. I needed to follow it. It was very strong and hard to ignore. I forced myself to do just that until the most dangerous parts of the mission were over. Once the slaves were freed, I could no longer ignore it. It was a very intense feeling. I went back inside to the throne room, and there was a door that I needed to go in, but it was locked. I looked for Nnej's hand, hoping it would be keyed for him. It was. It was a long set of stairs down into what was a dungeon or prison. There were a couple of guards that I easily dealt with, and I stole a key to the cells. I walked the cells until I felt the need to stop." She looks at me now. Worry in her eyes.

"Ronin, there was a Nlyaxian male in the cell. I still had my disguise on, but he said to me something like, 'who do we have here, not a Trogu.' He knew I was not who I appeared to be. The compulsion was telling me to let him out. He was very intimidating. He was bigger than you. Dirty though, like he'd been there a while."

My heart feels like it's stopped. I want her to say it, but at the same time, I do not. "When I unlocked the door, he attacked, but for some reason, I knew he wouldn't hurt me. He had me by the neck and pulled the seam apart on the hood. When he saw me, he was so shocked he stumbled back away from me and hit the cell. I still do not understand why I shocked him."

"Mate, please, what did this male look like?"

"I don't have to tell you what he looked like. I learned today who he is. Ronin. His name is Dax."

I stand quickly and set her on her feet. I walk to the windows. I do not understand how he can be alive. "Ronin, before I could stop him, he ran away from me. So fast. I couldn't catch up, and I knew I had to get to the shuttle. The compulsion was gone, so I ran for the shuttle. Ronin, at the time, I did not know it was Dax. I swear it."

"I do not understand. How is he alive? I... how?"

"I don't know, I'm sorry."

I hear the worry in her voice and look at her, "What's wrong? Why are you sorry?"

She starts pacing slowly across the room, "Ronin... I see him sometimes in my dreams. At first, I just thought my mind was making him up in my dreams since I had seen him, but in one, he acted like we had met before when we were young... and I remembered we had...I had dreams of a little boy who I now know was Nlyaxian. We used to play games and explore wild places. He was my friend. My only friend for a long time. In these current dreams, he was so sad and kept saying that I wasn't real. Today I laid down on a chair by the river to try and relax after the whole table thing. I fell asleep, and I saw him again in my dream. He saved me from a nightmare. A terrible one. I asked him his name, and he said it was Dax."

I turn back to the window. I am having trouble focusing.

"Ronin, are you angry with me?"

"No, my Mate. I am definitely not angry with you, but I am having problems with my emotions. I do not know how to handle the information you have given me. I am going for a walk. I will be back."

June

Ronin has been gone for a few hours, and I'm worried. I hope he's ok. I can't imagine what he's going through knowing his best friend is alive and imprisoned like he was. I hear the door open and stand. Ronin walks in, sits down, and holds out his hand.

He looks determined now, like he's made some sort of decision. I walk over, and he pulls me back into his lap. He grabs my face and pulls me into a long, slow kiss. My head is reeling when he's done.

"Thank you for saving my best friend and brother. Thank you so much." I nod, a little emotional myself. "Now I need some details. You said you remember him from your dreams?"

"Yes. Once he said it, the memories came back. He was so much fun to be with him in my dreams. He was my only friend for a very long time. He taught me new games and showed me a beautiful world with purple grass and trees with purple leaves. The grass was super thin, like hair. It was all so amazing to me. We played games and explored. He was so nice to me, and he was a bit of a tease. He used to pull my hair so he could win at games."

Ronin chuckles and then closes his eyes. When he opens them, "You are his mate."

I jump off his lap, "No! I am your mate. Yours."

He stands and comes over to hold me, "Of course, I am your Mate. I mean, he is supposed to be part of our Triad. He is your mate and one of my Triad."

A little overwhelmed, "What... I don't understand."

He gives me a gentle smile, "You remember when I told you about Dax, how he was different from most of my people?" I nod, not sure where he is going. "I told you Dax had dreams even when he was young." Oh my god. "Yes, my beautiful Mate. Dax dreamed of his mate."

I knew... I'm not sure how but I knew he was meant to be mine.

"I have a few more questions, Pillut. You said he did not believe you were real. What happened?"

"The first time he appeared in my dream, he was so sad, Ronin. He touched my face and said I had grown and was more beautiful than he could imagine, but then he got angry because it had been so long since I had been in his dreams. He accused me of being there to torture him too."

Ronin's head drops to his chest for a minute, "He has had a very difficult life."

I nod, "The next dream, he asked why I kept pulling him there. I'm not sure how we kept ending up in each other's dreams. My body reacted to his deep voice, and he got close to me and said, 'your body calls to me,' but then backed away and said I wasn't real. I really needed him to believe I was real, so I cupped his face and asked, please believe I am real. He touched my breast, rubbing my nipple. I moaned at the sensation. Then his hand dropped, and he said, 'see, you are not real because no female would react the way I did to his touch.' Ronin, I'm sorry I reacted to him..."

Ronin interrupts me, "No, my Mate. No. It makes me very happy you are drawn to Dax. We told each other long ago if we meet our mate, that the others automatically get permission to court her. I am very happy. I am worried about Dax. His behavior in these dreams is worrying. I worry for his state of mind."

"Today, in the nightmare, he saved me. He said he felt my fear and came for me. After he saved me, we were back in the valley. I was naked, wrapped in a blanket. We talked for a bit, but he couldn't resist touching me."

I can feel Ronin is hard. His voice is low, "Where did he touch you, my mate?"

"My breast." He pulls off my shirt and bra. "Like this?"

He caresses my breasts, then asks, "What else did he do?"

"He touched my nipples." His finger rub and circle. I can't help the moan that escapes.

"What else?"

I am panting now, "He... ran his fingers down my stomach and ran his fingers through my pussy." He growls, and I shiver. He stands me up and takes the rest of my clothes off. He sits me on his lap, my back to his front, and moves his hands down my stomach till his fingers move through my folds expertly, making my fire burn hotter and hotter.

"Ronin, Please!" He pinches my clit, and I come apart. He picks me up and sets me on my feet again. In seconds he grabs me, spins me around, and pulls me into his lap. I wrap my legs around his back as he lowers me onto his cock. We both groan. I start moving my hips, making sure to move across his lateral ridges, and grind my clit against his ridges at the base. Taking my pleasure from his body. My climax is building and the sensations are making it hard to focus. "Ronin... please"

We are now on the floor, and Ronin is using me the same way I used him. Focusing on the feeling my pussy creates on his cock going faster and faster, deeper and deeper. My orgasm washes over me, and I feel my pussy lock down on his cock. He roars as he releases, and his sprili unfurl and vibrate immediately, which sends me into another mind-blowing orgasm.

I'm not sure when he rolled us, but I'm now sprawled on his chest, and he is running his fingers up and down my back. "June, do you want Dax as part of our Triad?"

I don't even need to think about it, "I do."

He kisses my forehead, "I am happy about that. Dax needs you. From what you have told me, he is struggling deeply with his emotions and confidence. Make him see you. Show him the love and caring you have shown me. Maybe we can find him, or he will find us."

"I will. He is so sad, Ronin. It breaks my heart."

We are once again on the Emancipation on our way to Gamma station. Ronin seems distracted since I told him Dax was alive. Now I worry about them both, one because I want him safe with us and the other... I see the guilt he feels for not knowing that Dax was alive. I find this ridiculous because there is no way he could have known, but he is still processing the information. Most nights, he wanders the ship, unable to sleep.

We added intel on any Nlyaxians that might be wandering the galaxy free or slaves. I am hoping we encounter no problems, but the reputation of the station will keep me on guard. I hope Ronin's focus returns once we are there.

I lay in bed alone. I haven't dreamt of Dax since we were on the planet. I hope nightly to see him, but each morning I wake disappointed. I can't bring myself to wish for a nightmare; I cannot take them. I just can't. It seems Ronin is going to wander for a while, so I settle down to sleep, wondering if I will see him.

I'm dreaming, and I know I am. This is new. I'm standing in a forest on Earth. I loved walking in the national parks on Earth. I take a big breath smelling the pine needles. A pang of sadness hits me. There are things I miss.

I am naked again. I have to wonder what is going on in my subconscious; why am I always naked? Fear hits me suddenly, I start looking around for danger, but I see nothing. Then the pain hits. It is horrible, and I almost cry out. I stand breathing through it, but then I realize it is not my fear or pain.

It's Dax's. Oh no, not today, Satan. My Katana appears in my hands, and clothes now cover me. Yes. Let's do it.

I close my eyes and focus on Dax, on his fear, on his pain. I feel the change. I open my eyes. I am in a dark hallway. It has dark metal walls and floor, so I must be on some kind of ship. The ceilings and doors along the hallway are wider and taller than the Emancipation.

I hear a bellow of pain. I run toward the sound and have to stop and listen again. I hear something laughing. At least, I think that's what it is doing. It sounds more like shushing, and I creep forward to the open door it comes from. When I turn into the room, what I see is terrible.

There is an alien in the center of the room. It has six spindly legs attached to a large upright torso and two similar arms. One of those arms at the end is wrapped around some sort of cutting instrument. It steps to the side, and I see Dax. Fury, as I have never felt, erupts in me. He hangs limp by his arms and is covered in blood and wounds.

Most might think I would be scared of the fact that it looks like a fucking spider, but honestly, for me, it's fucking great. I am gonna take some revenge on some nasty mother fuckers.

I stalk forward as the spider turns and sees me. Strange, I assumed I would be ignored in a memory. It screams and tries to attack me with a blade, foolish.

I see Dax lift his head. I feel his terror at seeing me here, but I cannot comfort him. The spider is close, and its reach is long. Before its blade gets close, I sweep my blades and disarm it by removing its arm.

The pitch of its screaming changes, it's awful but I can deal with it. Surprisingly its tact doesn't change. It's still coming at me. It spits something at me, but I see it coming and am well out of the way, so it strikes the wall behind me. Gross. Ready to be done, I move into offensive maneuvers. I get in close and take off its head. Its tactics are awful. Whatever it was, it sucks at combat.

I turn to Dax and walk to him. This is a dream which means I control it. I wrap my arm around his waist and close my eyes. When I open them again, we are in his valley. His weight is too much for me, so we topple to the ground.

I land on top of him, and I realize I am once again naked. What in the actual fuck? Quickly I forget about that because I am slipping in his blood.

Dream, this is a dream. I close my eyes and put my hands on each side of his face and close my eyes. I imagine him healed. No blood.

I open my eyes, and he looks up at me in shock. "How did you do that? I have never been able to get out of their mind traps."

I shrug my shoulders, "Not sure. I just knew I could." I remember we are both naked, and so does my body. My nipples harden, and I become very wet. He closes his eyes, and breaths in. I can feel his hard cock against my lower stomach. "Dax, I want you to be part of my Triad."

His eyes spring open, focusing on my face. He rolls on top of me. His cock rubs up my folds. We both moan at the sensation. He refocuses on my face, "Who is your prime?"

I lift my hand to his face, "My prime is Ronin." A look of disbelief runs across his face, but he looks back at me and sees the truth.

He moves his cock to my entrance and thrusts into me. "Yes... Dax," I moan.

He grabs my hair, exposing my neck to him. He leans down to my ear, "Not good enough. It's time for you to scream my name."

Fuck, that's hot. He pulls me in for a hard, passionate kiss. He starts to thrust hard and fast. At the end of every thrust, he ensures his base ridges hit my clit. I am barreling toward my climax. He is focused on my face. Watching my reactions.

My orgasm explodes, "Dax!" I scream, and my pussy locks down on his cock. He moans and starts pounding harder and faster. I feel his sprili unfurl, "Yes!" At that, he roars his release, and the sprili start vibrating, sending me into another orgasm. "Dax!"

He lays on top of me. We are both trying to catch our breath. He lifts up to his elbows and starts kissing me gently. He lifts his head, "Truly? Ronin is your Prime? He is alive?"

I caress his cheek, "Yes, Dax. He is alive and knows you are now. He is very worried for you." He rolls us again, so I am on top. He has a faraway look on his face, "Does he want to see me? Is he disappointed?"

I sit up, pushing his cock deeper. We both moan, and he grabs my hips. "What could he possibly be disappointed in you for? He thought you were dead..." I pull myself up his cock and slowly back down. "He was in so much pain thinking you were gone."

Moaning, I keep my movements slow, moving up and down to ensure the most sensation against his ridges. "You are his brother in every sense of the word except blood."

He moans because of the sensations I am creating for us both. "He needs you, Dax." The conversation stops because neither of us can concentrate. His hands are roaming my body, but it's not until his thumb moves to my clit circling and thrumming, that I lose all control. I start moving up and down as fast as I can. When he pinches my clit an orgasm explodes through my body, my body locking down on his. He immediately reverses our position and sets a hard pace. Building me backup to another, then his sprili unfurl, and I am screaming his name as his release begins. The vibrations send me deeper into my orgasm. Dax disappears before I can scream his name again. Something must have woken him up. Fuck.

Dax

I am woken by someone yelling and banging on the door, "Time is up! Get out or pay more credits!"

My cock is still rock hard because of her. My mate... is it possible she is real? She pulled me from the mental torture of the Lutetian. I have never been able to do that. She was magnificent when she walked into the room. She was fury personified. I get dressed and head out. The way she fought, she is well trained in battle, and she moves like the flow of water. Her focus was also extremely impressive.

She said Ronin is her Prime. Is it possible he is alive? The joy I felt when she said that was almost too much for me to bear. Is it possible he wants to see me again? Will he be disappointed in what I have become? The violence I feel is all the time. Sometimes I cannot control it.

I shake my head; my mission has not changed, find the Lutetian who destroyed my people and kill them all. I move through the crowded markets at the station. I need information, and I intend to get it.

June

As I wake, Ronin is pushing into me. He shows me he knows I saw Dax and now is working to make me scream his name.

We lay in bed later, and Ronin quietly asks, "How was he?"

I struggle with how to answer that question, not because I don't want to tell him but because of what he'll have to hear. "He was in a nightmare that wasn't really a nightmare."

"I do not understand."

"I am confused as well. When I fell asleep, I felt his fear and his pain. I somehow knew I could find him, so I closed my eyes and pictured him. When I opened them again, I was on some kind of ship. I thought it was a dream. I found Dax," my emotions get the best of me, and tears escape, "He was strung up by his arms, and this spider-looking thing with six legs and two arms was... cutting him and laughing. Ronin, it was awful." He hugs me tight.

"I was furious. Then the strangest thing happened. The spider turned and attacked me." At his confused look, I continue. "If it was a dream, logically speaking, I should not have been able to interact with anything but Dax. The characters in his nightmare should not even acknowledge my existence. That's what happened in mine, Dax roared, and it disappeared. Why did the spider see me and try to fight me? It even spit at me." Ronin is shaking. I look up and see he is fighting his battle fury. I sit up, "What is it, Ronin?"

He quickly gets out of bed and starts stalking the room. "The spider is a species called the Lutetian, but that's impossible because we killed them all! What else happened?"

"I killed it. It was a terrible fighter. I walked over and wrapped my arm around him, and mentally pulled him back to our valley. I had to heal him in the dream as well. He was still covered in cuts and blood." I look up at Ronin, and he's giving me a look I cannot read. "What?"

"How did you heal him?"

"I don't know. I put my hands on his face and imagined him healed and the blood gone."

He continues stalking the room, quiet for around five minutes. "Ronin, what is it?"

He stops and looks at me. The battle fury is gone. "When we battled the Lutetian, when soldiers slept, they would sometimes wake with horrible wounds. Wounds that were not there when they went to sleep. They never knew how they were injured, and it always concerned me. It was rumored that Lutetian had strange mental abilities, but I never gave it a thought. The Lutetian would always get intel on our plans somehow, and we could never figure it out. What if they were pulling soldiers into this dream-like state, then torturing them for information? What if Dax is somehow different, able to remember these."

"Prior to rescuing Dax, I would've said it sounded crazy, but Ronin, it felt strangely real. I feel like if I had been injured there, I would have been injured here."

"If you ever see a Lutetian, never let their spit hit you. It contains a neurotoxin that paralyzes their victims but other than that, they are horrible warriors, which is why they create the mutated soldiers."

"What do you mean 'mutated soldiers'?"

"Forgive me. The Lutetian know their limitations well, so instead of fighting in battles, they use genetic manipulation to create soldiers to fight for them. Generally, they use the population of the planets they attack for this. It is a horrible thing. The people they mutate, their minds are gone because the process is done while they are awake."

"That is pure evil."

"It is, and it is why we started the war with them. We won the war. I do not understand how the Lutetian you saw even exists."

"I guess we have more intel to collect on the station." He sits back down in bed and pulls me to him.

We recline against the headboard. "What happened after you healed him?"

"I told him I wanted him as part of my Triad. He asked who my Prime was, and I told him you. Ronin, he thinks you will be disappointed in him for some reason. I told him 'no,' that he is your brother and that you need him."

Ronin rolls us, and we are now both facing the wall, one arm holding the headboard. His other arm is wrapped around my waist, not allowing me to move. I can feel he is hard again at my entrance, "Did he take you? This is very important."

I whisper, "yes..." he thrusts into me and roars, smiling. He continues pounding into me and yells, "We are two!"

He fucks me senseless for the rest of the night. In the morning, when we finally wake and ask, "So by two, you meant two males?" Ronin barks a laugh and slaps me on the ass as he gets up. "Yes, my beautiful Mate. Once you ask a Nlyaxian male to be part of your Triad, if he mates with you, he is one with the Triad."

"Now we just have to find him," this thought makes me sad. What if we cannot find him? Ronin, half-dressed, sits on the bed and pulls me into his lap.

"Do not worry, my Mate. He will be compelled to find us now. We will be looking for each other." He brings his mouth to my nipple while his finger moves through my folds. I arch my back and moan. They find my clit and begin to slowly circle, "Have no fear Pillut we will be fucking you together soon." Then he pinches my clit, and I explode.

I think it's time for more bed play, but he deposits me on the bed, "Come! We have more planning to do!" and out he walks, laughing as he goes. Fucking male. Two can play this game, and I reach for my Kokoro and stroke.

I look down and freeze. Ronin strides back in for revenge but stops at the look on my face and the tears on my cheeks. He looks at my arm, then yanks up his sleeve. Both of our Kokoro has a new symbol around the center that represents Dax. We both stroke the symbol with reverence.

Dax

My attempts at collecting intel on the Lutetian have been fruitless. I am moving to the next dive bar to feel out the beings there. Someone must know something.

I freeze, then move to an alleyway. I feel... I feel her, and I feel... Ronin. I pull up my sleeve, and there is a silver design on my arm forearm. It is a swirling design in the shape of a split circle with three segments with an intricate full circle in the center. The outer circle has two segments that are complete.

One segment has a design with Ronin's royal crest, the other has my beautiful valley, and the circle in the center has an image that looks like fire.

I am not sure how I know, but I can feel my Triad through this. I rest my hand on it, and I feel them even clearer in my mind. I feel their fear for my well-being, their joy at my joining the Triad, and their deep emotional connection to me. I close my eyes, overwhelmed by their feelings for me. They are real. I send my feelings for them across the bond and feel their joy at my response. So overwhelmed I remove my hand from the design. I am not used to being so close to others. It has been too long; back to my mission.

June

When he breaks the connection, I cannot help the tears rolling down my cheeks. Ronin rushes over and pulls me into his lap again. He holds me tight. "Ronin, he's so sad and so very alone. I cannot take it. He should be with us."

"I know, little Pillut. I know. It hurts me too, but I promise we will find him. We will be together." I nod. It's the only thing I can do.

Chapter 28

I'm on the bridge, staring at the display showing us getting closer to the station. As we get closer, I get more agitated. I don't know why but something is driving me crazy. I didn't feel well this morning when I woke, but after I ate, I was fine. I jump up from my chair, pacing the bridge. Ronin walks in a bit later and stops, "Mate? What is wrong?"

"I don't know!" I almost scream at him. I take a calming breath, "I'm sorry. I don't know, but the closer we get to that, the more agitated I become."

I turn and look at the screen again. I am frustrated, and I don't know why. I cross my arms, and as I make contact with the Kororo, I realize why. "Ronin!" I scream and spin. He looks at me, shocked. I point to the display, "He is there!"

Confusion crosses his face for a brief moment then understanding dawns. He rips his sleeve to get it up, then slaps his hand to his arm. His eyes take on a faraway look. When he refocuses on me, a smile lights his face. Quietly he says, "He is."

"You two want to let us know who 'he' is?" Doraj says, a bit annoyed. I'm guessing my bad behavior over the last hour is getting on his nerves.

I look at him and laugh, "Our second for our Triad. Dax is on that station."

A broad smile crosses his face, "Congratulations! What the hell is he doing there?"

Ronin is beside me and turns me to him. He knows how emotional I am right now. He puts his forehead to mine. "He is ok. We will have him soon." I nod because I can't speak.

Lessur speaks up, "Beginning docking procedures."

I whisper, "Ronin..."

He cups my face, "We will find him."

Ronin

My Mate's nerves are obvious. She is not her usual calm self in these situations. She has her disguise on to ensure we do not attract too much unwanted attention. She is heavily armed; she is distracted, not foolish. We stand at the cargo door with Lessur, Ekim, Elana, and Doraj, waiting for clearance to open the door.

Sia's voice comes over our coms, "You are cleared. Opening cargo door."

I am surprised to see the station dock manager standing waiting for us. "Hello, my friends. We are still gathering the supplies you requested, but I understand you plan to spend some time in the station?"

"Yes, we need to relax for a while." Giving him what he expected to hear.

"Good. Good! Spend some time and spend some credits, and all will be well!" His eyes get a faraway look for a few minutes, like someone is communicating with him. He looks at Elana and June, then back at me, "Ah. Mr. Nlyaxian, the station Mistress, would like to speak with you. You are to meet her on the 250th floor in her conference room."

I do not like this, but I have no choice. She can hold our ship and us until I meet with her. I glance back at my Mate. She gives me the barest of nods, signaling she understands the predicament we are in.

"Fine, but my crew will explore the station without me." Not really a question.

"Yes, yes, of course. You can join them when you are done. I will take you." I follow but cannot help my glance back at her. She will be fine. I will be back soon.

Dax

Once again, my old contact did not pan out. I am on edge for no real reason, and I do not like it. Something compels me to go to the market. I do not know what my next steps are, so I will follow it. The market is huge. It's seven floors of shops with an atrium in the center. The bottom is an area where shoppers can sit, eat and talk. Why anyone would want to do that is beyond my understanding. What am I looking for? Why am I here?

I am standing on the fifth floor, scanning the floors I can see and have a clear view of. What am I looking for?

Then I see a Torgu. I cannot possibly be her. It walks, looking cautiously around. The Torgu freezes, then slowly turns and looks directly at me. It is her, she is here. I look for Ronin, and I see a Nlyaxian a distance ahead of her. He has not noticed she stopped, but it is not him. I look back at her and she still stares at me. Is it her? She lifts her Torgu hand and lays in on the same exact spot on her arm where my design is. It is her. The joy I feel at finding her is amazing. My mind is not broken.

I notice movement over her shoulder. A Cruxlin is poised to stab her with a tranquilizer hypo. I ROAR ferociously, but it is too late. She collapses, and they put her in a bag and over their shoulder. I am running, sprinting to get to her. I leap from my balcony to the one above where they were. I swing over the balcony railing and come down on the floor. I look for indications of where they went then I smell her.

She smells of Pillut flowers. I sprint, following the scent. I realize we are headed in the direction of the docks. NO, NO, NO. They cannot get her off this station; I will never find her. I push myself for more speed, and the scent is getting stronger.

I hit the docks and continue at a sprint, then I see them. They are already on the ramp to their ship. I hear the other Nlyaxian far behind me, but I ignore him. Pushing myself more.

The vile Cruxlin sees me and panics. He races onto the ship, closes, and locks the door. The others of his species are stuck on the outside. I get to their door and can hear their engines turning up. NO!

I ram the door, and it does not budge. I start beating my fists against it, roaring my frustration at not getting to my mate. The door is damaged, but it still does not open. Through the window in the door, I see a Nlyaxian I do not recognize. He has a vile smile and holds her by the hair. He licks her face.

The rage I feel grows exponentially, and I start beating the door harder. The plates nearly buckle. Then ship pulls away from the dock. No. I stare at it as it leaves the station, unable to do anything about it.

The Nlyaxian catches up, "Is she on that ship?"

I look at him furiously and scream, "YES!" I think I may kill him. He was with her... he was supposed to protect her. He sees the murder in my eyes and starts to back away.

He curiously taps his ear, "Ronin, Cruxlin's took the Captain!"

Ronin. Why wasn't he here? Why wasn't he protecting her... maybe I'll kill him instead. Another Nlyaxian, Trogu, and Noinapmoc run up to back up the first. Let's have some fun first.

Ronin

When I hear Ekim say it, all my muscles lock up for a second. We had just entered the conference room. I do not even fight my battle fury for dominance. I let it take over. The roar I release rattles the windows in the room. I start to turn to run to my Mate when I see the look in the dock manager's eyes. I know he had a hand in this. I'm on him before he can utter a word. My hand has him up against the wall, his feet not touching the ground. Menacingly I ask, "What do you know of Cruxlin's stealing my crew?"

"Nnn-othing." I can see his lie. I can see all lies.

From behind me, a female voice says, "Do not lie. The prince of my people can see all lies." I growl, not caring who she is.

"Yes, yes." is all he can get out because he cannot breathe. I let his feet touch the ground and release my grip a fraction. "They showed up on the dock a few days ago. Said they'd give me a million credits if I notified them when two Trogu showed up. When you walked off your ship with two, well, I let them know."

I snap his neck and look at the female. She holds up her hands, "I had nothing to do with this." She is not lying. I turn and stalk out the door.

My battle fury is still in complete control. The beings on the station run the opposite way when they see me. As I reach the docks, I see someone fighting my crew and winning. I sprint across the docks and put myself between the attacker and my people.

I roar again, putting all my anger into it. A shocked look comes over his face then my mind registers who it is. Before I can do anything, he is screaming and throwing punches. "Why? Why were you not with her?"

He is right. I let him land the punches. They keep coming and coming. I am lying on the floor when they stop. I can no longer see because my eyes are swollen. I feel someone pick me up, "Where is your ship?" We walk, and after a bit, I am laid on a bed. I can feel Nalax's hands working on me.

I wake up sometime later and realize the swelling is down, and I look for him. I find Dax sitting next to the bed, his head rests on the bed next to me, and his hands are on my chest.

"Dax." My voice is rough, barely a whisper. His hands clench in my tunic.

I hear him whisper, "Thank the Goddess. I did not kill you. Forgive me."

"Dax. Look at me."

He lifts his face to mine. My best friend is here, alive. I can hardly believe it. The pain on his face hurts me. "Dax. It is alright. You are right. I failed her," I pause to get my emotions in check, "I should have been there."

"No, Ronin. It was unfair of me to say that. Your crew told me what happened at the dock when you got here. You had to go, and she was distracted...looking for me." His head once again rests on his chest.

"The blame is not yours if it is not mine, my brother. The Cruxlin are the ones who took her."

His eyes connect with mine, "It was not only Cruxlin. There was a Nlyaxian on the ship at the door when I got to it. He smiled at me and...he licked her."

Both of our eyes are black, "What did he look like?"

"I did not recognize him, but he was only slightly taller than June."

I cannot contain the growl that escapes, "Sitruc."

I hear Nalax gasp. "Ronin, he tried to force himself on her several times."

I cannot help the concussive roar that escapes me at her words.

"What are we going to do?" Dax asks as he paces the room.

With conviction, I say, "We are going to find her."

He looks me in the eyes for a few minutes, then nods.

I sit up and pull him into a very firm embrace, "I thought I lost you, my brother."

He wraps his arms around me, "When she said you were alive... I didn't want to hope, didn't want to believe because it would hurt too much if it wasn't true."

"How did you survive?"

"I was not there. I did not want to celebrate your sister's coronation. The Lutetian were regularly pulling me into their mental torture. I was at a supply station drinking myself to sleep. Hoping they could not get me while I was drunk. I was wrong. I did not learn of the fall of our homeworld until almost a week after it happened. I went crazy in my grief for you and Aanon. The station captured me and sold me off to pay for the damage I had done. I had been Negg's toy in his fight pits until our mate saved me."

He asks, "Will you tell me how you came to be alive and how you found our mate?"

I cannot say no to him. He sits back as I recount everything that has happened since the fall of our home.

He sits back, the emotional ups and downs of my story wearing him out. "Ronin, the guilt I feel for not trying to find you..."

"No, Dax. We both just lost our entire planet. The depression that took us convinced us that all was lost even though it was not. That is not your fault."

He looks like he wants to ask a question, "What is it, Dax?"

He looks at his hands, "I cannot help but wonder, I am alive, you are alive... do you think it is possible..."

I know what he is asking, and it hurts my heart, "Aanon." He nods. "I have hope now when before I had none, but the pessimist in me is still loud. He tells me Aanon would never miss the coronation of our new Queen. That he was on the planet...but I was convinced you were also on the planet so...I have hope. The Goddess saw fit to keep you alive and gift us with the female you dreamed about so it's not out of the range of possibilities." He nods. Neither of us can bear the thought.

"June would have adored him." He says sadly.

"Yes. She would have."

He nods but still looks upset, "Ronin, I was angry with June for a long time. I pushed her away in my dreams when we left for military training. Thinking that maybe everyone was right, that she was not real. She was so upset that day. She begged me not to abandon her. I was rude to her, mean even. Then when I was captured, I begged her to come back. I yelled and yelled for her to return, so she could help me survive, but she never came. I was so angry with her."

He pauses for a while, but I know he is not done, so I wait. "It was not till years later that I realized how childish I was. It was not her fault; I pushed her away."

"Dax, I wish to pose a question to you, how much of your life would you change if it meant losing her?"

He sits up, "Nothing. I would change nothing."

I smile at him, "The Goddess has gifted us a beautiful warrior mate. She is Her Chosen Warrior. Do you believe She would give Her Chosen to someone she did not care for, someone unworthy?"

He thinks for a long time, then gives me a sideways smile, "I suppose you are right, but it makes me wonder why her? why us?"

"June and I have asked that question of ourselves many times. We have yet to come up with an answer. Trust in Her. Trust in your Mate. We will find her. We will be with her again because," I chuckle, "that female was born to be ours. She was born to be in our Triad. I will spend the rest of my days worshiping her body in the ways the Goddess intended."

Dax smiles genuinely, "I cannot wait for that either, my Brother. I have not even touched her outside the dreams."

"Do not worry, my brother. Her sexual appetite is greater than even a Nlyaxian female. She is perfect."

"How are we going to find her?" Desperation is written across his face.

Sia says, "*I can help with that. I shot a tracker onto their ship before they exited the station doors.*"

"Sia..." I have no words. "Sia, set an intercept course and do what you can to mask our approach." I look at Dax, "Let's go find our Mate."

June

I wake, and I am thankfully clothed but restrained to another metal table. I do not open my eyes. "You can open your eyes whore. Since your last little stunt when the Cruxlin's had you, they added some safeguards to detect brain activity. You are fooling no one."

I open my eyes, praying I am wrong about who is speaking. When I see him, my stomach drops. Sitruc. "Yes. It is me. Are you surprised? I told you I would have you, and now, at least for a while, I will."

"Over my dead body." I say with as much malice as I can muster.

"Tsk, tsk, tsk, little whore. You will have no choice." He lifts his arm, and the terror that comes across my face makes him laugh. "Yes. Now you understand. The Cruxlin have excellent medical technology. I stole this from his quarters after that dung-headed prince took you to another room to sleep. Then I escaped in one of the pods."

I can't stop staring at his arm. I cannot process what I am seeing. On his forearm is a patch of skin that is obviously not his. On it, there are three gold dots.

I feel my body lock down and panic, but something is different. It's like parts of me are locked, then they release, and others are locked. It's glitchy. Good. You can try fucker, but I will kill you if you do.

"Time to put you back under but do not worry, little whore, I will make sure you are awake so you can enjoy it when I am pounding my cock into you."

We shall see fucker. We shall see.

I wake, and this time I don't bother to hide it. I am once again naked but lying on a cot in what looks like a cell of some kind, except there are no bars, just walls, and a door. There is what looks like a toilet and a sink in the corner. So much for privacy.

I sit up on the bed and take inventory. Nothing is broken, and it doesn't feel like I have been violated in any way, so I guess that's good. I get up and feel along the walls for a weakness, vent, or anything I might be able to use.

I see where the door is and start feeling around it to see if I can pry it open, but no luck. I knew it was a long shot.

I'm left alone in my cell for a night cycle. Food is dispensed in a little unit by the sink, but I can definitely say they are not worried about my culinary pallet. The food it gives me is like a cube of jello but with no flavor. I have to assume it's nutritionally packed, so I eat it.

I am pacing the cell when the slave tats lock down kind of; one leg and the opposite arm cannot move, but the other two I control. I need to keep that little fact in my back pocket for use.

The door opens, and Sitruc walks in with a look of victory on his face. "I am going to fuck you senseless now."

I laugh at him, "I'm not sure about senseless because the last time I saw it, I'm not altogether sure I'll feel it when it goes in." Keep your enemy emotional and off balance.

His eyes go black. I feel the push of the slave tats and follow along. I back to the wall and put my arms above my head. He undoes his pants and pulls out his cock.

I laugh again, "It's a lot smaller than even Kaxlins."

He roars. It's then I notice that the slave tattoos lose control when he does. Interesting. He then up against me, I can feel his cock on my stomach, and it makes me want to vomit. He grabs my ass and starts to lift me, and I feel it throb in anticipation. It's now or never.

I bring the knee I control up to connect with his balls while I use my one arm and hand to gouge his eyeballs. He bellows and falls back. Blood drips from both his sockets. He is blind. I have full control, for the moment, and attack. I deliver blows to his head, neck, and abdomen. He is screaming and swinging, trying to get me. One of my arms locks down, but nothing else.

"*Bitch*! I will kill you for this." Spittle flies from his mouth.

I laugh, "You have to find me first."

He turns in my direction and barrels toward me. I step out of the way, and he runs directly into the wall.

I laugh again, taunting him, "Awe, what's wrong, Sitruc? Can't control the slave tattoos? You must not be as strong as Kaxlin was."

He roars and charges again, but I am no longer where I was. This time his head hits the wall, and I think I heard his skull crack. He is moaning on the floor. Time to end this.

The door opens, and five guards file in. The last is a doctor or lab tech, and he shoots me with one of those damn darts.

I fall to the ground. "Take that idiot to the infirmary. Take her as well. I need to make sure the embryo is still intact. The Lutetian will be furious if she loses the child!"

What? Am I pregnant? That's not possible. "no," I slur.

The doctor or whatever comes over, "We had to change the meds in the darts because we do not know the effects it will have on your embryo. We will have new sedation by the end of the cycle today, so you will be sedated soon."

He says this as if it will relieve me, but it does not. "no child," I manage to get out.

He laughs, "Oh, yes! Congratulations! You are with child. It is healthy, but its progress seems to be in some sort of stasis. We do not understand why." He continues to chat with me like we are friends as I am wheeled to the infirmary. "It is most fascinating. The embryo is around two weeks gestation and perfectly healthy, but the development stopped and entered some sort of stasis. We have seen this in other species but never humans."

"what do with me?"

"Oh well, I am sorry to tell you, but the Lutetian have paid a very large sum of credits for you because you are mated with the prince, and when they found out you are with child, they quadrupled the credits! So you are going with them." He actually gets a bit of a remorseful look, then smiles.

"why"

"Why? Oh, why do they want you? My theory is they are building their new army, but I do not know that for sure. I do know they want the prince very badly. That is why we were sent after you, so they could get him. That fact that you are carrying his child made them very excited." He shrugs and leaves my side because we are now in the infirmary.

I am pregnant with Ronin's child. Nalax said three years, but it's not even been one yet. I'm guessing human biological differences but... what will I do? A tear escapes. I will do everything in my power to keep our baby safe, but that is becoming more and more difficult. If the Lutetian get their hands on me, what happens? Why do they want Ronin?

Ronin told me about the ways they develop their armies, and it terrifies me. What do they plan to do to Ronin and our baby? Tears are now flowing into my hair, and I am nearly hyperventilating. I wanted Ronin and Dax to find me, but now I fear it.

"Ah, we have a new med that will sedate you and not harm the embryo. Time to sleep." He sticks me with the hypo, and darkness envelops me.

End book 1

Appendix

Glossary/Info:

Ahmya - Human best friend

Kaxlin/Dlanod - Nlyaxian Pirate Captain

Tanto - Japanese short sword

Katana - Japanese long sword

Leena - Nlyaxian slave girl

Nalax - Noinapmocian ex-slave for Kaxlin. Role is now a physician.

Doraj - Noinapmocian engineering slave, Mate to Nalax

Craxlin - Yellow aliens working with human to buy women for sale to Lutetian

Lutetian - Mystery bad guys.

Sitruc - Kaxlin's 2nd in command. Nlyaxian. No slave collar.

Sia - Ship AI

Pillut - Small Nlyaxian flower with green petals, term of endearment

Ferin - Reclusive species . Excellent fighters and followers of the Goddess

The Goddess - Immortal being that teaches logic, compassion, strength of will, independent thought and science driven

Trogu - Alien disguise June wears

Kokoro - Nlyaxian mate symbol

Expalita - Ferin aura

Amabo, Karab, Ellechim - Elected leaders of Haven

A professional nerd, AL Carter has spent the last two decades in the tech industry supporting the infrastructure, websites and software the world runs on. She loves science, reading, and making just about anything sparkly in her spare time. She gets great joy from writing science fiction romance novels giving her female characters strength and purpose! Her heroines do not need saving but they love to create steam with their partners!